MW00344933

THE HEARTS
WE TRUST

Trust your heart !

Annell St. Charles

ANNELL ST. CHARLES

THE HEARTS WE TRUST by ANNELL ST. CHARLES., ©
Copyright 2021 Annell St. Charles. All Rights Reserved and
Preserved. No part of this book may be reproduced or transmitted
in any form or by any means, electronic or mechanical, including
photocopying, recording, or by information storage and retrieval
systems, without written permission of the Publisher with
exceptions as to brief quotes, references, articles, reviews, and
certain other noncommercial uses permitted by copyright law.

For Permission requests, write to:
YBR Publishing, LLC
PO Box 4904
Beaufort SC 29903-4904
contact@ybrpub.com
843-900-0859

ISBN-13: 978-1-7349515-5-4

Front cover photograph ©2021 Annell St. Charles

YBR PUBLISHING, LLC

Jack Gannon – Co-Founder, Production Manager
Cyndi Williams-Barnier – Co-Founder, Production Editor
Bill Barnier – Senior Editor
Loreen Ridge-Husum – Art Director

Also by the Author:

It is only with the heart that one can see rightly; what is essential is invisible to the eye.

Antoine de Saint-Exupéry

DEDICATION

As always, to the heart I trust most in this world: my husband,
Costas Tsinakis.

FORWARD

I introduced the Gullah language in my third novel, "The Chances We Take". As I explained in the forward to that book, the word "Gullah" refers to a people, their culture, and their language thought to have originated in Angola, on the west coast of Africa. From the 1500s to the 1800s, thousands of West Africans were enslaved and brought to the United States to work on plantations and private settlements on the eastern Sea Islands, including Hilton Head Island. Reports indicate that as many as 20,000 enslaved Africans were brought to South Carolina by the mid-1700s. Their descendants can still be found today along what is called the "Gullah-Geechee Cultural Heritage Corridor", which extends from North Carolina to Florida.

The use of the name "Geechee" was adopted after many of the African slaves settled along the Ogeechee River in South Georgia. Presently, the word *Gullah* is used to refer to those who live in South Carolina, while *Geechee* indicates those who live in Georgia. The Corridor has been designated a Federal National Heritage Area to help preserve and interpret the traditional cultural practices, sites and resources associated with the Gullah-Geechee people. In this book, I refer to their descendants as "Gullah" because the setting for the story is Hilton Head Island, South Carolina.

The Gullah/Geechee language technically became known as an English-based creole language in the mid-1700s. Research has uncovered a strong connection between the Gullah language and the Krio language spoken in Sierra Leone and was adopted by the second generation of Blacks. Presently, the language is kept alive by a relatively small number of descendants of the formerly enslaved Africans, some of whom still live on Hilton Head Island. By including the language in this book, my hope is that I can contribute in some small manner to keeping it alive.

Most of the letters used in Gullah have the same sounds as English words. However, there are changes in some sounds, some consonant shifts, and some sounds that are unique to Gullah, but resemble the Black dialect.

General Rules
"v" is always substituted with "b"
"th" is always substituted with "d"
the "h" is dropped in most cases
An apostrophe (') is used to show where a letter, word, or group of words is omitted. It can also show where two words are pronounced as one (mekum = make them).

I included an extensive Gullah-English dictionary in the back of "The Chances We Take". That dictionary can be used to aid in understanding the Gullah dialogue I have included in this book. In addition, I recommend reading the Gullah sections out loud because (according to some of my teacher friends) that may help ears unfamiliar with the language understand it better.

ACKNOWLEDGEMENTS

I would like to express my gratitude to the following groups and individuals:

The Gullah-Geechee community on Hilton Head island: those who are an integral part of it; those who are by choice associated with it. The events, celebrations, works of art and artistry, talks and tributes, have helped expand my knowledge of your history, and open my heart to your messages of inclusivity and freedom for all.

My Hilton Head friend, Jane Hilson, for reading the first draft of this novel and making valuable suggestions.

The Coastal Discovery Museum, especially Natalie Hefter and Jennifer Stupica, for carrying my books and allowing me to post a promotional video on their Facebook page.

Nadia Wagner at The Harbour Town Lighthouse Museum for including my novels in the gift shop.

3 Sisters Resale and More on Palmetto Bay Road: a store run by three actual sisters who are keen on supporting local authors and artists (in addition to stocking an amazing array of intriguing "finds"). They have carried every one of my written works since 2016.

David Martin at the Coligny Plaza Piggly Wiggly: the epitome of a true neighbor and consistent supporter of island activities. I appreciate you allowing me to place a couple of my books for sale in your store, and for tolerating my fictitious use of a character based upon you in this and the previous novel. My depiction doesn't do you justice!

Erika Waronsky, owner of the Sandbar Beach Eats Restaurant, for your willingness to host a book event for my last novel (even though Covid-19 bashed that plan!).

Parnassus Bookstore in Nashville, Tennessee for allowing this humble local author to hold a live book event upon the release of my first novel, to be included among those you virtually supported on your Facebook page in 2020, and for carrying my novels in your store.

St. Bernard Academy, Nashville, Tennessee: my high school alma mater. I extend my deepest appreciation to Principal Chuck Sabo and Sydnie Hochstein, the Director of Events, for suggesting and hosting a virtual book event to replace the live event that would have occurred at the school had it not been for the pandemic. Your kindness was overwhelming.

Judy Manley Elliott, for featuring me via zoom on her "Lifestyles for Women" TV show. She was one of the first media folks to reach out during the pandemic with a creative suggestion for how I could promote my third novel, "The Chances We Take".

To YBR Publishing: Bill Barnier, Cyndi Williams-Barnier, and Jack Gannon. I believe it was kismet that I met Cyndi and Jack at a book event a few years ago, and subsequently signed on with the Company. Your help with the editing, promotion, and production of this novel and the previous ones has been invaluable. Not only are my books much improved as a result of your efforts, but I have personally learned a lot from you. I have grown to value you as friends as much as business partners.

Finally, to all my readers: it is not an easy task to expose one's heart and soul by putting traces of them in print. I appreciate each of you who have taken the time to reach out to me to let me know how my books have affected you.

CHAPTER ONE

A shimmer of pale gold, tinged with streaks of rose and deep purple, was just beginning to paint the sky as I slipped out the back door. I had lingered a little too long over my morning cup of coffee, forcing me to hurry my steps as I made my way the short distance from our house on Dune Street to Coligny Beach. There weren't many situations where I felt the need to hurry to do anything since Jon and I moved to Hilton Head Island. But when it came to catching the sunrise, I was willing to rush a bit.

I stepped onto the sandy shore and paused to take in the spectacle before me and allow my thumping heart to still. The "always special but never the same" quality of the sunrises on Hilton Head was one of the first things I fell in love with when Jon and I joined our friends, Julie and Harry, for a week's vacation on the island four years earlier. It felt strange to realize it had been that long since I first visited Hilton Head. So much had transpired since then. I met the ghostly spirit of Miss Bessie Barnhill in a cemetery on the island and helped solve the mystery of her grandfather's death. Jon and I were married upon our return to Nashville after our vacation trip. Jon's company was sold by his father, causing him to reconsider his career path. Jon and I bought a house on Hilton Head and ended up moving here permanently, and we became close friends with Henry and Mary Palmer, a sweet, Black couple we met during our first trip to the island.

The Palmers ran a little store on the main road that led onto the island. They were descendants of the original Gullah people who had been brought to Hilton Head, known then as Trench's Island, from West Africa in the 1700s. That history alone was enough to spark some fascinating, albeit challenging, conversations between the four of us. The Palmers both spoke with a strong Gullah dialect that was oftentimes difficult for Jon and me to understand. But our communication was about much more than words. They were kind and gentle people whose gift of friendship was a treasure.

"Hey, Georgia. I thought I'd find you out here."

I turned to spot Jon emerging from the sandy path that ran between the dunes in front of our house. The sight of him warmed my heart and brought a smile to my face, which grew even bigger as he sat down the little bundle he was carrying.

"Mommy, Mommy! Daddy say de dolfs be swimming dis morning. Can I see de dolfs?"

That was another thing that changed in my life since our move to Hilton Head. Shortly after we purchased the house on Dune Street, I discovered that the frequent stomach upsets I had been experiencing were not due to food intolerance, anxiety, or any other mundane matter, but heralded the pending arrival of our son. Jonathan Franklin Barnett, or Frankie as we called him, became part of our lives in April of 1976, almost nine months after Jon and I returned to the island to finalize the purchase of our house. Frankie was born on the island during one of our return trips, after I went into labor a few weeks before my due date. Luckily, the local hospital was completed the previous year preventing me from having to call on one of the local midwives to assist with the birth. You could say that Frankie was an island baby through and through, which explained his total fascination with dolphins, or *dolfs* as he called them, and anything else associated with life by the ocean.

I crouched and held my arms open as his little legs churned through the sand. We celebrated Frankie's third birthday the previous weekend and, like most three-year old's, he tended to run everywhere he went. Especially when it involved a beach adventure. As he reached me, he launched himself into my arms, causing me to topple over backwards.

"I'm sorry, Mommy." His little face curved into a frown as he peered down at me.

I quickly pulled myself into a sitting position "You're getting so big and strong!" His frown turned into a huge smile as he stood up straight with his hands on his hips. I gave him a quick hug and stood, brushing the sand from my clothes. "I think I saw a pod of dolphins swimming just offshore. Why don't we see if we can find them?" I offered him my hand.

He grabbed it eagerly, turning to look over his shoulder at Jon. "Come on, Daddy. Mommy and me going tuh find de dolfs."

Jon took Frankie's other hand, and the three of us strolled northwards along the beach, scanning the waves for the sleek gray backs of the dolphins. It didn't take long to spot them. Their appearance in the shallow water near the shore had drawn a sizable crowd of spectators who pointed excitedly in their direction. Frankie began to jump up and down between us. "The dolfs are here! The dolfs are here! I want tuh pet one!"

I looked down at him with a smile. "I don't think that will be possible. They're very fast. But if we hurry, we'll get as close to them as we can." We released his hands and watched as he ran swiftly in the direction of the crowd, stopping only when his legs were immersed up to his knees by the incoming tide. "That's far enough, Frankie. The tide's coming in." He looked down and began to giggle as the receding water bathed his bare feet.

"The water's cold!" He hopped in place as the waves flowed forward and back.

Jon bent and lifted Frankie from the water, turning him so he was facing the path of the dolphins. "What's dat one doing, Daddy?" He pointed to where one of the dolphins had rolled onto

3

its side with one pectoral flipper raised high. Others from the pod joined in as they swam in a circle, splashing their tail flukes.

Jon looked where Frankie was pointing. "Most likely they're circling a school of fish so they can grab a quick meal. It's something called pinwheeling."

Frankie looked at him with disbelief. "Fishes go tuh school? Do they have tuh learn dere ABCs?"

Jon laughed and squeezed him affectionately. "They're in a different type of school where fish go so they are less likely to get picked off by predators."

Frankie continued to watch the actions of the dolphins with a quizzical look. "I don' tink dese fish are very smart, cos' the dolfs going tuh eat dem."

I was listening to their exchange with curiosity. It had occurred to me more than once that Frankie's speech sounded a lot like the unique dialect of the Gullah people, and I wondered if spending a good deal of time around Mary, Henry, and their grand and great-grandchildren, had rubbed off on him. I tucked it away in the back of my mind to speak to his Daycare teacher about it, returning my attention to the present.

"Speaking of eating, are you two ready for breakfast? We have some of those muffins left over from the Coligny bakery, and I could scramble some eggs to go with them."

Jon smiled at me and turned Frankie so he could look at him more directly. "Sounds good to me. What do you say, Frankie? Are you ready to eat?"

Frankie nodded vigorously as he squirmed to get down. When his feet were once more firmly planted on the sand, he flopped down on his side with one arm in the air while his legs churned. "I swimmin' like de dolfs! Goin' tuh catch some fish for breakfast."

I shook my head at him in a pretense of disapproval. "The only thing you're going to catch, young man, is a cold. Hop up from there so we can go home and wipe the beach off you."

He pushed himself into a standing position before trotting off in the direction of the path that led to our house. Jon put his arm around me and pulled me close. "I think we've got our hands full with that one."

"That's an understatement," I said. "He has more energy than both of us put together."

Jon bent and planted a firm kiss on top of my head. "Maybe it's a good thing a second one hasn't come along."

We both grew silent for a moment, lost in our private thoughts of the failed attempts at a second pregnancy. Frankie was a surprise. Not an unpleasant one, but a surprise, nonetheless. After he was born, we decided to wait a couple of years before trying for another baby, but since then we'd done nothing to prevent it. For whatever reason, the cards just hadn't seemed to be stacked in our favor. I tried not to dwell on it much, choosing instead to believe that whatever was meant to be, would be. It wasn't as easy for Jon. He longed for another child, believing that Frankie would benefit from a sibling, and that it would round out our family circle in a positive way.

For the past few months, I began wearing the amulet Miss Bessie gave me back when I first met her in the cemetery. The amulet steered me in the right direction during the time I was trying to sort out what happened to Miss Bessie's grandfather, and since then it served as a beacon of light, directing my choices in many other areas of my life. I lost the habit of wearing it once Frankie was born. As an infant, he always seemed to latch hold of it, causing me to worry he would one day stuff it into his mouth. As he grew older, I began wearing it again, hoping it would help me sort out whether or not I would have another baby. So far, it remained silent on that matter.

I decided a few days earlier to talk with Mary about my worries. She was like a grandmother to me, or at least a wise old Auntie. Talking with her never failed to ease whatever doubt was weighing on me or help me gain perspective about what I was feeling.

I squeezed Jon's side where my arm encircled him. "Let's be thankful for what we have. Besides, I'm not sure I have enough energy for another child if it's anything like Frankie."

Jon nodded somewhat reluctantly. "It's just that he reminds me of myself when I was his age, and I remember how excited I was when my little sister came along. I guess I'd like him to have someone special in his life like she has always been for me. Brothers and sisters have a unique relationship that's at a different level than that of a parent and child. Or even a best friend." He suddenly stopped walking and turned to me with a look of concern. "That was thoughtless of me. I forgot for a moment that you're an only child. I hope my comments didn't make you feel bad."

It was true. I was an only child. But given the nature of my relationship with my parents, I wasn't sure it would have been fair to wish for another child to go through what I had grown up with. The rule in our house was children should be *seen and not heard.* My parents kept their distance from me, except when they deemed it appropriate to correct something I said or did or didn't do. It wasn't that they were intentionally unkind. They just weren't particularly good at parenting. It took me a long time to figure out that their behavior had little to do with who I was, and a lot to do with who they weren't.

"It's okay. Sometimes I envy the closeness you share with Jen. Luckily though, I have Julie."

Julie had been my best friend since high school, and we remained close to the present day. Leaving her behind was one of the most difficult things about moving from Nashville to Hilton Head Island. She and her husband Harry had been making regular visits to the island every summer since we moved here, and occasionally Julie hopped a plane to come see us by herself. There was a small, local airport on the island, but it was only used by private jets. There was talk about adding commercial service, but in the meantime, air travel from Nashville to Hilton Head required a stop in Atlanta before continuing on to the airport in Savannah. As visitors to the island increased, a local company began offering shuttle service between the Savannah airport and Hilton Head, making the one hour ride each way a little easier to manage.

Julie had been invaluable when we first moved into our house on Dune Street, visiting numerous secondhand furniture stores with me, and making suggestions about the décor. Those visits had become far less frequent in the last couple of years following the birth of her twin daughters, Ashley and Emily. The twins were born a few months after Frankie, and their proximity in age was another reason I hated to live so far away. It would be a great joy to watch our children grow up together. When Julie discovered her pregnancy would result in twins, she took it in stride, having been well seasoned in the nuances of living with twins by the presence of her sisters, Sherry and Carey.

"Mommy and Daddy, come ON! I'm hungry!" Frankie was waiting for us on the back porch of our house, his little arms folded across his belly. In moments like this, he reminded me acutely of Jon in one of his less patient moments.

"We're coming, sweetheart. Just hold your horses," I said.

He looked around in bewilderment. "No horses, Mommy. Jes' Ebie." He pointed toward our black cat, Ebie, who stood watch just inside the screen door. Ebie had been with me since she was a kitten. She and Jon became fast friends when he first began to frequent my doorstep. It took her a little longer to warm up to Frankie. In the beginning, she looked at the newborn with curiosity that quickly turned into alarm when he erupted into one of his frequent crying jaunts. As he grew older, but no less quiet, she tended to skitter away, only coming close when he was asleep to peer at him inquisitively.

She began to mew insistently when Jon pushed the screen door open. "I think someone else is hungry, too," he said.

I grabbed a beach towel we kept on a hook by the back door and rubbed Frankie clean of the sand and water that clung to him. Once freed of my ministrations, he ran directly to the living room where he scooped up his stuffed dolphin and began to imitate the antics we had watched on the beach. "My dolf is hungry, too!"

Jon and I made our way into the kitchen. He pulled out eggs and butter from the fridge, handing me a half empty can of

7

cat food in the process. After I filled Ebie's bowls with food and water, we started preparations for our own breakfast, working easily in tandem. Truthfully, Jon was a better cook than me. I was always happy to turn the cooking duties over to him when he was available. Since it was Sunday, his schedule allowed him a little more flexibility than the other days of the week when his time was mostly occupied with growing his real estate business. When we bought the house on Dune Street, our plan was to renovate it for resale. When we discovered I was pregnant, we abandoned that idea and Jon decided to join one of the local real estate companies so he could continue to pursue his newfound interest. So far, he did well in the business. Well enough to provide a comfortable life for us. His business dealings mostly involved working with retirees who were intent on making Hilton Head their new home. I could tell he was itching to expand into other unexplored areas of the marketplace. I wasn't sure exactly what that meant since he hadn't been ready to talk with me about it yet, but I felt certain that, knowing Jon, we were in for an exciting ride.

CHAPTER TWO

I often thought of life on Hilton Head as divided into three categories: family time, which was confined to the time Frankie, Jon and I would spend together; me time–those rare hours spent in blessed solitude; and friend time, which might include a visit from Julie, or one of my other Nashville buddies, or a social call to one of the local folks I had grown close to over the past few years. Mary Palmer was at the top of that list. On this particular day, since Jon was at work, and Frankie was occupied at the Daycare Center operated out of one of the island churches, I had my choice between "me" and "friend" time. I chose the latter and decided to seek her out.

Mary and Henry lived in a house on Brams Point in Spanish Wells. I first visited their home with Julie during our girls' trip to Hilton Head in the summer of 1974. Since moving to the island, we saw them regularly, for an impromptu visit; to get together at one of our houses for dinner, or to bring Frankie to play with one of their great-grandchildren. I knew Mary's schedule pretty much by heart. Monday through Saturday, she went to Henry's store around lunchtime to bring him something to eat and tidy up the place. She attended church on Wednesday nights and

Sunday mornings. The rest of the time she was usually at home. Since it was Monday, and nowhere close to lunchtime, I decided to head for her house after I dropped Frankie off at Daycare.

I drove down the now-familiar street, admiring the view across the marshes on either side before turning into their sandy driveway. I stepped out of the car and was greeted by the excited barking of their new dog, Beau. Beau was a border beagle, which meant he was a mix between a border collie and a beagle. He was a cuddly, playful, and smart dog whose only vice was jumping on people when he was excited, which was most of the time. Beau wandered into Mary and Henry's yard one afternoon and never left. He wasn't wearing a collar, and no one ever came looking for him. The way his eyes followed them with absolute devotion, it was a fair guess he had been abandoned and was thrilled to find a home.

"Hey there, Beau. What a good dog you are!" I bent to hug his neck, receiving slobbery kisses in return. "Is your mom home? Take me to her." Beau hopped in a circle before stopping to look over his shoulder at me as if to say *are you coming?* I followed him to the porch just as the screen door opened to reveal Mary wiping her hands on a dishtowel.

"Heard de car, den saw Beau light out. Uh jis' put on de kittle. Cum' inside, chile." I stopped to give her a hug as I entered, receiving a warm embrace in return. Mary's hugs felt like being enveloped in warm sunshine, and I never passed up a chance to accept one.

"I hope it's not a bad time to stop by."

She waved her hand. "Nebbuh bad time fo' see oonuh. Uh jes' need tuh mek 'Enry's lunch tuh tek ober dere later. Got time tuh sit and bizzit now." She indicated I should take one of the chairs facing the fireplace as she sat in the other. "'Enry mek dis fire 'fo' 'e leabe. Feel nice tuh me bones."

I nodded. "It's still a bit cool in the mornings, but I don't mind because it's a good excuse to enjoy the fireplace. I'm so glad Jon suggested adding one to our house as part of the renovation."

Mary poured both of us a cup of tea from the kettle. We sat quietly for a few moments, enjoying the warmth from the fire and the contentment that comes from sharing silence with a good friend. Eventually, she set her cup down and shifted so she could face me.

"Wuh hebby een oonuh min'? Uh kin see de wheels turn'n'."

I smiled at her perceptiveness. "You know me well, Mary." I paused to collect my thoughts. "You know Jon and I have been hoping to have another child. I've been wearing the amulet lately to see if it's going to happen, but I'm not getting any messages. I wonder if I'm not using it in the right way."

She stared into the fire. "De chaam don' always wu'k lukkuh 'spect 'e tuh. Sometime hab tuh wait fuh 'e tuh cum clear. Bes' t'ing kin do is hab patience and trus' oonuh fin' ansuh w'en time right."

It wasn't what I was hoping to hear. I took a slow sip of my tea. "I know you're probably right, but I was wishing you'd have a different answer for me."

She patted my knee. "If wishing could mek 'e so, we all be sitting in dey lap ub luxury!" She laughed joyously. "Good t'ing we don' hab dat kin' majic. De debble fin' 'e weh tuh us den. Mmm huh. 'E sho' nuff would!"

"I guess you're right. I just need to be patient and trust whatever is meant to happen, will happen. I'm just not particularly good at waiting when it's something I really want."

She looked at me through squinting eyes. "Uh 'membuh wen oonuh een he'lt' wid Frankie. Uh seen de signs 'fore dat, but t'ink 'e bes' say nutt'n'. Den w'en oonuh know, tek time tuh tell Jon. Attuhw'ile, say what know be true, but face look strick. Uh 'spect oonuh habn't study 'e head 'bout babies 'fo' dat. 'Ventually, Jon so happy 'e rub off joy on oonuh. Joy real attuhw'ile, but not tuhreckly. Maybe oonuh not sure 'bout dis one yet either. How oonuh husbun' feel 'bout 'e?"

I still found Mary's peculiar language difficult to understand at times, even after knowing her a few years. I gathered she was telling me it took me a while to come around to accepting and feeling happy about my first pregnancy, and that it was primarily Jon's excitement that rubbed off on me and changed the way I felt.

"He would love to have another baby. Jon is close to his younger sister, Jen, although they don't see much of each other these days. I think he would like to give Frankie a sibling to grow up with so they could be close like he and Jen used to be."

Mary nodded sagely. "Dat nice. Uh like w'en menfolk tek care ub dey siblin's. 'E mek dem mo' uh man een my eye." She stood up and brushed the wrinkles out of her apron. "Got tuh finish dey bittle fo' 'Enry lunch. Oonuh welcome tuh stay. Won' tek long."

I joined her in standing and shook my head. "Thanks, Mary. I'd love to stay, but I need some time to myself before I pick up Frankie. There are a lot of thoughts running around in my head that I need to try to sort out. I don't expect I'll manage to do that today. Once Frankie is around, I won't have a chance to think about anything but keeping up with him."

She laughed heartily. "Dat boy be a han' full, sho' be true! 'E got mo' energy dan all we gran'chillun an' great-grans put tuhgedduh. 'Cept maybe Neesie. Dem two mo' like dan not!"

Neesie was her youngest grandchild. I first met her when Julie and I came to dinner at their house. I remembered her as being so quiet at times she was almost invisible, yet so full of energy at other times it was like watching a small whirlwind. She was ten years old now. A lot older than Frankie, yet they seemed completely comfortable in each other's company.

I thanked her again as I left, accepting once more her bosomy embrace. Being wrapped in one of Mary's hugs was balm to my soul, and I lingered there for an extra few seconds.

I could feel her watching me as I made my way to my car, with Beau trotting beside me. I bent to rub my hands on either side of his head before opening the door. "Take care of that sweet woman, Beau." He whimpered and licked my hand. I waved goodbye to Mary and she lifted one hand in reply.

I glanced at my watch as I pulled out of their drive. I didn't have to pick up Frankie for another hour, which left me with an unexpected block of time to myself. The temperature had warmed considerably, so I decided to drive to a nearby beach. I headed in the direction of Fish Haul Beach, located on the "Achilles Heel" of the foot-shaped island, only a short distance from Mary's house. I first discovered this particular beach after attending a function with Mary and Henry at the First African Church on Beach City Road. The beach was located off the same road and could be reached by traveling a dirt road through a maritime forest abundant with Palmetto and Live Oak trees. The beach was also just northeast of the historic Mitchelville.

Mitchelville was established in 1862 by a Union soldier, General Ormsby Mitchel. It was created to serve as a freedmen's camp to shelter escaped slaves who were known at the time as "contrabands of war". It quickly evolved into a township with its own roads, houses, schools, churches, and local government. It was also recognized as the only known freedmen township to exist in the United States before the signing of the Emancipation Proclamation, and the more inclusive thirteenth Amendment to the Constitution.

I slowly made my way to Fish Haul Beach, being careful to avoid the frequent potholes marking my route. I stopped to park my car next to a leaf strewn path that I knew led to a boardwalk ending on the beach.

Unlike Coligny, where I spent the majority of my beach time, the beach at Fish Haul was fairly narrow, especially at high tide, making it less popular as a destination to haul beach chairs and blankets. It also wasn't very amenable to swimming given the swiftly flowing tide pools and underwater rock hazards. It was, however, a Mecca for spotting shorebirds of all types, or collecting shells of various sizes left behind with the receding tide. Fish Haul was also known for its seafood-rich shallow waters, which is likely what contributed to its name, as well as its popularity as a fishing spot for both birds and humans.

I stepped onto the sandy shore and paused to look up and down the beach. There were only a few other beachgoers visible, which allowed me the promise of the solitude I sought. I removed the light jacket I was wearing and tied it around my waist before heading north along the shore, picking my way carefully along the slightly sloped, rocky, and shell-strewn shore.

I walked for several minutes before reaching a spot where the beach rose upward to create a makeshift hill. I made my way to the top, stepping carefully over the beach grass until I reached a large rock. I settled into a concave groove on the rock face, turning toward the water so I could gaze out at the view. There were a few fishing boats visible in the distance, including one shrimp trawler easily recognized by the nets that protruded from either side like giant wings.

I once asked Henry to explain how the trawler works, and he told me the nets are suspended from outrigger or boom masts that are either dragged along the ocean floor or held midway depending upon where the most shrimp are thought to be located. Sometimes the nets rake in other things like prawns and fish. Unfortunately, sea turtles are also routinely caught up in the nets, often causing them to drown when they are unable to reach the surface for air.

I read somewhere that a couple of men were working on developing turtle excluder nets that allowed a captured turtle to escape when caught up in the ropes. As far as I knew, these devices were not widely used, which was likely because the shrimp catch would suffer as many of them escaped along with the turtles. I sympathized with the shrimpers who were only trying to make a living, but my stronger allegiance was with the sea turtles.

I shaded my eyes against the midday sun in order to scan the water more carefully behind the trawler. Trawlers were dolphin magnets. Since the nets are not particular about what they rake in, the fishermen on board are forced to sort through the catch, discarding the creatures they choose not to keep. As a result, the boats are popular with dolphins and a variety of shore birds who wisely follow along behind the boats waiting patiently to scoop up the discards.

There was a bevy of sea birds visible above the aft of the trawler. I couldn't make out what they were since they only appeared as dark images in the glare of the sun. I could also detect the rolling backs of a few dolphins in the water to the nearside and aft of the boat. The thought of Frankie and his fascination with dolphins prompted me to glance at my watch. I would have to hurry to be on time to pick him up. I rose reluctantly from my rock chair and walked quickly in the direction of my car.

CHAPTER THREE

It has been said that the weather in May on Hilton Head Island comes in like a lamb but begins roaring like a lion with the approach of June. I didn't really find this to be true. To me, the transition from Spring to Summer was subtle. The temperatures typically ranged from the low 60s to mid-80s in May, only warming by a few degrees with the arrival of June. Both months brought plenty of opportunity to enjoy the outdoors without much discomfort, except for the occasional spike in temperature, or the rarity of a rainy day. Sometimes, I welcomed rain on Hilton Head. It gave me an excuse to take care of indoor chores that, on a sunny day, seemed to rob me of time I would rather spend outside enjoying the natural beauty of the island.

The most noticeable difference between May and June was the increase in visitors to the island. I often heard the locals expressing disdain for the onslaught of tourists but having been one myself in the not-too-distant past, I tended to be more forgiving of their arrival. After all, without them, the businesses that depended upon their revenue would be hard pressed to stay afloat. I did find it somewhat challenging to cope with the recreational cyclists who grew in numbers as Summer approached. More times than I wanted to remember, I barely missed a head-on collision when one of them veered into my path or took a blind corner too fast. I added a bell to my handlebars shortly after moving to the island hoping it would be useful for alerting other riders of my presence. Unfortunately, it usually only served to make the other rider turn their head (and their bike) in my direction.

I developed a fondness for bicycling on the island during my first trip in 1974. At that time, the bicycle pathways were limited to those that lined the roads leading into and inside of Sea Pines and a few other private communities. Since then, the biking routes were expanded to include many more private and public areas. Bike riding along much of the 12 miles of beach was also an option, and one that I often preferred. This was especially true at low tide when the sand was wide and firmly packed. Of course, being mindful of which way the wind was blowing was essential. In the beginning of my beach bike riding days, I was tricked more than once into believing my round-trip ride would be easy because of the gentle breeze facing me as I headed out, not realizing that a strong headwind awaited me for the return trip.

On this particular June day, the blue sky overhead, and promise of a calm day in the mid-70s, had me pulling my bike out of our storage shed and heading for the beach. It was a rare mid-week "me" day, since Frankie's Daycare Center was taking the children on a field trip to the nearby island of Daufuskie.

Daufuskie Island was located between Hilton Head Island and Savannah, Georgia. Reaching Daufuskie required a ferry or private boat ride across the Calibogue Sound since there was no bridge connecting Daufuskie with Hilton Head, or any other location on the mainland. The island was mostly ignored prior to the publication of the memoir *The Water Is Wide* by author Pat Conroy in which he described his experiences teaching there in the 1960s. A lesser-known fact about Daufuskie is that it was the center of the "live oaking" trade in the late 1700s. This practice involved using timber from huge live oak trees to construct ships. I found it fascinating to learn that the USS Constitution, or "Old

Ironsides" as it is known, was constructed from live oaks harvested from Daufuskie Island.

Daufuskie Island was only 5 miles long and approximately 2.5 miles wide, with 3 miles of beachfront making it less than a third of the size of Hilton Head Island. It was also mostly undeveloped with few inhabitants and even fewer roads. Getting around on the island was on foot, on horseback, in carriages drawn by horses or cows, by bicycle, or in golf carts. There were a few cars, but they were used infrequently. Frankie's teacher had arranged for two golf carts to transport them to their beachfront picnic spot, located below the Bloody Point Lighthouse on the southern tip of the island. Its ominous name referred to several Indian battles which took place there in the early 1700s, although the lighthouse itself wasn't built until 1883. My one glance at the structure during a boat ride between Hilton Head Island and Savannah, revealed that it looked nothing like the lighthouses I was familiar with. It resembled a normal looking house, except a large dormer window jutted out from the roof. The tour guide on the boat ride explained how the dormer was opened at night, exposing a fixed reflexor lens that transformed the building into a lighthouse.

The lighthouse was originally located beachfront, but in the late 1890s, beach erosion caused the structure to be moved further inland. In the 1950s, part of it was converted into a small winery. Since that time, the lighthouse has been privately owned, and with no public dock nearby, it was necessary for a private tour to be arranged in order to view the grounds. The head teacher at Frankie's Daycare Center had family roots on Daufuskie, giving her an "in" to arrange the ferry ride, transportation to the former lighthouse, and a beachside picnic for the children. Frankie had been beside himself with excitement for the past week over the upcoming outing, and I had been inwardly jumping for joy at the unexpected day to myself.

I loaded the basket attached to the handlebars of my bike with a thermos of water and some snacks, then pushed it along the sandy path to the beach. Beach umbrellas were lined in a row on the sandy shore, their flaps indicating the direction of the wind. Since they hung still with barely any motion, I decided it was safe to expect an easy ride in either direction. I decided to head North, which I knew to be the quieter end of the beach. The location of the Holiday Inn and Sea Pines Resort to the South guaranteed a larger crowd, whereas the North was mostly populated by private residences.

The morning paper indicated that low tide would occur at approximately 11:15 a.m., with the high tide to follow about six and a half hours later. I knew from experience that the beach would be optimal for biking at least two hours before and after each low tide, which meant my 10 a.m. start would give me at least three hours of optimal riding time. I pulled my baseball cap more snugly onto my head and pushed against the pedals. The cap gave me added protection against the glare of the sun beaming down on me. The day was warm, with a forecast of reaching the mid-80s by early afternoon. I didn't mind the heat, especially since biking created its own natural breeze. But I was glad for the extra water I brought, and the sunscreen I had amply applied before leaving home.

I passed a few of the "regulars", as I thought of them, and greeted them with a wave. I didn't know any of them by name but recognized them from their usual beach routines. There was the newspaper man who walked back and forth from the Holiday Inn each morning holding a rolled-up newspaper. The dog people, a man and a woman who did not seem to belong to each other but who met regularly on their walks as their dogs trotted alongside. Then there was the yoga lady who was always perched in the same spot on a dune in front of the Sea Crest Motel, legs folded into a lotus pose as she gazed serenely out at the ocean.

I wondered if the regulars had a made-up name for me as well, and I briefly entertained myself imagining what it might be. Biking girl, or dolphin watcher were two of my favorites. It was just as likely they never thought of me at all, which suited me just fine. When I was off on one of my solitary beach outings, I much preferred to remain invisible, except to the shorebirds and sea creatures who allowed me to share their habitat.

About twenty minutes into my ride, I arrived at the part of the beach known as "The Folly". The name referred to an inlet of water south of the Folly Field community that cut a swath across the sand between Singleton and Burke's beaches. The Folly was impassible except at low tide, unless you didn't mind wading through knee deep swiftly moving water. There was still about six inches of water in the Folly when I reached it. I knew the water would soon recede leaving it mostly dry, and I calculated how long that would allow me to bike on the other side before the path would become swamped again. I decided to chance it and pedaled my way carefully across the stream. My bike was old and somewhat corroded from my numerous encounters with salty water, but I still made a mental note to thoroughly rinse it off once I returned home.

The beach on the other side of the Folly was spotted by several people who had staked out their space with an umbrella, sand chairs, and a cooler. A few cyclers were visible up and down the shore, as well as the usual shell seekers. I continued my ride for another thirty minutes until I reached the point where a sandbar stretched out across the expanse of water. At high tide, it was invisible except for the birds that chose to rest there. But today it stuck out of the surf like a long, narrow island.

I noticed two men standing along its length holding fishing poles, and three women walking in the exposed sand at the beginning of the bar, their bodies bent at the waist searching for treasures. I stopped and straddled my bike, pulling the thermos from the basket. After downing most of it, I grabbed a handful of nuts and raisins from a plastic bag, enjoying the comforting scene of life on our special island. A young boy ran past, laughing giddily as a man ran after him, grabbing him by the waist swinging him in a circle. The image of the two reminded me of Frankie and Jon, which made me smile. Jon was such a good father. Stern when he needed to be, but never without an undercoating of love and affection.

I realized I would need to head home soon. Jon offered to pick up Frankie since the Daycare outing would have him back at the Center around the time Jon would be leaving work. That left me plenty of time before they arrived at the house, but time and tide would fill the Folly if I didn't cross it within the next 45 minutes.

I pushed my bike South on the beach a short distance, allowing my eyes to drink in the view before hopping back on for the return trip.

When I reached the path in front of our house, the sun was directly overhead, and the temperature had warmed considerably. I pulled off my cap and ran my fingers through my damp hair. I glanced in the direction of the Tiki Hut beachfront bar in front of the Holiday Inn and made a sudden decision to delay my return home, deciding instead that one of their icy beverages was just what I needed to top off my bike ride.

I pulled up to a rack on the side of the bar and locked my bike securely before walking up the ramp to the Tiki Hut. There was a good-sized crowd already gathered. Most of them had claimed seats either at the rectangular wooden bar or at tables placed to take advantage of the shade from the thatched roof. I made my way to an empty seat at the bar. A bartender spotted me and came over to take my order.

"Hey there. What can I get for you?" He asked.

I wasn't usually what you'd call a day drinker. Alcohol in the daytime just made me sleepy, but I felt like treating myself to something special. "How about a Pina Colada?"

"Don't mind if I do." He gave me a wide grin as he wiped his hands on a dish towel. "I'll have that right up."

I shifted my stool so I could watch the volleyball game in the sand just in front of the Hut. A lot of the time, the sandy courts at the Tiki Hut drew a serious crowd of players, but today the four players just seemed intent on smashing one another with the ball before lapsing into a fit of laughter.

The sound of music wafted over me from the back of the Hut where a group of musicians was beginning their set. The bartender returned with my drink and I took a deep sip. Brain freeze! I had forgotten how much pain could be produced by drinking the frosty concoction too quickly! I pressed my hand against my forehead while I waited for the pain to subside.

"That always happens to me, too."

I turned to the lady sitting to my left. "I'm sorry. What did you say?"

"Brain freeze. Happens to me every time I try to drink one of those frozen things. That's why I stick to beer." She waggled her bottle before offering her hand. "Savannah."

I hesitated before returning her greeting. "Georgia."

"You're kidding, right?"

I took another small sip of my drink, remembering to press my tongue against the roof of my mouth to avoid the same fate as last time. "No, my name's really Georgia. Funny coincidence, huh?"

"You can say that again." She took a long swallow from her beer. "This your first time on Hilton Head?"

"No, I live here with my husband and our son. We have a house just down there." I pointed in the direction of the Sea Crest Motel.

"I live on Tybee. In case you don't know, it's an island just East of Savannah. I was born in Savannah, which is why my parents thought it would be cool to give me that as a first name. Were you born in Georgia?"

I shook my head. "My parents were big fans of the song *Georgia On My Mind*."

"Oh yeah! I have a record with Willie Nelson singing it. I love that song!"

"Me, too, but they fell in love with the version Hoagy Carmichael recorded. I believe that was in the 30s. Billie Holliday released her version in the 40s, followed by Ray Charles in the

60s. His recording is probably the most famous, but I love listening to Willie sing it, too."

We sat in silence for a couple of minutes, sipping our drinks and listening to the live music.

"Where did you live before you moved here?" She asked. "I'm assuming you moved here from somewhere else since that's true for most people I've met. It's not like the Savannah area where you can still meet a lot of locals whose family connections to the city date back many years. Hilton Head is more of a *came for vacation and decided to stay* place."

I swirled the straw in my drink. "That pretty much describes what happened to us, although it took a few trips here before we took the plunge to move. I was born in Nashville, Tennessee and lived there my whole life, until we moved here. I met my husband, Jon, when he moved to Nashville from Washington D.C. for work, and we were married about four years ago.

"We first came to Hilton Head in 1974 when some friends invited us to join them. I pretty much fell instantly in love with the place, though my husband took a while to warm up to it. Eventually, I guess he saw something about it that drew his interest. At least, from a business perspective. When his work situation in Nashville changed, he came up with the idea of getting into the real estate business here. At first, he was just going to go the buy-then-resell route, but the birth of our son caused him to rethink his plans. Now he works for one of the local real estate companies."

She nodded thoughtfully. "Makes sense. The housing market here has had its ups and downs, but it's supposed to be on the rebound now."

"He's been doing pretty well. Selling mostly to people from Northern states looking to relocate to a warmer climate. He seems to be getting a little restless lately. I suspect he'll be expanding into some other aspect of real estate before long."

We sat quietly for another minute before she turned to me abruptly. "Say! I know someone your husband might be interested

23

in talking to. My uncle–my dad's brother–has an investment company. I heard him tell my dad the other day they're awfully close to acquiring a large development that could prove to be extremely profitable for everyone involved. Apparently, one of his partners bowed out of the deal because he had to move back North. He said he wants to add another sharp and motivated realtor to replace that guy. Someone with an eagerness to dig into something new. I've never met your husband, but it sounds like he might fit the bill."

I flagged down the bartender and asked for a piece of paper and a pen. I placed them in front of Savannah. "Could you write down his name and number? I'll give it to Jon and see if he's interested in talking with your uncle."

"Sure." She tore the sheet in half and jotted down her uncle's info before handing both halves to me. "I put my name and number there, too. Why don't you write down your name and your husband's and the best phone number to reach both of you?" I did as she asked, returning my half of the sheet to her. She glanced at the paper before tucking it in her back pocket. "Well, I guess I'd better be going. I'm supposed to meet some friends in Savannah for a little shopping before I head back to Tybee, and I'd like to miss the off-island exodus." She climbed off her stool and tossed two dollars on the counter. "It was really nice to meet you, Georgia. Give me a call sometime if you want to get together. I come over to Hilton Head at least once a week, and the Tiki Hut is always on my list for a midday stop."

"I'd like that. And thanks for the suggestion about your uncle. I'll give his information to my husband."

She waved a final goodbye before heading for the parking lot. I finished my drink and listened to a couple more tunes from the band before settling my bill. What an interesting coincidence meeting Savannah, I thought. I couldn't wait to tell Jon about our conversation.

CHAPTER FOUR

I arrived home with a couple of free hours still ahead of me before Jon and Frankie were due to return and decided to treat myself to a relaxing bubble bath. Ebie stood watch from the edge of the tub as the water level rose. She seemed fascinated by the bubbles, which she kept trying to take a swipe at with one curved paw, almost toppling into the water in the process. When the tub was filled, I eased in and closed my eyes as the warmth enveloped me. I lay quietly for a few minutes until I heard a meek mew next to my ear. I opened my eyes to find Ebie perched on the back of the tub and leaning over my shoulder.

"I wouldn't do that if I were you. You're going to end up in the water, and I promise you won't like it." I pushed gently against her chest causing her to jump to the floor, before walking purposefully out the door. "You'll thank me later!" I called after her, chuckling at her ability to treat every situation as if it were all about her.

I settled back into the tub, allowing my mind to wander over the events of the day. The bike ride had been completely satisfying. Just enough of a challenge to leave me feeling pleasantly tired but not exhausted, and with sights and sounds that filled me with delight. *I'll have to tell Frankie about the shrimp boat,* I thought.

The bath water grew cooler, so I reluctantly pulled the chain to remove the plug from the drain. I grabbed my towel from the nearby bar, rubbing my skin vigorously.

I quickly dressed in clean clothes and padded barefoot into the kitchen to study the contents of the refrigerator. Finding nothing that appealed to me, I decided to walk to the Red and White to pick up some steaks and ingredients for a salad. Buying steaks meant Jon would likely take over the cooking duties once he arrived home, since he was the self-proclaimed grill master. I pulled on my sandals and closed the door behind me, admonishing Ebie to stand watch over the house. She opened one eye from her prone spot in a patch of sunshine before tucking her head under her front leg. "Okay, I get the message. I'll bring you back something special, too."

I learned to avoid grocery shopping on Saturday afternoons and Sunday mornings when the store filled with tourists hunting for things to tide them over during their vacation stay. But since it was Wednesday, I figured a shopping trip would be safe. There were a few people roaming the aisles when I arrived. Grabbing a shopping cart, I waved at one of the cashiers named Jody, whose cousin had sold our house to us. I headed for the produce section, selecting what I would need for the salad before heading to the back of the store. I added three T-bone steaks to the cart then pushed my way to the seafood counter where David, the owner's son, could usually be found. When I first met him, he was working part-time at the store during school breaks. Since graduating, he had been taking a more active role in the everyday activities of the store.

I spotted his baseball-cap covered head peeking up from behind the seafood case and waved in greeting.

"Miss Georgia! How are things today?"

"Great! I took a nice bike ride, then had a drink at the Tiki Hut. Just came by to pick up some things for dinner."

He walked around the seafood counter and peered down into my shopping basket. "Looks like Mr. Jon will be doing the cooking tonight." He looked up at me with a mischievous grin. David had been to dinner at our house a couple of times and knew the grilling duties were always Jon's. "You might want to consider some fresh fish to replace those T-bones, or at least add to them. A local guy brought in some Redfish he caught this morning from the in-shore grass flats. It's as fresh as you can get."

I walked over to the display case with him and examined the fish he mentioned. I also noticed a good number of gray-brown shrimp in the other end of the case. "Are the shrimp local? I thought the season didn't start until later in the Summer."

"That's true for white shrimp, but the brown ones start showing up in May. The white ones are large and tender with a milder flavor. Brown shrimp are smaller, with a firmer texture and stronger flavor. A lot of folks prefer the white, which is why they cost more."

"I saw a trawler off Port Royal beach this morning."

"Must have been Brandon on the *Carolina Girl*. That's where the shrimp came from. He brings them in the afternoon, and heads back out early the next morning. Unfortunately, he's known for pulling in a load of roe and immature white shrimp mixed with the brown. Makes the other shrimpers mad."

His comment puzzled me. "Isn't roe the same thing as fish eggs?"

He smiled. "Not exactly. It's true that fish eggs are called roe, or caviar if you buy it in those little tin cans or jars that cost a small fortune in specialty shops. Fish carry their eggs inside, whereas shrimp roe is on the underside of their bodies. The male shrimp mates with a female and transfers sperm to a sac on the female's abdomen. That's called spawning. Between six and twenty hours later, the female begins to produce roe. After they develop, the fertilized eggs are released and hatch into larvae. The larvae go through several transformations for a month to month and a half, after which they become tiny shrimp. They don't fully mature for another four to six months. That is, if they manage to

27

live that long. Brown shrimp typically spawn in the Fall and mature in time for the Summer season. White shrimp spawn in the Spring for the Fall season. If a trawler rakes up the roe or the immature white shrimp with the rest of the haul it could greatly impact the seasonal profit for all the shrimpers."

"I can see why that would make the shrimpers pretty upset. So, why does Brandon do that? Trawl so early he risks the catch for everyone?"

He shrugged. "Some say greed, but my bet is he's just trying his best to scrap out a living. The whole industry has suffered in recent years because of imported shrimp, and most captains have to hold off-season jobs to get by. The number of shrimpers has been in a slow decline for years as captain after captain has given up the trade. Brandon is one of the ones who has hung on, but he's barely getting by. He's a good guy. I don't think he'd intentionally do anything to harm the season unless he didn't see any way around it."

I turned my attention back to the display case. "I'm sure the Redfish are great, but I have my heart set on steak, and I think both would be a bit much. How about a pound of the shrimp, though?"

"Surf and turf. You can't beat that." He moved behind the counter and scooped shrimp into a plastic bag before weighing it on a metal scale hanging nearby. His years of experience were evident as he only added a couple more shrimp to reach a pound. He closed the bag and wrapped it in brown paper, marking the price on the outside. "Don't forget the lemon, and tell Mr. Jon I said hello." He handed me the package with a smile. The first time I met David, he was working behind the seafood case, and he admonished me to remember to buy lemon to go with my shrimp. It had become a running joke between us since then.

I waved the bag at him and headed for the produce section.

It was late afternoon by the time I returned from the store. Jon and Frankie would be home around four, so I set about peeling and deveining the shrimp before cutting up the vegetables for the salad. I was wiping off the countertop when I heard the front door open.

"Mommy, Mommy! Look what I drew!" Frankie ran into the kitchen waving a large sheet of paper. I studied it carefully. It was a drawing of a house, with a porch lined with rocking chairs, and one large window protruding from the roof. Stick-figure children covered the yard. Some appeared to be playing ball, while others held hands in a circle. A taller, female figure stood in the middle of the yard.

"Why, this is wonderful, sweetie! Are you in this picture?"

He nodded emphatically and pointed. "Dat's me ober dere. See? I'm next to the tree."

There was a figure with tousled, black hair sitting under a tree. I could tell it was meant to be Frankie because he was wearing his favorite Superman t-shirt. He appeared to be looking away from the house. I started to ask him about the drawing when Jon entered the room.

"I'm starved! What are we having for dinner?" He walked up beside me and drew me into an embrace. I could smell the musky sweatiness of him, mixed with his particularly unique scent of leather and aftershave.

"I picked up some steak and shrimp from the Red and White. I thought you could grill them while I finish the salad."

"That sounds great. Just let me clean up a little first. I've been tromping all over the island today showing beachfront houses to a couple from New Jersey. They weren't satisfied just seeing the inside of the houses. I must have logged twice as many miles showing them each and every beach from Port Royal to Land's End. If I'd known what they had in mind, I would have worn my boots." He lifted one foot to display his sand crusted leather dress shoes.

"I'll fix us a drink while you change. Scotch okay?"

"You know it. I'll be back in a jiff. Frankie, slip off your sneakers. I'll take our shoes out back and try to get the sand off."

"Just leave them at the back door. I'll use the whisk broom to clean them before I start on the drinks."

The guys pulled off their shoes, leaving them in a sandy pile in the kitchen before heading down the hall to the bedrooms. I smiled at the sandy trail that stretched from the front door to their shoes before heading to the pantry to get a broom and dustpan.

By the time I returned to the kitchen, Jon had changed into a pair of khaki shorts and an untucked white polo shirt. He was standing at the counter filling two glasses and a plastic cup with ice. He took a pitcher of lemonade from the refrigerator and placed it next to the cup. "Gin and tonic? Extra lime?" He looked at me.

"Yes, thanks. Sorry. I didn't have time to fix our drinks yet."

"No need to apologize. I'm the one who left you with our mess. We should have taken off our shoes before coming into the house. Frankie was so excited to show you his picture, he was in the door before I could stop him." He took the Scotch and Gin from an upper cabinet and reached into the refrigerator for the tonic and a lime. I leaned against the kitchen counter watching him, remembering the first time I tasted what was now one of my favorite summer drinks. We were at a restaurant in Nashville called Ireland's. It wasn't the first time we had gone out together, but it was the first time we called it an official date. Jon suggested I try a Gin and Tonic, and I was delighted at the refreshing taste. He ordered it with extra lime, which had since become our private saying for remembering the evening. It suddenly occurred to me that at least two of the special events in my life had been marked by citrus fruits! I smiled at the thought.

"Did Frankie seem to have a good time today? I didn't get a chance to ask him."

"I think so. They had a picnic near the Bloody Point Lighthouse. His teacher told the children a ghost story about how the lighthouse got its name, which Frankie thought was so cool. The sentiment wasn't shared by all of the kids, however. A few of them broke down in tears and refused to go into the house, even to use the bathroom. The teacher had to take them out back in the woods, which Frankie thought was hilarious. He kept talking about a man he met there, too, although I don't recall seeing any other adults when they arrived back at the Daycare Center. It must have been someone who worked at the Lighthouse. You know it's privately owned these days."

I nodded. "I read about that in the *Island Packet*. It was part of an expose about Pat Conroy, the author. You know he used to teach school on Daufuskie."

"Yeah, he wrote a memoir about his teaching experiences there. What was it called?"

"*The Water Is Wide*. It was adapted as a film around the time we first visited Hilton Head. It was called *Conrack* because that was what his students called him. Julie and I saw it at the Belcourt Theater in Nashville after we returned from that trip. It opened my eyes to the racism he had to deal with in the public-school system. Not that I was completely unaware of it. I was just surprised to see how strong it was, even in a school that tiny, with only Black students."

"Not unlike a lot of other places at the time, especially in the South." He placed my drink on the counter beside me and took a sip from his own. "Umm. That hits the spot." He grabbed a plate from the kitchen cabinet and unwrapped the steaks, adding a generous dose of salt, pepper, and garlic powder to each side. "I'm going to fire up the grill while the steaks are resting. Come on out and join me when you're ready."

I finished placing the salad ingredients in a large bowl and set it aside before unwrapping a sheet of aluminum foil from a box I kept in the pantry. I carefully placed a loaf of Italian bread down

31

its center, marking cuts partway through the bread every couple of inches then inserted a chunk of butter into each cut before loosely wrapping the loaf in the foil. I had just placed it in the oven to warm when Frankie ran into the room.

"Oh! Honey, you startled me! Where are you rushing off to?"

"I need tuh give something to you, Mommy. The man said to, but I forgot." He held both hands up for my inspection.

I leaned forward in order to better see what he was holding. It was a small, opaque glass bottle with a screw top. I held it up to the light. "What's in it?"

"De man say it's oil for you to rub on that little red sack you hab. He said de sack is hungry and dis will feed it."

I almost dropped the bottle as his words sank in. The sack he was referring to must be the amulet the ghost of Miss Bessie had given me years earlier. *But who was this man, how did he know about the amulet, and more importantly, how did he know Frankie was my son?* A shiver ran up my spine.

"Frankie, who was this man? Did he tell you his name?"

He stood on one leg and fiddled with the hem of his t-shirt. "I don't think so. He was in the woods where we were playing. I went to fetch my ball, and he grabbed me by the arm. I thought he was going to get mad at me for losing the ball, but he just pressed this into my hand and told me to give it to you and what you was to do wid it." His round eyes looked up into mine. "Are you mad at me, Mommy?"

My heart nearly broke at seeing his concern. "No, Sweetie. I'm not mad at you. But it worries me that you went into the woods by yourself. Did you tell your teacher about the man?"

He shook his head. "I was 'fraid to. She told us not tuh go into the woods by ourselves, but I forgot. I just wanted to get the ball."

I crouched down so I could look him in the eyes. "It's important for you to listen to your teacher and do what she says. Something bad could have happened to you, and your Daddy and I would have been very, very sad."

His lips formed a pout. "I sorry, Mommy."

I pulled him into my arms for a hug and then stood. "What did the man look like?"

He began to swing his arms from side to side. "Big. Like Daddy. Only he was dark, like Uncle Henry. His hand felt rough where it held my arm, but his eyes was sweet, like Aunt Mary." He stopped swinging and smiled. "I wasn't 'fraid, Mommy. He was real nice."

His description relieved some of my concern. There was still the issue of how he knew who Frankie was, and that I had the amulet. I decided not to say anything else about the matter to Frankie. "Why don't I pour you some lemonade, and you can go watch TV for a little while before dinner?" I took the plastic cup of ice Jon had prepared and filled it halfway with lemonade before handing it to Frankie. "Be careful it doesn't spill." He held the cup in both hands and walked slowly in the direction of the living room.

I waited until he was out of sight then unscrewed the top of the bottle, taking a sniff of the contents. It smelled strongly of lemon with an overtone of something slightly sweet and musky, almost like wet soil. Frankie said it was supposed to feed the amulet. I wasn't sure what that meant, but it sounded ominous. I screwed the cap on tightly and placed it in the kitchen cabinet out of Frankie's reach before going to join Jon on the deck.

CHAPTER FIVE

The questions I had about the man in the woods and his odd gift continued to nag me for several days. I finally gave in and called Mary. She told me she was planning to be at Henry's store later that afternoon and suggested I stop by. I did my best to distract myself until it was time to meet her, but by the time I arrived at the store, I was a bundle of nerves. I quickly made my way inside and looked around for Mary. She was nowhere in sight, but I spotted Henry bent over the metal drink cooler, placing bottles into its depths. He straightened up when he heard the screen door close and smiled at me warmly.

"Glad fuh see oonuh! Mary be right back. 'E jes gone tuh see 'bout dey fish we grandson ketch dis mawnin'." He gestured in the direction of the cooler. "Why don' oonuh hab sump'in' cold tuh drink? De day gone hot."

I walked to the cooler and studied its contents, pulling an icy bottle of orange soda from the case. Henry nodded his approval and took the bottle from me so he could pop the top off on a metal opener attached to the front counter. He handed the bottle back to me and I took a swig, relishing in the sweet, refreshing flavor.

"Umm, that's nice. Thanks, Henry."

He studied me for a moment. "'Peers dere's sum'tin' hebby een oonuh min'."

I nodded. "Something happened to Frankie when his teacher at the Daycare Center took the class on a picnic to Daufuskie Island. I was hoping to talk it over with Mary. With you, too, if you have the time."

His eyes squinted in concern. "Always hab time fuh oonuh." He looked up as Mary entered the back door. Her face broke into a huge grin as she held her arms out wide.

"Blessit chile! Cum gib Mary a big hug!"

I walked into her waiting embrace. She swung me gently from side to side before releasing me, holding me at arms' length while she looked deep into my eyes. "Les go tuh de porch where dere's a breeze. 'Enry, bring sum col' water wid oonuh." She eyed my soft drink. "My di'betes won' 'low me tuh 'joy dem sweet ones, but col' water go down jes' fine."

Mary and I made our way out to the porch where we settled into the two worn rocking chairs on either side of the door. Henry joined us, dragging a third chair across from where we sat. He handed Mary her water and eased onto the seat. The three of us sat quietly for a minute sipping our drinks and looking out at the cars that passed along the road in front of the store. Finally, Mary broke the silence.

"No need tuh worry 'bout wha' een oonuh min'. Jes let de words cum loose."

I cleared my throat. "There was a man in the woods near where Frankie's class was having a picnic over on Daufuskie. It was in front of the Bloody Point Lighthouse. Frankie ran into the woods to get a ball, and the man grabbed him by the arm and handed him a little glass bottle filled with some sort of liquid. He told Frankie he should give it to me to feed my amulet. I sniffed it, and it reminded me of a mixture of lemon and wet dirt. I wasn't sure what I should do with it." I reached in my purse and pulled out the bottle, holding it up for their inspection.

Mary leaned forward and took the bottle from my hand. She unscrewed the top and sniffed the contents before handing it to Henry. "Dis wha' dey call cawndition oil. Mos' likely mek wid lemon verbena and patchouli. Root doctors use 'e tuh feed de mojo bag, de amulet. Bags lose strengk ober time. Sum'tim pour liddle w'iskey on de bag to keep 'e strong, but de oil wu'k better."

I frowned at her description. "Okay, you lost me there. What is a root doctor, and does that mean this is made from roots?"

"Root doctor also caw'd jujuman, conjure man, or witch doctor. We tink of dem as sum com'nation ub reb'ren' an' doctor. Dey kin work magic fo' ebil or good. Wen only do good, call by name *Nganga*. Mek cawndition oil wid roots, plants, oils, herbs, udder tings. Wha' dey use depend on wha' magic dey try tuh mek."

What she was describing was completely foreign to me, but I was getting used to feeling that way whenever we talked about spirits or Gullah ways. "The man told Frankie that what's in the bottle will help the amulet regain its strength. I guess that means it can start doing what it's supposed to do. What I don't understand is how it could lose strength? Did I do something wrong?"

"Eef tetch too much, 'speshily by folks not de ohnuh ub de bag; ken lose strengk. Ober time, eben do nuttin', still lose strengk. De oil act luk bittle fo' de bag. 'Ventually get strengk 'gen."

Henry nodded his agreement and handed the bottle back to me. "All kin' cawndition oils. Dis one all-purpose protekshun. Wha' oonuh ask ub de bag, 'e ansuh mo' clear attuh feed wid de oil."

I studied the bottle in my hand. I wondered if that was why the amulet had been so silent in recent months, even when I asked it repeatedly to tell me if I was to have another child. The thought that the contents of the bottle might help me with my dilemma gave me a sense of hope. But it was tainted by the unanswered questions surrounding the appearance of the man in the woods.

"Do you think the man who gave this to Frankie was a root doctor? Frankie said he wasn't afraid of the man. He said he seemed kind. But the whole idea that a stranger knew about my having the amulet, and that Frankie was my son, just gives me the creeps." I shivered in spite of the heat of the day.

Mary slowly rocked back and forth. "Uh huh. 'Spec' 'e would. Uh heard 'bout uh root doctor ober 'Fuskie. 'E 'sposed tuh hab strong Hoodoo. 'Fren down de chu'ch say 'e meet 'e once. Wen' tuh 'Fuskie fo' healin' time attuh 'e lose 'e hus'bun. Root doctor gib 'e oil wid honeysuckle, rose, cinnamon. 'E called Come to Me oil. Few weeks go by, 'e fin' lub 'gin. Haa't still miss hus'bun, but now 'e not so hebby."

"But how did this Root Doctor know about me? I've never even been to Daufuskie."

"Don' need tuh tek steps weh 'e lib fo' 'e tuh know oonuh haa't. Root doctors conjure t'ings from de wind. Hear t'ings een de trees. Smell 'e een de lan'. 'E likely hab knowledge ub oonuh f'um Miss Bessie, too. Sperrits communicate aw kinda ways. Een dis worl' or next."

Henry stood and rested his hands on the back of the chair, looking at Mary, then me. "Lot's ub t'ings can't 'splain 'do' still true. Uh bleebe 'e mek gift tuh oonuh. Don' know why de chil' in de middle, but sho' dere good ansuh. Oonuh 'member wha' Bessie say? Jes trust de heart. Dat wha' uh t'ink best 'vice 'gen."

Yes. That's what Miss Bessie said to me in the cemetery just before she disappeared for the last time. Jes trust de heart. Sometimes I managed to remember her advice and follow it, but just as often I found myself doubting what I felt.

"Good advice; hard to follow." I looked at Mary and Henry for confirmation.

Mary nodded. "Dat sho'nuff be true. 'Specially wen 'e be 'po'tant."

Henry slapped the back of his chair. "Got sumpin tuh gib oonuh. Be back tuhreckly." He opened the screen door and went inside, returning soon with a small paper-wrapped item in his hand. "Jes 'membuh uh hab dis. Gib tuh me lon' time 'go by conjure 'ooman. 'E tell uh gib luck wen seem gone. Neber use 'e since den. Tink maybe 'e be fuh oonuh."

I took the item from his outstretched hand and carefully unwrapped it. There was a small stone inside that fit neatly into the palm of my hand. It was nearly black in color and rough in texture. Tiny bits of what looked like metal threads clung to its surface in spots. I could feel a slight tingle in the tips of my fingers when I touched them.

"Caw 'e lodestone. Hab magnetic power. Mos' folks use dem tuh collect nails and udder metal t'ings. But hab power tuh hep wid spells. Keep 'e near oonuh mojo bag, 'e gib mo' strengk. Jes nebbuh put een watuh. Wash een w'iskey if need tuh, or sum dat oil in de boddle. Cum full moon, lay een de light till mawnin'. Grow stronger dat wey."

I studied the rock a moment longer before wrapping it back in the paper. "Thank you, Henry. I can't tell you how much it means to me that you gave me this. Both of you are always so kind to me. I'm still not sure what to make of what happened to Frankie in the woods, but you've given me some sense of relief that whatever happened was meant to be helpful." I glanced at my watch and stood. "I'd better be going. I've taken enough of your time. I need to pick up Frankie soon."

Mary laid one hand on my arm. "Oonuh gib dat liddle boy a big hug fum me. 'E special. Fact dat 'e meet dis conjurer show de trute ub dat eben mo'."

I smiled and rested my hand on top of hers. "I think that's what scares me the most: why Frankie is a part of this, whatever this is."

Henry took my arm as we walked to my car. "Tell Jon us need tuh talk soon. Hab uh notion ub sumt'in' 'e might fin' useful."

I squeezed his arm and reached to open my car door. "I will. I'm sure he'll give you a call."

I arrived at the Daycare Center just as the children were collecting their things to leave. Frankie ran to me shouting something I couldn't quite hear.

"Slow down, Sweetheart. I couldn't understand what you were saying."

He paused a moment to catch his breath. "I made a new friend, and I want you tuh meet him." He turned and looked over his shoulder, waving frantically at a boy who stood near the entrance to the Center. "Tommy! Come here and meet my Mommy!" He kept waving until the boy began to make his way in our direction. He stopped a few paces from where we stood and regarded us with a shy smile. Frankie took his arm, pulling him closer. "This is Tommy. Him and me hab the same birfday!" He grinned at his new friend.

"Is that right? Well, that's certainly a special coincidence."

What's a quinsedance, Mommy?"

"It means something good happens by accident."

He nodded sagely. "Kind of like when you and Daddy met?"

We told him the story several times of how Jon and I met at the Belle Meade Mansion ball, and how what seemed at first to be a fiasco, turned into a special twist of fate. "Yes, kind of like that. Tommy, have you lived on Hilton Head Island very long?"

Tommy shuffled his feet and shook his head. "No Ma'am. We moved here from Ohio last month. My daddy worked for the 'lectric company. A man came around asking if anybody wanted to live in a warmer place. Daddy said no, but my momma told him he'd better change his mind, or she'd have to move here without him."

I laughed at his story. "Smart woman." I placed my hand on Frankie's head. "Sweetheart, can you wait here a few minutes with Tommy? I need to talk to Miss Browne." Miss Browne was Frankie's teacher at the Daycare Center.

"Okay, Mommy. Can Tommy and I go over to the swings?"

"Just be sure you don't leave the schoolyard." They ran off hand in hand.

I looked around the yard to locate Miss Browne and spotted her standing with a small group of children a short distance away. She waved as I began to walk in her direction.

"Hello, Mrs. Barnett. How are you today?"

"I'm fine, Miss Browne. Do you have a minute? I need to talk with you about something."

"Certainly. Why don't we speak over here?" She gestured toward the side of the building away from any other listeners. When we were settled, she turned to me with a curious look. "What can I do for you?"

"It's about the trip to Daufuskie. Frankie told me he met a man in the woods. I wondered if you saw a man near where the children were playing?"

She looked at me with alarm. "A man? No! There weren't any other adults there that day except for me and my assistant, Jean. What did he say about the man?"

"Frankie ran after a ball that went into the woods. He ran into a man there, who took him by the arm, and handed him something to give to me. Frankie said he was nice. He wasn't afraid of him, but it troubled me. I was just wondering if you knew anything about it."

She shook her head. "I'm so sorry. I clearly told the children NOT to go into the woods. I was concerned about them coming across a snake or alligator, but certainly not a man. Did Frankie describe what he looked like?"

I thought back to what Frankie said. "Tall and dark-skinned, with kind eyes. That's all he told me about him. He gave him a little bottle of liquid, saying I should use it to strengthen an amulet I've had for a few years." I hesitated to tell her that last bit of information, but I felt it could be important.

"An amulet, you say? Where did you get it?"

I paused before answering. "Let's just say it was given to me in an unusual set of circumstances."

Her brow furrowed as she nodded slowly. "I see."

I waited for her to say more, but she remained silent.

"What are you thinking?" I asked.

"Nothing, really. I was just remembering something I heard some time ago from one of my relatives. My family has roots going back several generations on Daufuskie Island. An uncle told me about a man who was considered a healer. He used potions of various herbs and oils depending upon what ailed a person. Some folks called him conjure man. More generally, he was known as a root doctor".

Her comments reminded me of what Mary and Henry had said. "Could that be the man Frankie saw?"

She shook her head. "He's been long dead by now. Although, I suppose it's possible he could be related to the man in the woods. That is, if the man Frankie met is also a root doctor. The healing powers tend to be passed on within families." Her expression grew thoughtful. "You said you were given the amulet under unusual circumstances. Was the person who gave it to you alive or dead?"

Her question surprised me. "At first, I thought she was alive, but I finally understood I was seeing her spirit; her ghost-self. It took me a while to believe that was true, but eventually there was no denying it."

"I see. What did she tell you to do with the amulet?"

"She said it would help me know what to do. I thought she was referring to my relationship with Jon. He's my husband now, but we were just dating then. Later on, I understood she was referring to other matters in my life, as well. I've been trying to use it lately to help me with something, but it hasn't seemed to respond. I'm hoping the potion Frankie passed on to me will help." I wondered what she would make of what I was saying, because it sounded bizarre even to my own ears.

She twisted a strand of hair behind her ear and stared at the ground. "This might sound crazy, but it's quite possible the spirit you communicated with has been in touch with the man your son saw. Root doctors don't just make potions to help the living, they also receive messages from those who have crossed over. Quite often, the deceased lets the root doctor know what kind of help is needed. That enables the conjure man, or woman, to concoct the right potion."

"That's hard for me to swallow, but no more so than when I first met the ghost I mentioned. Some friends recently reminded me of the last message I received from her–the ghost, I mean. Her name was Bessie. She said I should trust my heart. That could relate to a lot of different things in my life, but I guess it must mean, whatever the issue, I should get out of my head, and look inward for guidance." I looked off in the direction of the swings to assure myself Frankie was okay. "I'd better collect Frankie and head home. I really appreciate you taking time to talk to me."

She shrugged with a smile. "It's not every day someone asks me to interpret an encounter of this type. It helps me remember there's more going on in this life than just what is obvious. My belief in these things used to be strong. But more recently I find myself having more doubt than trust in their validity. I guess I need to work on that."

I called to Frankie. He looked at me reluctantly. "Can't we play a little longer, Mommy?"

"I'm sorry Sweetheart, but we need to go. Maybe I can talk with Tommy's mother sometime and arrange for him to come over to our house."

The boys grinned at each other. We climbed into the car and started for home with Frankie waving frantically out the window until Tommy was out of sight. It warmed my heart to see him so happy.

"You and Tommy really seemed to hit it off."

"He's my BEST friend. I want him to come live wid us."

I looked at him in surprise. Frankie was the type of child who made friends easily, but I never heard him proclaim such a special fondness for anyone before Tommy.

"I'm happy you've made a new friend. I know it's hard to say goodbye, but at least you'll see him at the Center tomorrow."

He frowned. "Are you and Daddy going to have a baby?"

His question startled me. "Where did you get that idea?"

"I heard the two of you talking 'bout it. Daddy said he wanted one 'cos it would be good for me to hab a sister or brother."

I would have to remind Jon about Frankie's stellar hearing, especially when we were discussing something we didn't really want him to hear. "We've thought about having a baby, but that's not something we can necessarily control. Sometimes mommies and daddies want a child, but it doesn't happen. All we can do is wait and see."

He reached across the front seat and lay his little hand on my arm. "That's okay, Mommy. Tommy can be my brother, and I don't really need a sister. Girls are weird!"

I smiled at him. "Oh really? But Mommy's a girl."

His eyes grew big. "No, you're not. You're a mommy. That's different."

I pulled into our driveway and turned off the car. Jon's Mercedes was already parked under the carport.

"Daddy's home. Why don't you go say hello to him, then wash up for dinner?"

He hopped out of the car and ran up the steps to the front door.

I remained in the car for a couple of minutes, allowing my mind to rehash my conversation with Henry and Mary; the discussion with Miss Browne; and Frankie's comments about wanting a sibling. Life sure had a way of getting complicated when I least expected it. This day had certainly proven that to be true.

CHAPTER SIX

I awoke the next day to the sound of rain drumming against our windows. Rain had been scarce through much of May, but it returned with a vengeance during the first week of June. I looked out the back door, considering whether or not to venture out for my usual early morning walk, finally giving in to common sense with only a little regret. Sometimes, a rainy morning gave me a good excuse to break my routine. I decided to surprise Jon by making coffee and getting a head-start on breakfast. Both tasks usually fell to him, since he typically awoke around the time I left for my morning walk.

I pulled on my robe and headed for the kitchen. It wasn't really chilly in the house, but the rain gave the impression of coolness. I started the coffee and set out cups and bowls for cereal. I removed a bowl of fresh cut fruit from the refrigerator, setting it on the table along with a carton of milk, three spoons, and a glass of orange juice for Frankie.

A sleepy Jon appeared. "Good morning. I guess the rain kept you inside today."

"Yeah. I thought about going out but decided against it. I'm hoping it will let up a little later so I can still get in a walk." The coffee had finished brewing, and I lifted the pot. "Coffee?"

"Please." He opened the front door and snagged the plastic covered morning paper off the top step. He tossed the wrapping in the trash and sat at the kitchen table, unfurling the paper.

When we first moved to Hilton Head, I wrote a column for the local paper that focused on the lives of local and regional personalities. Most of the people I interviewed were involved in education on some level. The column was an idea cooked up by Jon and Thomas Bookman, my former boss at Belmont College in Nashville. Thomas was a keen advocate of New Journalism; a style of reporting that makes nonfiction read like a good short story. The column was intended to serve as an avenue for bringing attention to this journalistic style, while heralding the activities of notable educators across the South.

My work with the paper fizzled out after Frankie was born. Not only because raising him took a great deal of my time, but I also realized my heart just wasn't in the work. In a rare moment of clarity, I had decided to jis' trus' de heart, and with Jon's blessing, terminated my column. I hadn't found anything to replace it yet. Not that I was trying very hard. I guess I was still searching for my calling, as I sometimes thought of it. But I didn't worry so much about what that was anymore. Life on Hilton Head was good, and it was reward enough just to spend time exploring the island.

Jon looked up from the paper. "I can give Frankie a ride to the Center this morning."

"Oh, great. What do you have going on today?"

"Not much. There's a meeting at the Town Hall I want to attend. They'll be addressing plans for developing some of the vacant land on the island, and I thought it might be worth listening. A little later, I'm meeting a couple of prospective buyers to show them some property. They seem to be more interested in looking than buying, but I'm hoping I can change their minds."

His comments reminded me of Henry's request. "I forgot to mention that Henry wants you to give him a call. He said he has an idea you may be interested in."

He squinted at me over the top of the paper. "Hunh. I wonder what that's about."

I shrugged. "That's all he said. I also met a woman at the Tiki Hut the other day, and she gave me the name of her uncle and a number you can use to reach him. Apparently, he has some sort of real estate venture he's been exploring, and he's looking to add another realtor to his roster." I walked into the bedroom and retrieved the paper where she had written the information, handing it to him.

He glanced at the paper before tucking it in the front pocket of his shirt. "I'll check it out." He took a sip of coffee.

Frankie walked into the kitchen clutching his stuffed dolphin and climbed onto his chair. I brushed the hair from his face and kissed him on the cheek. "Good morning, sleepy head. Did you sleep well?"

"Uh huh. But Dolf said the rain woke him up." He placed his stuffed friend on his lap and picked up his glass of juice.

I filled his bowl with cereal and topped it with some of the fruit before adding milk. He dug in and began crunching his way through the bowl. I waited for Jon to finish his cup of coffee before pouring cereal into his bowl. I did the same with mine and added fruit to both. Jon picked up his spoon and looked over at Frankie, who had made fast work of finishing off his breakfast. "Frankie-boy, go brush your teeth and meet me back here in a jiff."

Frankie jumped from his chair and trotted off in the direction of the bathroom.

Jon finished his breakfast then carried his and Frankie's dishes to the sink. "What do you have planned for the day?"

I stretched my arms overhead and grinned at him. "Since I have an unexpected free morning, I think I'll take a leisurely bath, then read a while."

He walked behind my chair and planted a kiss on top of my head. "Sounds grueling. Are you sure you have enough energy for all that?" His mouth twisted into a smirk.

"If not, I just may have to take a nap, too." I added another scoop of fruit to my bowl. "Do you want me to pick up Frankie this afternoon?"

He considered my question. "That's probably a good idea. I don't know how long I'll have to be with the prospective buyers. I'll give you a call when I finish up."

Jon disappeared down the hall just as Frankie re-entered the kitchen. "Mommy, kin Tommy come over to play this afternoon?" His eyes looked up at me hopefully.

"I need to talk to his mother first. Maybe we can see her when I come to pick you up."

"'Kay." He ran to the living room, returning with his rather bedraggled gray dolphin. "Miss Browne say'd we kin bring something to show and tell today. I want to bring Dolf."

"Are you sure you wouldn't rather bring your bear or that cute dog Aunt Julie gave you?"

He shook his head vigorously. "Dolf is my best one. I told Tommy I'd bring 'em."

I started to voice my concern about the appearance of the stuffed animal, but Jon stopped me with a hand on my shoulder. "That's one you won't win, I'm afraid. Best to just let it go." He clapped his hands. "Ready, Frankie? Head 'em up and move 'em out!" Frankie grinned and ran for the door, yelling yay! as he left.

I waved at Jon and smiled as he caught up to Frankie. Taking him by the hand as they made their way down the front steps.

The house felt blissfully quiet in the aftermath of all the morning activity. I walked to the coffee pot for a refill, then went to start the water in the tub. I added some relaxing lavender bath salts to the tub. Settling into the water, I closed my eyes in pleasure as I settled my head against the back. Ebie stared at me from the open door at one point, but wisely chose not to repeat her near miss of nose diving into the tub on the last occasion of my bubble bath. When I finished my soak, I dried off and rummaged in our bedroom closet for my most comfortable sweat suit then walked back into the living room.

There was a slight chill in the air, so I decided to light a fire in the brick fireplace. When we first discussed renovating the house, I balked at Jon's suggestion of adding a fireplace, thinking it would be unnecessary in a beach house. Luckily, his persistence paid off, and we enjoyed many days and nights in front of its warm glow. It was most welcome during the winter months, but I also appreciated it on days like this when the air was chilled by the lingering rain.

I lit a match to the waiting logs and settled onto the sofa with a novel. I hadn't even finished a page before the telephone demanded my attention.

"Hello?"

"Hey, Georgia. You want some company?"

I recognized Julie's voice immediately. "Sure! I'll just put on another pot of coffee, and you can grab a Coke out of the fridge." Julie didn't like the taste of coffee, and caffeine gave her the jitters. But she loved the taste of Coke.

"A glass of wine would be more like it."

I frowned. "In the morning? That's not like you."

"No, it's not, but it IS like me in the evening, which is when I'll be arriving."

I sat up straight. "You're coming here? Tonight?"

She laughed. "I know! It's a big surprise to me, too. Harry has a meeting in Savannah tomorrow. His boss–my dad–just sprung it on him, and Harry suggested we drive down with the girls and pay you all a visit. Harry will have to head back over to Savannah in the morning, but then he'll come back, and we can stay for the weekend. That is, if it's okay with you."

"It's better than okay! We have the extra space, as you know. It will be great to see all of you."

Another part of our home renovation involved adding an upstairs to the formerly one level house. The renovation added two small bedrooms and a bathroom to the second-floor space, which could easily accommodate Julie, Harry, and their twin daughters.

"Oh, good! I hoped you'd say that. The girls have been asking about Frankie every day. I think they really miss him. At least, Emily does."

Her twin daughters, while identical in appearance, were polar opposites in personality. Emily was what was commonly called a *Tom Boy* because of her fondness for sports, climbing trees, and other pursuits that were typically preferred by the male species. Ashley, on the other hand, was a girly-girl through and through. She preferred to play dress-up or share pretend-tea with her dolls. Frankie didn't seem to know what to make of Ashley, but he gravitated towards Emily like a piece of metal to a magnet.

"I'll get your bedrooms ready. Oh, I can't believe you're really coming! It will be SO good to see you!"

"Me, too. I'd better be going so we can get ready. See 'ya."

I hung up the phone with a big grin. Julie was coming! I jumped up from the sofa and looked around the room, wondering what I should do first. I would need to put sheets on the guest beds, and stock up on groceries. Oh, and I needed to tell Jon! I decided calling him better be my first order of business.

Luckily, Jon was as thrilled with the idea of the Simpsons visiting as I was. I spent the day getting the house in order and loading up on enough food and drinks to easily fill a small army. It was nearly two by the time I finished everything, which left me just enough time to change clothes and drive to pick up Frankie.

When I pulled into the Daycare Center parking lot, I spotted Frankie talking to his new friend Tommy, and a woman who I guessed was Tommy's mother. I parked the car and made my way over to them. Frankie saw me before I had a chance to introduce myself.

"Mommy! Mommy! Dis is Tommy's mommy." He grabbed her hand and began pulling her in my direction.

"Slow down, Sweetheart. You're going to pull her arm off!" I looked at her apologetically.

He looked at her hand in alarm and released it quickly.

"It's no trouble," she said. "You must be Mrs. Barnett. I'm Betty Sanders. Tommy's mommy."

I appreciated her sense of humor at picking up on Frankie's inadvertent rhyme.

"Please call me Georgia. Tommy said ya'll moved here recently from Ohio?"

She nodded. "We moved from Toledo a few weeks ago. It's been quite a change for us, but a good one, for the *most* part."

I wondered at her use of the word most but decided not to address it. "A lot warmer, I'd imagine."

"Absolutely, though there are still chilly days like today. I was wishing our apartment had a fireplace, or at least a heating unit that worked well. We're just renting a small place over near the Ocean Gate entrance to Sea Pines while we look for something more permanent. I'm afraid it leaves a lot to be desired."

"I understand. When we bought our place, it had to be almost totally renovated because of a leaky roof, and mold that had intruded into the walls. Luckily, we still had our home in Nashville to return to while the work was being done. I can't imagine how difficult it would be to move so far away and have to live someplace you're less than thrilled with. I hope I'm not out of line in mentioning this, but my husband is a realtor. If you and your husband would be interested, I'm sure he could help you scout out some potential places to live. When you're ready, that is."

"Oh! That would be great! Hal, my husband, has been so busy settling into his new job that we haven't really had a chance to look. Maybe you can give me your husband's card."

I looked at the two boys, who were standing a few feet away studying Frankie's stuffed dolphin with what appeared to be total absorption. "I have an even better idea. Frankie has been begging me to let Tommy come over to play sometime. Perhaps we can arrange an evening when you can all come for dinner. We have house guests arriving from Nashville tonight, but they'll be gone by Sunday. Maybe some night next week?"

"That would be lovely. But only if you let me bring something."

I rummaged in my purse for a pen and paper. "Let me get your number. I'll call you toward the end of the weekend to arrange it."

She wrote down her information and handed it to me. "I'm so happy we ran into each other. I look forward to your call."

The boys trotted over and looked up at us expectantly. I smiled at Tommy. "Your mom and I have been having a nice chat. We're going to arrange a night next week when you all can come to our house for dinner. Would you like that?"

Tommy's eyes grew wide. Both boys nodded vigorously.

"Why can't Tommy come over now?" Frankie asked.

"Well, your Aunt Julie called, and she and Uncle Harry, Emily and Ashley are coming for a visit. They'll be here this evening and will stay through the weekend. I thought it would be best to wait and have Tommy's family over after they leave."

His little mouth formed a pout. "But why can't Tommy come play wid all of us? Two girls an' two boys."

I had to admit that what he was suggesting made sense. "You know what? I think you're right. Why not have Tommy over to play while the girls are here." I looked at Betty to gauge her reaction.

She lifted her shoulders. "That's fine by me. Tommy hasn't really made friends with anyone before he met Frankie. He's had to spend a lot of time just hanging out with us grown-ups. I think he'd enjoy a chance to play with some other children."

"Okay, then. I'll call you later this evening once our friends arrive and arrange a time for you to bring Tommy over. We'll figure out the details when we speak."

She waved, heading toward their car.

Once Frankie and I were on our way, I glanced over at him. His face was covered with a big grin that seemed to stretch from ear to ear. "I'd say you're pretty happy that Tommy will be coming over tomorrow."

"Yeah. It's gonna be great!"

I hoped he was right. I hadn't run any of it by Julie and Harry, or Jon either, for that matter. I decided to trust my heart and believe that only good could come from expanding Frankie's circle of friends. That thought made me extremely happy.

CHAPTER SEVEN

Jon phoned in the late afternoon to tell me his prospective buyers finally made the transition to actual buyers. That was great news for our pocketbooks, but it meant Jon would be delayed returning home until close to the time the Simpsons would arrive. I kept busy tidying up the house and starting dinner preparations until I heard the crunch of tires in our gravel driveway.

"Frankie? Run out front and see if that's the Simpsons' car." My hands were covered in flour from the pie crust I was rolling out.

He sped by me and yanked open the front door. "They're here!" Before I could stop him, he was running down the steps. I quickly rinsed my hands and wiped them dry on a dish towel before following him outside. Harrys' red station wagon was parked in the drive. When the girls were born, he'd traded in his red pickup truck for the more family-friendly wagon. I suspected the trade wasn't something Harry was thrilled about, but Julie said he had taken it in stride.

Julie emerged from the car and opened the back door so the twins could get out. "We made it! Boy, that drive between Macon and I-95 is so LONG!"

Harry stepped out and headed for the trunk. "It's not really that long. At least not any longer than any other part of the trip. It just feels like it because it's so boring." He opened the rear door of the car and began unloading suitcases.

I quickly made my way down the steps and threw my arms around Julie. "I've missed you so much."

She returned my embrace. "I know. It feels like forever since I've seen you."

The twins skipped up next to us. "Hi, Aunt Georgia. Where's Frankie?" Emily asked.

I looked around to see where he had disappeared to. He was standing at one corner of the yard, staring down at something. "Frankie, what are you doing? Don't you want to come say hello?"

His grim little face looked at me. "Dere's a dead bird in the yard, Mommy." Julie, the twins, and I, walked over and looked where he was pointing. There was, in fact, a dead bird laying on top of a palmetto frond. I leaned closer so I could study it. There was no obvious sign of injury. In fact, it looked as though it had been carefully laid on its resting place.

"It's a sparrow," I said. "I wonder what happened to it?"

Julie crouched down for a closer look. "It's a female. I can tell by the coloring." She stood and wrapped her arms around her chest. "Poor thing."

"Hey. I could use some help over here!" Harry had emptied the car and was loaded down with suitcases and beach bags. I took a final look at the sparrow before we all rushed over to give him a hand. The kids each grabbed a small bag, while Julie and I picked up the rest. Once we had deposited everything on the living room floor, I faced the kids.

"Frankie, why don't you take the girls out back and play? Don't leave the yard, though. I'll call you when it's time to wash up for supper."

Frankie grabbed Emily by the hand, and they rushed for the back door, with Ashley following demurely behind.

I turned to look at Harry and Julie. "It's so good to see you both. You must be exhausted from the long drive. Why don't you take some of your things upstairs to your bedrooms while I fix us all a drink? White wine okay?"

"White wine's good for me." Julie looked at Harry for confirmation.

"You wouldn't happen to have a beer, would you?" He asked.

I had forgotten that beer was Harry's go-to drink of choice. Luckily, we always kept a few in the refrigerator. "Of course! Coming right up."

By the time they came downstairs, I had filled a tray with our drinks and an assortment of cheese and crackers to tide us over until dinner. I added a small pitcher of lemonade and some plastic cups for the kids.

"Let me get that." Harry reached around me and picked up the tray. "If one of you will open the door, I'll take this outside."

Jon and I added a small patio to the back of the house as part of the renovations. There was a round umbrella table surrounded by four chairs, flanked by two lounge chairs. Harry sat the tray down while I closed the umbrella. The rain had stopped midday, with the clouds slowly following, revealing a bright blue sky. It was nearly sunset, and the trees to our South provided all the shade we needed.

I walked to the edge of the patio to call the kids. "Hey, you three! There's cold lemonade here if you want some."

They looked up at the sound of my voice before returning their attention to something on the ground. "Huh. Guess they're not thirsty," I said.

"Well, I am." Harry took his cold beer and drank deeply. "Ahhh. That hits the spot!"

Julie poked him in the stomach. "This spot? I think maybe you've had a little too many of those." She grinned at him playfully.

Harry rubbed his tummy with a grimace. "Guess I am getting a little soft in the middle. Too many long days at work, and not enough play."

She wrapped her arms around him and looked into his eyes. "Maybe we should take more vacations. I bet you'd lose that little paunch in no time."

He pecked a kiss on her nose before taking another swig of beer.

I handed Julie a glass of wine and picked up my own. "More vacation sounds like a great idea. I know a beach house that has extra room."

"We're so lucky you and Jon didn't mind us crashing here for a few days."

"We love having the four of you here. I just wish you could stay longer."

Our exchange was interrupted by the arrival of Frankie and Emily. "We're thirsty. Kin we hab some lemonade?" The hopeful look on Frankie's face was mirrored on Emily's.

"Of course." I poured each of them a cup and looked around for Ashley. "Emily, where's your sister?"

She shrugged. "She said she wanted to stay with the bird."

Her comment puzzled me. "She's in the front yard?"

She shook her head. "She's with the other bird. The one that's over there." She pointed to the far corner of the back yard. Ashley was sitting cross-legged on the ground. Her elbows rested on her legs staring intently at the object in front of her. Julie, Harry, and I exchanged a look of confusion.

"I wonder if that's another dead sparrow? How odd if there are two of them in our yard at the same time."

The three of us began to walk to where the dead bird lay. It clearly was a sparrow, and this one lay on top of a palmetto frond in a similar fashion to the one in the front yard. "Doesn't it strike you as odd that there would be TWO dead sparrows in our yard at the same time? And both of them look as if they've been carefully laid to rest on those palmetto fronds."

Julie raised her shoulders and clasped her arms across her chest. "Strange doesn't begin to describe it." She glanced at Ashley who still sat motionless. "Ashley honey, why don't we go up to the patio? Aunt Georgia made some lemonade for you kids."

Ashley looked up as if she had just noticed us. "The bird is dead, Momma. Just like the bird in the front yard. Why are they dead?"

Julie placed her hand on Ashley's head. "I don't know, sweetheart. Sometimes things happen that we don't have an explanation for."

Ashley seemed to consider her comment. She nodded her head slowly before standing to join the others. "Okay."

Julie and I exchanged a surprised look. "Sometimes it scares me how grown up that little girl seems."

"I was just thinking the same thing."

We linked arms and made our way to the house.

Jon arrived home about an hour later. He was in a jovial mood, likely fueled by his real estate sale, and the prospect of a fat commission check. He and Harry fell into their usual droll exchange that left Julie and me in stitches as they tried to outdo each other with witty quips. Their friendship had been slow to develop, but it had grown deeper after the four of us took our first Hilton Head vacation together four years earlier. Harry helped advise Jon on the purchase of our home on the island, which bloomed into the real estate business Jon now enjoyed. It gave me pleasure to see how easily they related to each other, which made it even more possible for Julie and me to continue our long-standing friendship.

After we put the kids to bed, the four of us decided a nightcap was in order. We carried our drinks into the living room so we could hear sounds from the rest of the house. I thought it might be a little difficult to get Frankie settled, since he was so excited to have two playmates for a few days. But all three children went right to sleep shortly after we tucked them in. The sea air had a way of doing that. Even to grown-ups. It wasn't long before the rest of us were yawning. We were all headed to our respective bedrooms when I remembered my promise to Betty Sanders.

"I almost forgot. Frankie met a new boy at his Daycare Center, and they've become fast friends. I spoke to his mother earlier today, and we decided it would be nice to get the two of them together for a play date. I mentioned to her that you all were coming, and that it might be possible for us to have Tommy over while the girls are here. If you don't think it's a good idea, I'm sure I can push the get-together off until after you leave."

Julie smiled. "I don't see any problem with adding one more kid to the mix. Since Harry has to go to Savannah tomorrow, why don't we invite Frankie's new friend to come play sometime in the early afternoon?"

"That's what I was thinking. I did suggest to his mother that we'd have her and her husband over sometime, too, but I think it's best if we wait on that. I'll just give her a call and try to set up a playdate for the kids."

I said goodnight to everyone before heading for the phone in the kitchen. Betty answered after the second ring, and we arranged for her to drop Tommy off after lunch the next day.

Satisfied that all was right with the world–at least the small bit of it that I had some semblance of control over–I headed for bed, as well.

The next morning brought blue skies and plenty of sunshine. Harry left the house shortly after daybreak to head for Savannah, and Jon set out a short time later to meet his new buyers to discuss some final details about their purchase.

I had just poured myself a second cup of coffee when Julie appeared. To be as close as we were, we were still quite different in a lot of ways. For one thing, I was an early riser by nature, whereas Julie liked to linger in bed as long as possible. Her routine had been turned upside down by the arrival of the twins, but whenever she had the opportunity, she fell comfortably back into her former pattern.

"I slept so well! What is it about the beach that makes it easy to relax?"

I grinned as she dug around in the refrigerator for the Coke she knew I would have stocked in anticipation of her arrival. "I think it's the air. It feels lighter here, and the sound of the waves–at least when the windows are open–is like our own personal sound machine. You know, one of those things they sell to help people sleep."

She filled a glass with ice and sat at the kitchen table. "Well, whatever it is, if you could bottle it, you'd make a fortune." She sipped her fizzy drink and purred like a cat. As if she could read our minds, Ebie chose that moment to appear. She'd been oddly absent the night before; likely feeling ostracized by our decision to ban her from the patio to avoid her dashing out to discover the dead bird. She sidled up to Julie's legs under the table and began butting them with her head.

Julie reached down to rub a hand down her back. "'Morning, Ebie. Did you sleep well, too?"

Ebie answered her with another head butt before sauntering over to her food bowl She sat in front of it with her back to us, making her point quite clear. I reached into the cabinet for her food and shook some into the bowl, then checked to make sure she had plenty of water. She dug her face into the dry kibble, still purposefully ignoring me–at least that's what I assumed she was doing. Truthfully, I sometimes tended to give Ebie human powers she might not actually possess.

"Just before I went to bed last night, I was thinking about the dead birds, or *The Sparrows Tale*, as Harry so glibly called it. I wonder if this isn't something to run by Henry and Mary?"

I looked at her with surprise. "Why? Do you think there's more to it than meets the eye?"

"I really don't know, but I think it's worth finding out. As you well know, there are hidden meanings behind all kinds of things around here."

59

I knew she was referring to my ghostly encounter in the Braddock's Point cemetery when we first came to Hilton Head. What she DIDN'T know was that a man–possibly a Root Doctor–had given Frankie a bottle of oil for me to revitalize my amulet.

"More than you know. When Frankie's teacher took his class to Daufuskie Island for a field trip and picnic, he met a man in the woods who gave him a little bottle to give me. It turns out, the man was what they call a conjurer, or Root Doctor. The bottle contained some mixture of plant oils and herbs that's supposed to be able to restore power to amulets. At least, that's the explanation Henry and Mary gave me."

"Wow. Then I DEFINITELY think you should tell them about the dead sparrows. For all we know, there could be a connection between the two, or I guess it's three."

I frowned as I let her words sink in. "I suppose I should. Maybe I could ask them to come over here. That way, they can see the birds and how they look. No one moved them, did they?"

She looked uncomfortable. "Harry and Jon picked them up while we were getting the kids ready for bed. They were afraid they'd attract rats or some other type of vermin. They put them in a plastic bag and put it in the garbage can. Jon said the trash is picked up today, so it should be okay to leave them there overnight."

We looked at each other in alarm as we jumped up and hurried outside. Luckily, the trash had not been picked up yet. I removed the bag and laid it on a shelf in the storage shed, out of reach by critters, but accessible for inspection should the Palmers come over.

We went inside and I headed for the telephone. I reached Henry just as he was about to leave for the store. Luckily, his nephew was opening the store for him that morning, and he said he and Mary would drop by our house shortly.

By the time they arrived, all three kids had been fed, and were settled in front of the television. Frankie was over the moon about the pending visit by Tommy, although the girls were less enthused. Emily seemed miffed at having to share Frankie's attention with someone else, while Ashley just didn't care for the company of another member of her less favorite gender. I was hopeful their moods would improve by the time Tommy arrived, but I knew we were possibly in for a rocky time.

I escorted the Palmers into the kitchen where Julie was waiting. After they all exchanged hugs and heartfelt greetings, I told them the story of the dead birds. As I spoke, I became aware of how quiet they'd become, and the pointed looks they gave each other. When I finished, Henry leaned back in his chair and gazed at the ceiling, while Mary tut-tutted and fanned herself with a napkin. Finally, Henry stood and walked in the direction of the back door.

"Oonuh say de bag wid de burs een de shed?"

I nodded and followed him out the door with Julie and Mary trooping behind us. Henry lifted the plastic bag off the shelf and carefully placed it on the ground. He grabbed a beach chair from against the wall and unfolded it in front of the bag, before slowly lowering himself into it. He unwrapped the clasp on the bag and peered inside before turning the bag so the contents could tumble to the ground. The birds had fallen off their leafy beds but were still intact and looked much the same as they had when we first found them.

"Weh dey lay, an' how dey look?"

I described the location of each and how they had been carefully laid on top of a flat palmetto frond, each one mimicking the appearance of the other.

He nodded slowly as I spoke, then used a branch to push the birds back into the bag.

"Mary? Wha' oonuh t'ink?"

"Look like sum kin' omen. Sum folks tink dead bur mean death be comin'. Udders t'ink it sign of new beginning. Sparrow 'present t'roat an' heart. Fin' dem near tuh home, mean bird hep open de heart. Sparrow also symbol ub need tuh tek t'ings slow. Watch fo' wha' cum."

Henry nodded his agreement. "Fin' two sparrow, 'specially at front an' back do', mite mean need tuh pay attention tuh wha' in past and future. An' sparrow bery social bir'. Remin' us tuh hol' fast tuh dose close tuh we."

A symbol of the throat and heart. Open the heart. Have courage but be cautious. Pay attention to the past and future. Keep our loved ones close. These were the messages Henry and Mary shared with me, as I understood them.

"Do you think finding these birds has anything to do with the bottle the root doctor gave Frankie?"

Mary began fanning herself more energetically. "'Spec so. Mos' likely dey connected."

I sighed. "More mysteries. I thought I had my fill after my encounters with Miss Bessie."

Henry chuckled. "Bessie mo' 'volved wid dis den oonuh t'ink. Got huh handwriting all ober 'e."

Mary agreed. "Uh huh. Jes 'member wha' 'e say: Trus' de heart. 'E hep oonuh wen need tuh."

Henry pushed up from his chair. "Time tuh go tuh de sto'. Nephew hab uder job een ebening. Need sleep 'fo' den."

I offered them a cold drink before leaving, which they both declined. Julie and I stood on the front steps watching as they drove away.

"Man, Georgia! You have the most interesting life of anyone I know!"

I couldn't disagree with her, but I wasn't sure if that was a blessing or a curse.

CHAPTER EIGHT

Tommy and his mother pulled up in front of our house just before one PM. Frankie had been growing increasingly restless, to the point that I was about to put him in time-out for a while just to give the rest of us a break. When he spotted Tommy, he began to jump up and down and clap his hands.

"He's here! He's here! Can I go outside, Mommy?"

"Okay. But be careful you don't knock him down in your enthusiasm."

He rushed down the stairs.

Julie looked at the twins. "Girls? Would you like to go outside with Frankie?"

Emily's face turned into a pout as she vehemently shook her head, while Ashley pretended she didn't hear. Julie looked at me with a sigh. "Maybe I should take them upstairs for a little while."

I nodded my agreement and went out to greet Betty and Tommy. The boys had already disappeared, and I looked around in confusion. Betty gave me a slight wave as I approached.

"The boys went to look at something in the storage shed."

I rolled my eyes. "We'd better go head that off. There are a couple of dead sparrows in the garbage, and I wouldn't put it past Frankie to scoop them out."

"Tommy's the same way. Must be a boy thing."

We reached the shed just as the boys were lifting the garbage bag onto the ground. "Hold on, Frankie. I don't want you taking those dead birds out of the bag. Put the bag back in the garbage." Frankie gave me a look of complete exasperation as he dropped the bag into the can.

"I want tuh show de birds to Tommy!"

"I know, but that's not a good idea. Why don't you show Tommy your room instead?"

He looked at Tommy eagerly. "Come on. You can play wid my army men. They've got real guns and everything!" The two ran up the stairs hand in hand.

Betty and I shook our heads as we watched them leave. "Do little boys ever walk anywhere? I swear I think Tommy started running before he could crawl."

"Frankie was the same way. I dread to think how it's going to be when he's a little older. There'll be no containing him." We began walking in the direction of the house.

"It's really nice of you to invite Tommy over. I hope it won't be any trouble having him here. I take it the two girls were less than thrilled at having another boy around?"

I was a little surprised by her insight. "How'd you guess?"

"I grew up with two brothers. They were almost more than I could take, but when either of them had a friend visit, I used to hide in my room until they left. I imagine it would be especially hard for your friends' twin girls since they aren't used to having even ONE boy around."

"Funny. I hadn't thought of it that way. Emily and Frankie have always seemed to enjoy playing together, but Ashley, her twin, is the exact opposite. Emily seems a little jealous at having to share Frankie. I imagine she's worried he'll ignore her. Ashley...well, there's no telling what she's thinking, if she's giving the boys any thought at all." We stopped next to her car.

"Why don't you come in for a cup of coffee or something? You can meet my friend, Julie, and it will give us a chance to see if the kids will be able to find some common ground to help them relax around one another."

Julie was in the kitchen when we entered. "You won't believe it." She looked at me and then Betty. "The boys came upstairs and asked the girls if they wanted to play army. I guess Emily was getting a little bored because she agreed right away, but only after telling him they'd have to add her plastic horse collection to the game. Ashley looked like she'd rather do anything BUT play with them, but she reluctantly followed them downstairs. The last time I looked, all four of them were sitting on the floor of Frankie's room discussing which horses went with which army men."

"I'm so glad. Julie, this is Tommy's mother, Betty, and this is my friend Julie."

Julie extended her hand to Betty. "I'm so glad to meet you, Betty. Georgia told me Frankie and your son have become good friends."

Betty accepted her handshake with a smile. "Yes. Tommy has been pretty miserable since we moved here from Toledo. Once he met Frankie, he's been a lot more chipper. How old are your daughters?"

"Not quite three. They were born about three months after Frankie came along."

"It must have been interesting for you and Georgia to be pregnant at the same time."

Julie rolled her head from side to side. "Kind of. Unfortunately, Georgia moved here shortly after she discovered she was pregnant. We didn't really get to share the experience in close proximity to each other, although maybe that was a good thing. I was pretty miserable most of the time. Carrying two babies instead of one was quite a challenge."

"I can only imagine. I've never known anyone who had twins."

"Julie has twin sisters, so at least she's experienced in the nuances of their unique connection," I said.

"You can say that again! My sisters, Sherry and Carey, were like two peas in a pod most of the time. Except on those rare occasions when they disagreed about something. Then it was like World War II in the house. Emily and Ashley aren't nearly as identical in their personalities as my sisters. I suspect we'll be in for a very stormy time with those two!"

"Let's take our drinks out to the patio. Betty, would you prefer coffee, tea, or Coke?"

"Coffee would be great. With a little milk, please?"

We collected our beverages and settled around the patio table.

"You have such a nice place here. And the location can't be beat." Betty looked around admiringly.

"That's what sold me on the place. You wouldn't believe how shabby the house was when we first saw it. We had to make a lot of renovations due to a mold and water leak issue, which was a good excuse to make some other changes we had in mind. Sometimes, I can't believe how lucky I am to be living here."

"Hal and I," she glanced at Julie. "That's my husband. Would love to find a place near the beach. We've only started looking, but most things seem out of our price range."

"As I mentioned, my husband, Jon, is a realtor. Once you and Hal have a chance to talk to him, I'm sure he can scout out some places that will match your budget."

"I hope so. The two-bedroom unit we've been renting is so depressing. It has made me question my insistence that we relocate here, although I love the rest of the island." She glanced at her watch. "Well, I'd better be going. What time should I stop back by to pick up Tommy?"

"How about three-thirty or four? Hopefully, they'll all get along fine for that length of time. If not, Julie and I will find some way to separate the girls from the boys."

After she left, Julie and I decided to check on the kids. To our delight, we found them still playing happily on the floor of

Frankie's room. "You kids doing okay? We thought maybe you'd like to go outside for a while. Maybe take a walk on the beach."

Frankie hopped up from the floor. "Yay! I can show Tommy the dolfs."

Emily stood and looked annoyed. "I want to see them, too."

Frankie looked at her with surprise. "Course you can, Em. But Tommy's never seen the dolfs. At least not on MY beach. You've seen 'em plenty of times." He took her by the hand." Come on. We can show him together." Emily's face lit up with pleasure.

As the two walked out of the room, Ashley and Tommy eyed each other shyly. "Do you like the beach?" Tommy asked.

Ashley seemed to consider his question. "Sometimes. I like to watch the birds and things, but I don't like to get all sandy."

"Okay. If sand gets on you, I'll wipe it off." He offered her his hand, which she took hesitantly. Julie and I exchanged a look of amazement as the two of them went to join Frankie and Emily.

"If that don't beat all! I don't believe I've ever seen Ashley warm up to someone as quickly as she did Tommy. Are we witnessing young love in the making?" Julie's eyes grew wider.

"Oh, I hope not. It's way too early for that. But at least we're seeing the beginning bud of friendship." We followed the kids downstairs and out the back door.

The rest of the day was uneventful. Unfortunately, there were no dolphins visible on the beach, but the kids entertained themselves chasing seagulls and splashing barefoot in the surf. Even Ashley slipped off her sandals and walked in the shallow water, with Tommy close by. Eventually, they grew tired of the sun, and we headed back to the house for some refreshments. By the time Betty returned, they were camped out on the floor of the living room watching Sesame Street. She collected Tommy, and we made plans to talk later in the week to plan a night for them to come over for dinner.

Julie and I wandered into the kitchen. "She seems nice. I hope Jon is able to help them find a house."

"Me, too. It must be awful to move to a new place and have to live somewhere you're not comfortable with." I opened the refrigerator and peered inside. "Hum. What do you feel like having for dinner? We could grill some burgers or order pizza and make a salad to go with whichever one we choose."

"I vote for pizza. The guys always enjoy manning the grill together, but they'll have more time for that tomorrow night."

"What time will Harry be back?"

"He said the meeting should be over by 4, so he should be rolling in around 5. What about Jon?"

"Around the same time. I guess we should make the salad before they get here." We turned to look back inside the refrigerator before making a simultaneous decision. "Nah! Let's have a glass of wine first."

We removed a chilled bottle, collecting some cheese and crackers to accompany it before carrying everything outside. The temperature had grown quite warm as the day progressed, and I unfurled the umbrella on the patio table before sitting.

Julie poured both of us a glass and handed mine to me. "Tell me more about the mystery man with the magic potion, and what Henry and Mary said about the dead sparrows."

I sipped my wine and took a piece of cheese. "As I mentioned before, he's what they call a root doctor. They make all sorts of potions depending upon what a person needs. Mary and Henry suggested that Miss Bessie–you remember, the ghost from the cemetery–probably communicated about me with the root doctor, which directed him to make my particular potion. They also felt the fact that the dead birds had been carefully placed in both the front and back yards meant I should pay attention to the past and future and keep those I love close to me. There was something about my throat and heart, too, but I didn't quite follow what that meant."

She shook her head in amazement. "Like I said before, you live the most interesting life! Strange, but remarkably interesting."

"Sometimes it just feels overwhelming. At least, since I first set foot on this island. There's something special about the place; mystical even. What I really don't understand is why these things keep happening to me. I mean, I didn't grow up believing in ghosts or spirits; even the ones the nuns tried to force down my throat. Oops! I guess I shouldn't say that!"

We grinned at each other as we said in unison, "What would the nuns think?" It was a standing joke between us to refer to anything we thought the nuns who had taught us for four years of high school would disapprove of, which was pretty much everything. I was raised in the Catholic faith, whereas Julie slid in the back door due to her parents' desire to give her a good education.

"You know, when they used to try to teach us about the Holy Ghost, I never paid much attention to it. I always thought they were just talking metaphorically. These recent events have given me a whole new perspective on the afterlife and things that aren't apparent in this world."

She gave me an impish look. "Maybe you should write an article for the Tennessee Register and describe your experiences with Miss Bessie. I'll bet that would gain you a whole host of Hail Mary's and Our Father's."

The newspaper she was referring to reported on all-things-Catholic in the Nashville area. "Let's just say I'm more open-minded now than I was ten years ago. Goodness! Can you believe it's been that long?"

"What's been that long?" A male voice chimed in from behind.

We turned to see Jon walking out the back door with Harry close behind. Both men had drinks in their hands.

"Oh! Hey you two! We were just reminiscing about high school," I said.

The guys pulled the remaining two chairs out from the patio table and sat.

"Whew! What a long day!" Harry drank deeply from his beer and set it on the table. "I've heard more than I ever wanted to about mergers and acquisitions."

Jon looked up in surprise. "Are you kidding? I thought you lived and breathed that stuff."

"Speaking in the past tense, you'd be correct. These days, I'm getting a little tired of hearing about companies failing and being taken over by larger corporations that usually only pay a fraction of what the company is worth. It makes me ill, to tell you the truth." It was unusual to see Harry so dejected, and I wondered what was really at the bottom of it.

"Something obviously rubbed you the wrong way today," I said.

He looked directly at me before answering. "What would you say if I told you that this place you love, at least a big chunk of it, is in danger of being sold?"

I looked at him askance. "Hilton Head Island? What are you saying?"

He squirmed in his seat. "There was a lot of talk at my meeting about a group of investors who want to buy Sea Pines. Or at least the Company that's behind it." He looked at Julie. "They've been in contact with the main office of our bank in Nashville to request assistance. Your dad got wind of it and sent me to find out what it's all about. I figured that might be a good idea seeing how invested Jon and Georgia are in this place."

His words struck a chord of alarm in me. "How could that even be possible? Isn't Sea Pines owned by the Town of Hilton Head?"

"No. Sea Pines is a privately-owned resort development. It's owned by the Sea Pines Company that was formed by Charles Fraser, his father, and his brother back in 1957."

Jon jumped into the conversation. "When I was at Harvard, I heard about this guy from Georgia who was a staunch proponent of environmentally sensitive land development back before most folks gave it a second thought. He wasn't a Harvard man. He had the audacity to attend Yale. However, he redeemed himself by hiring eleven MBA graduates of Harvard to help him realize his dream. A lot of people don't realize that Fraser moved to the island in 1956 when it was little more than mosquito infested swamp land.

"At the time, his father owned a timber company on Hilton Head, and Charles was appointed vice-president of what was known as the Hilton Head Company. He was only 26 years old when he drafted a land-use plan for the southern end of Hilton Head Island. The following year, he bought out his father's interest in the Hilton Head Company and began developing the land into the Sea Pines Plantation. That same year, the Hilton Head Company built a pontoon bridge to the island, which helped make tourism a feasible replacement to the timber business."

The conversation switched back to Harry. "The way I heard it, the board members of the Hilton Head Company wanted to mimic the development of Hilton Head on the pattern of popular beach towns like Myrtle Beach. That would have meant focusing on a grid-like pattern of multi-story hotels, condominiums, and houses on the beach, sometimes directly on top of bulldozed dunes or filled in wetlands. Charles Fraser argued that the company should emphasize a new type of coastal development that would draw high-end clients by limiting development and maintaining the island's natural beauty. Luckily, his father listened to his arguments and broke away from the Company, retaining 3,400 acres on the southern tip of the island for his use.

"Fraser's father sold that land to Charles, who formed the Sea Pines Company. He hired a landscape architect who developed a master plan that would give the island's natural environment a starring role. The plan involved staggering home sites and placing them far away from the beach; hiding the homes in groves of trees; mandating that homes be painted in earth tones;

and fining builders if too many trees were removed during construction. He employed planners who laid out winding roads that skirted key landscape features, built miles of bike trails to reduce automobile traffic, and imposed regulations restricting the use of signage. He even allocated over 1,000 acres of land to remain forever undeveloped.

"From 1965 to 1975, construction was nonstop, and home sales followed suit. During that same time, the Sea Pines Company began to branch out and buy acreage for development in other places, such as Puerto Rico and Florida. Unfortunately, that's the same time the recession hit, which caught Fraser and many other developers off-guard. Prime interest rates jumped from 6 to 11.75 between 1973 and 1974, and the Sea Pines Company fell into trouble. Their only way to ward off a complete financial disaster was to begin to sell off assets. As a result, by the time the crisis ended, the Company was much smaller."

Jon took over the conversation again. "Fraser was able to regain management of the company in 1976, but that was after the Sea Pines Company lost control of the Hilton Head Plantation at the Northwest end of the island, as well as many of their other holdings. Since then, Fraser and his partners have been scrambling to undo the damage the recession created, but there's still a lot that needs to take place before things are on an even keel again."

Harry nodded. "At the meeting I attended, there were rumblings about selling the Sea Pines Company to the highest bidder; a sentiment that is apparently not shared by the landowners."

I frowned at his description of what appeared to be a disaster waiting to happen. "What does Charles Fraser have to say about all of that?"

"I take it he's getting tired of being caught in the middle of a financial whirlpool. I've heard it said that he claims he's just an architect who wanted to see his dream of blending buildings with nature realized. A great idea, most people agree, but pretty unrealistic to think you could pull it off without a lot of attention to the financial side of things. Not that he was oblivious to it.

Luckily, he was a strong believer in the need for writing deed restrictions and covenants that would protect both homeowners and the environment. That just may be his saving grace."

There was a lull in the conversation as each of us allowed ourselves to digest everything. Finally, Julie spoke up. "You guys sure know a lot about this. I'm impressed."

Jon and Harry exchanged a look before Jon replied. "Yeah. Maybe we should go into business together. Find a way to turn some of this around to everyone's advantage."

I laughed out loud before I spotted the sober look on their faces. "You guys are serious, aren't you? Have you been talking about this?"

Jon's expression suggested the discussion had moved into an area he was uncomfortable with. "Let's don't get ahead of ourselves. Harry and I have just been keeping in touch about the real estate business on the island, and what appears to be happening in the financial sector. Anything else would be sheer speculation."

Harry nodded. "I totally agree. I only brought it up because everything I heard today was weighing heavy on my mind. Sorry."

I stood and pushed back my chair. "I think it's high time for us to order pizza. Julie, why don't you and Harry look in on the kids while Jon and I call the pizza place? I'll just order the usual." The four of us had shared pizza so many times we knew one another's preferences by heart.

"You'd better add a plain cheese to that order. Ashley has decided she won't eat anything on her pizza except cheese now." Julie offered.

I rolled my eyes. "Got it."

Julie and Harry headed in the back door. I was about to follow them when I felt Jon tug on my arm. "Wait a sec'." He turned me to face him. "You know that number you gave me from the woman you met at the Tiki Hut? I called it and spoke to her uncle. Apparently, he's a key player in these discussions Harry mentioned about possibly buying out the Sea Pines Company. I didn't want to say too much about it until I had a chance to talk to Harry, but the guy implied things are moving rapidly in the direction of a take-over."

"That's terrible! And her uncle is in the middle of it?"

"I'd say he's one of the ring-leaders. Anyway, I just wanted to warn you in case you see or hear from his niece again. What was her name?"

"Savannah. I'm glad you told me." Something she said occurred to me. "Did you tell this man you might be interested in joining him in whatever he's working on?"

"No. But I may have implied I was interested in learning more." He smiled. "You've heard the old saying about keeping your friends close and your enemies closer?"

"Yes, but which category are you putting her uncle in?"

"Let's just say I'm not sure he has the best interests of the island at heart."

He held the door open for me. I stepped inside, then remembered something else I wanted to ask him. "Say, did you talk to Henry?"

"Um hum, briefly. I'm going to stop by to see him tomorrow. I thought I'd invite Harry to join me. You never know what that ole' guy has in mind. It could be something both of us would want to hear."

CHAPTER NINE

I got up early the next morning and went for my usual sunrise beach walk. The sky was free of clouds and lit with warm orange and yellow tones as the sun rose out of the water. I breathed deeply of the warm, salty air and smiled. I couldn't think of a better way to start the day than to drink in the beauty of a sunrise on the beach.

When I returned to the house, the kitchen was empty except for Jon. The newspaper was laid out on the table in front of him, as usual, and he leaned over it as he sipped from a mug of coffee. I wrapped him in a hug.

"What's new in the world?"

He patted my arms and gave them a squeeze. "Just the usual. One of the things I've noticed since we've been living here, is the local news is usually full of happy stories about retirees who've fallen in love with their new home. Some days, I actually wish for something more catastrophic to read about, or at least less boring." He folded the paper and pushed it to one side, pulling me down onto his lap. "How was the beach this morning?"

I wrapped my arms around his neck and kissed him gently. "Wonderful! I love this place."

"No kidding." He grinned as he returned my kiss, lingering until I could feel the smoldering heat between us. "How about we go back upstairs before the others wake up?" His eyes darkened as he looked deep into mine. I was seriously considering his suggestion when I felt a tug on the hem of my shirt.

"Mommy? Can we have pancakes for breakfast?"

I looked behind me to find Frankie standing there. I nudged Jon and pointed over my shoulder. "I guess our nap will have to wait." His eyes showed their disappointment as he slowly pushed me up from his lap.

"Frankie, why don't you help your mom set the table in the dining room while I start breakfast. Are the girls awake yet?"

Frankie shook his head. "I tried tuh wake 'em, but they yell at me to go 'way."

I reached down and caressed his cheek. "That's okay. It will give us time to get everything ready." I opened a drawer and pulled out a handful of silverware, then grabbed a stack of napkins, handing the latter to Frankie. "Please take these into the dining room. I'll be along in a minute and show you where to put them." He clutched the napkins in both hands and trotted from the room. I took a stack of plates from the cupboard and put the silverware on top.

Jon moved to the stove where he was turning on burners and taking out pans. "Do you want some help with the food?" I asked.

"No thanks. But you might want to wake the others before I get started."

"We're awake." Julie and Harry walked in the kitchen with the twins in tow. "What can we do to help?"

"Good morning! I was just about to help Frankie set the dining room table. Maybe you could grab some glasses while I take these plates to the other room. Girls, would you like to help, too?" They nodded, and I gave them each a handful of silverware.

Once the table had been set for seven, Julie and I settled the kids in front of the morning cartoon show and returned to the kitchen. In our absence, Jon had whipped up the batter for the pancakes while Harry cracked a dozen eggs into a bowl. Julie and I stopped at the door and smirked at each other. "What a lovely sight! You guys will make some lucky ladies' great husbands. Oh, wait. WE'RE the lucky ladies!" Julie snickered behind her hands.

"I wouldn't be so quick to make jokes if I were you. You never know what strange and unusual ingredients might make their way into your eggs." Harry picked up a jar of pickles and pretended to open the lid.

"I don't know about you, Georgia, but I think dill pickles in scrambled eggs would be a nice touch. Kind of like deviled eggs, but without the mayonnaise. Say, Harry. Why don't you add a dollop of mayo to those eggs?"

Harry's eyes opened wide as he stared at her. "You're kidding, right?"

Julie laughed at his shock. "Only a little. I actually think the combination sounds delicious."

Harry shook his head at her and put the pickle jar safely out of reach.

"Anyone want bacon? I could throw some in a skillet while the rest of this is cooking." Jon raised an eyebrow in question.

"Why not." I walked to the refrigerator and took out a carton of milk and another of orange juice. "Julie, do you want a Coke, or is juice enough?"

"Juice'll do. The kids are being awfully quiet. I think I'd better go see what they're up to."

A short while later, we were all gathered around the dining room table enjoying the breakfast feast Jon and Harry had prepared. When everyone had eaten their fill, we sent the kids to wash their hands and brush their teeth so the adults could have a few minutes alone. We knew we were taking a risk letting the four of them tackle this chore unsupervised, but we counted on Ashley to keep them all straight. Julie and I had noticed more than once that she tended to fall easily into mother-mode when there was no adult around. "I think she gets that from me." Julie offered. "I used to think it was my job to keep my four siblings straight, even when there WAS a parent close by. I've been trying to break Ashley of that habit, but she still becomes a little mother when I'm not nearby."

Julie and I exchanged a look, and I knew we were both remembering how many sessions it took with her psychologist before she began to make a dent in her efforts to change that particular tendency in herself. I decided not to voice our mutual concern.

"Jon mentioned that he's planning to visit Henry today and invite Harry along. Why don't the rest of us visit Mary? Their house is always a lot of fun for the kids, especially if some of her great-grandkids are visiting."

"That sounds like a great idea. Maybe we can stop at the Coligny Bakery on our way and bring her something. I know she can't eat sugary things because of her diabetes, but she might enjoy one of their homemade rolls."

I looked at her skeptically. "Are you sure you're not just looking for an excuse to go there? I know how much you love their sweet rolls and cookies."

She smiled. "True. But that's the LAST thing I'm thinking of after those pancakes which, by the way Jon, were fantastic!"

I nodded. "Almost as good as the Pancake Pantry's." The Pancake Pantry was a long-standing Nashville restaurant famous for its pancakes that came in more varieties than I could name. A waitress shared with Jon and me once that buttermilk was the ingredient that made them so delectable, and Jon had added it to his recipe from that day on.

"I'd say they're better," Harry added. "But then I think Jon's burgers are as good as Rotier's, too, so what do I know." He grinned. Rotier's was another Nashville icon, famous for its cheeseburgers on French Bread.

"I can't disagree with you, Harry," I said. "When are you two planning to visit Henry's store?"

Jon looked at his watch. "I'm thinking we should head over there soon. Catch him before the lunch rush. Ever since he started selling bologna sandwiches at lunch, it's become pretty much impossible to have a private conversation with him from Noon until around 1:30 or 2:00 PM."

Julie and I stood and started collecting the dirty dishes. "We'll take care of these. It's the least we can do since you guys cooked."

"Sounds fair. Harry, let's meet at the car in about fifteen minutes."

The guys went their separate ways, while Julie and I set about clearing the table and filling the dishwasher. "I never thought I'd be happy about having one of these things. It seemed such a waste for just two people, but once Frankie came into the picture, I don't know how I ever managed without one."

"I know what you mean. How can one or TWO kids accumulate so many dirty dishes? Some days, I just stick to paper plates and cups so there's less to wash up."

We finished wiping off the counters and hung the dish rags over the oven door to dry. "How long do you need to get ready?" I asked.

"It will probably take me a half hour to get the girls cleaned up and dressed."

I glanced at my watch. "Okay. Let's meet back here around 10."

When we had all three kids ready to go and stopped by the bakery to pick up some treats, it was close to 11 AM. We pulled into the Palmers' driveway just before 11:30, and were greeted by their dog, Beau, and two of their great grandkids. Frankie hopped out of the car as soon as I pulled to a stop and hugged Beau around the neck, giggling as he was treated to a tongue wash. The twins left the protection of the car more slowly, glancing nervously at the dog, while taking cautious looks at the great grandkids.

The screen door slammed as Mary appeared on the front porch. "Come 'ere, Beau. Leabe dem chillun 'lone!" The big dog gave a final tongue swipe to Frankie before he loped off in Mary's direction. "Enry say de men gonna bizzet tuhday. Uh hope dat mean uh see oonuh sumtime." Julie and I walked into her embrace, turning aside so she could see the children. "Got all tree ub dem wid ya. Dat nice. Dis be Ben an' Mary. She name fuh me." She touched the head of each of her great-grandchildren as she said their names. "Liddle Mary, tek dese chillun een de house an' gib dem sum ub dat lem'nade f'um de col'box."

Ben and Mary began walking slowly toward the house, picking up speed as Frankie started to run past them. "Come on, Ben," he yelled as he ran past. "Let's beat the girls inside." The boys took off at a sprint as the girls hurried to catch up.

Mary shook her head as we watched them go. "Sum t'ings nebbuh change. Boys all-time got tuh show how quick dey mobe; how strong dey are. Try tuh impress dey gurls eben w'ile preten' don' care. Jes de way ub de worl'." She wiped her hands on her apron and examined Julie and me. "Sumt'ing een oonuh min'. Uh kin feel 'e be so." She waited for us to speak.

"Maybe we could go sit on the porch?" I asked.

She led us in that direction, motioning for us to sit in the well-worn rocking chairs that rested along the expanse. "Uh fetch us sum col' watuh tuhreckly, but talk now 'fo' de chillun cum back."

She rocked slowly back and forth as she waited for us to speak. Finally, Julie leaned forward.

"Harry attended a meeting in Savannah yesterday. He said there was a lot of talk about the financial struggles Sea Pines Resort has faced in recent years. There was even some suggestion that the Resort, or the company that runs it, might be bought out. We were wondering if you knew anything about that."

Mary continued rocking as she stared up at the sky. "'Enry and uh been praying 'bout jes dat. 'E hear sumt'ing een de sto'. Two men talk. Say: 'Dat lan' wu't mo' dan jes de houses 'e hab.' Say dey wan' tuh mek big bizzness ub 'e. 'Enry hear 'e all, but man ac' like 'Enry not dere. Gibe 'e notion dat 'e plan tuh cause sum misery." She looked up at Julie. "Wha' 'arry t'ink?"

"He was worried that some of the men at the meeting were planning a takeover of the Sea Pines Company. Charles Fraser was also at the meeting. Harry said he seemed frustrated."

"Uh t'ink dat wha' 'Enry wan' talk wid Jon 'bout. Bes' us leabe 'e tuh dem fo' now."

Her suggestion that we stay out of the discussion and let the men talk it over both confused and surprised me. I had never known Mary to stay out of ANY business if she thought it was important. She certainly wasn't someone who made a point to suggest that women had any less right to be involved than men.

"I don't understand. Why would you suggest we should let the men figure this out? Maybe we could do something to help."

Mary squinted her eyes and seemed to look deep into me. "Mo' going on dan 'parent. Berry 'paw'tun don' projic' wid de bidness till 'cum clear. Uh know dat hard fo' oonuh. Hard fo' me, too. Hab tuh know w'en tuh lay low an' wait."

I sighed deeply. Waiting was never easy for me, and this felt like something extremely important. Especially if the odd occurrences involving the root doctor and dead sparrows had anything to do with it. I decided I needed to address that with Mary.

"But what about what the root doctor gave me, and the two dead sparrows in our yard? What if they are somehow related to this business with Sea Pines?"

Mary frowned. "Eef dat be so, cum clean 'ventually. Got tuh trus' de heart."

There it was again. Everyone keeps telling me to trust my heart, but my heart was clearly telling me something was wrong. "That's what I've been trying to do, and my heart's telling me something's off about this whole thing."

Mary nodded. "Trus'in' de heart don' hab tuh mean do nuttin'. An' don' hab tuh mean light out tuh do sump'n'nuttuh. Heart tell story like twisty river: don' rush tuh go nowhere, but 'ventually get where spose tuh be. Hab tuh open both heart an' min' 'fo' know weh dat be."

What she said made sense. Sort of. "Okay. I think I understand what you're saying. I just hope I can find the patience to wait. That's never been a strength of mine."

Mary nodded sagely. "Uh know 'e true, but oonuh hab more strengk den 'e know. Jes 'membuh wha' happen wid Miss Bessie. Mos' 'portan' mus' don' fly een Gawd face. 'E guide we straight'n fuh trute."

Julie had been listening to us quietly. She pushed up out of her chair and stood with her hands in the pockets of her shorts. "Mary? Can I ask you something?"

"'Co'se, chil."

I was wondering if you could advise me about something. I think Harry is unhappy, but I don't know why. I've tried to ask him, but he just tells me it's nothing. Should I insist he talk to me, or leave it alone for now?"

"Uh 'spect 'e hab lot een 'e min'. May not wan' tuh talk 'bout 'e till he clear een 'e own head. Men like dat. Uh know oonuh lub 'e, an' 'e crazy 'bout oonuh. Why not b'leebe 'e doin' de bes' 'e kin. Gib 'e time, 'e cum 'roun'."

Julie rocked back and forth on her heels. "I know you're right, but it's like Georgia said. Sometimes it's hard to have the patience to wait. Especially when it comes to Harry. We've always shared everything, and it throws me for a loop that he's holding something back from me now. At least, I think he is."

Mary smiled at the two of us. "Sum t'ings tek time cum clear. Cyan' hurry de trute, but 'e show 'ese'f 'ventually."

Julie looked unconvinced. "I guess you're telling me to trust my heart like you're always telling Georgia." She sighed. "I just have to remind myself I can trust Harry because he IS my heart."

The screen door swung open as little Mary stepped out. "Gran'mammy, kin Ben and me take the udder kids down to de barn? We want tuh show dem the new baby calf."

"Dat be fin'. Mek sure don' leebe de do' open to de baa'n." Little Mary called over her shoulder for the other kids and they breezed past us. Mary shook her head. "T'ink 'e smaa't we tek uh walk. Go down tuh de baa'n wid de chillum."

We nodded our agreement and followed her into the yard.

That evening, we decided to take the whole crew to dinner at a local restaurant known for its fresh seafood and water views. Hudson's had been in business since 1967. It started out as an oyster factory and seafood processing plant in the 1920s before opening the restaurant at its present location. It consisted of a long, single story building on the east bank of Broad Creek, facing Pinckney Island. There was also an outdoor deck that drew a huge crowd in good weather and boasted some of the best sunset views on the island. Julie and I first visited the restaurant when we took our girls' trip to the island a few years back, and it became a favorite spot for all of us. Not only did they have the freshest fish on the island because fishing boats docked at their pier, but also their hush puppies were practically world famous, at least according to Julie, who considered herself somewhat of a hush puppy connoisseur.

We pulled into the parking lot a little before six PM and managed to find a parking spot right in front of the door to the restaurant. Harry hopped out to put our name on the waiting list while the rest of us walked around to the deck bar. Julie hurried to snag a round table on the railing by the water, while Jon and I headed to the bar. We placed our drink order with a waitress who promised to deliver them to our table. Harry returned by then, and was helping Julie situate the kids, which was no small task given that Frankie and Emily seemed determined to stick their feet under the rails.

Julie looked up as we returned. "I guess it wasn't such a good idea to sit so close to the water."

I looked around at the crowd of people on the deck. "I'd say we were lucky to find anywhere to sit. Boy, what a crowd!"

Jon and Harry grabbed each of the kids by an arm and shifted them to the other side of the table, settling themselves on either side as a barrier against their likely attempts to escape. Frankie looked at Jon with a pout, but a stern look from his daddy had him quickly turning his frown into a mischievous grin.

"The hostess said they should have a table for us in about twenty minutes. We got lucky because a party of six just decided to up and leave before they even ordered any food. Something to do with a faucet left running in a bathroom."

I grimaced. "That could be a disaster! At least they remembered it, which is good fortune for them, and apparently, for us, too."

The waitress arrived with a tray of drinks. "Hey everybody! Who had the white wine? "Julie and I held up our hands, and the drinks were placed in front of us. "Beer?" That one went to Harry. "So, I suppose this last one is for you." She placed the remaining alcoholic beverage in front of Jon. "One of our other servers will be here shortly with the soft drinks you ordered. Can I get you anything else for now?"

"How about a double order of hush puppies?" Julie piped up.

"Coming right up."

I looked out at the horizon. It was just beginning to show a change in color as the sun moved lower in the sky. The mood on the deck was lively, which made for a festive atmosphere, but cancelled out any chance of holding a serious conversation. That was fine with me. I felt like being quiet. My head was still full of the things Mary said, and I needed some time to process it all. A musician was playing guitar and singing at one end of the deck, and a few people were shuffling in time to the music as they waited for their names to be called for a table. I began to sway gently in time to the music, drawing a questioning look from Jon.

"What's the name of that song?" He asked.

"I'm not sure. I believe it was recorded by John Denver, but I can't remember what it's called."

Julie listened intently for a minute. "That's *Back Home Again*. It's one of my favorites."

She began to sing quietly along with the chorus. "Hey, it's good to be back home again. Sometimes, this old farm feels like a long-lost friend."

Yes, it does. I thought. If I replaced the word farm with island, he could be singing about me.

I looked around the table at my friends and family, and friends who I considered family, and smiled. Yes, it felt like home.

CHAPTER TEN

The Simpsons left two days later. We parted with the usual promises to stay in touch and visit again soon, but I still couldn't stop my eyes from filling with tears as I watched them pull out of our driveway. Jon wrapped me in a hug.

"It's too bad they live so far away," he said.

I nodded against his shoulder. "I wish they would move here. Wouldn't that be great?"

"Yeah, it would." He squeezed me once more before pulling gently away. "I have to make a phone call. After that, maybe you'd like to take a walk on the beach?"

"I'd like that."

We walked up the front stairs and into the house. Frankie had disappeared shortly before the Simpsons left, and I went to look for him. I found him lying across his bed, holding an army man in one hand and a horse in the other.

"Is that one of Emily's horses?"

He nodded. "She said I could keep 'em." He rolled onto one side, so he was facing me. "Mommy, why'd dey have to go away? It makes me sad."

I sat on the bed next to him. "It makes me sad, too, sweetheart. But you know they live in Nashville."

"Yeah, but why do they have to live there? They could live here." He moved the army man so that its plastic arm was caressing the horses back. "We could play all the time then." The grim set of his lips tugged at my heart.

"Say. Why don't we call Tommy's mother and see when they can come over this week?"

He sat up on the bed and nodded vigorously. "Can we?"

"Absolutely! Let's go in the kitchen and call them right now."

He jumped off the bed and skipped down the hall.

Luckily, the Sanders were at home. Betty and I spoke and arranged for the three of them to come to dinner the following Wednesday. Frankie wanted them to come sooner, but that was as early as they were available. We agreed Tommy could come home with Frankie that day so they would have more time to play together, which elicited a happy dance from him.

I hung up the phone and turned to him with a smile. "Okay, we're all set. Now, how about you and I get ready to go to the beach. Daddy suggested we go, and I'll bet he's ready by now."

He ran down the hall to his room while I headed to the living room to find Jon.

"I spoke to Betty Sanders and invited them for dinner this Wednesday. Tommy will come home with Frankie from day care, and then Betty and Hal will join us around 6:00 PM."

His eyes seemed far off. "What's that? Oh. The Sanders. That sounds good. I should be able to get home early that day."

I studied him curiously. "Everything okay? You seem distracted."

"Just some work stuff. Are you ready to go to the beach?"

"I just need to put some sunscreen on myself and Frankie."

He nodded, but his attention seemed to have drifted off again. I decided not to pursue it as Mary's advice popped back into my head. I was determined to give whatever was weighing on him time to become clear and trust he would share it with me when he was ready. My heart told me that was the right thing to do, but my mind was trying hard to disagree.

I didn't have to wait long to find out what was on Jon's mind. We decided to stop by the Tiki Hut at the end of our beach walk and, as fate would have it, Savannah was there. She spotted me, as we walked up from the beach, and eagerly waved us over.

"Hey, Georgia! I've been hoping I'd run into you again." She glanced at Jon. "You must be Jon. My uncle told me he spoke to you on the phone a couple of times."

Jon offered her his hand to shake. "That's right. It's nice to meet you." Frankie butted his head against Jon's leg. "And this is our son, Frankie." Frankie pushed his hand out in imitation of his dads' gesture. Savannah smiled and shook his offered hand.

"What a gentleman you are!" She looked around. "I'm afraid there aren't any empty seats at the bar, but we could move to a table. That is, if you'd like to. I don't want to intrude on your family time."

I looked to Jon for an answer, hoping he would find a way to decline her invitation. I had enjoyed talking to her when we first met at the Tiki Hut, but my gut was having the opposite reaction now. Unfortunately, Jon didn't seem to have the same response.

"Sure. Let's sit over there." He indicated a vacant table at the far end of the patio.

Once we were seated, Savannah leaned over to me. "My uncle told me your husband has been a godsend. Apparently, they've been conspiring over some deal he claims will turn Hilton Head on its head."

"Oh really? In what way?"

"It's too early to talk about at this point. We've just been batting around some ideas." Jon was wearing his best poker face.

Savannah considered his reply. "Hum. Well, that's not how my uncle described it. He seems to think you're some kind of real estate miracle worker. The whole idea that one investment might make a million-dollar difference in profit is pretty doggone impressive, any way you look at it."

Jon flagged down a waiter. "Why don't we order. Georgia, what would you like?"

I wanted to say, "What I'd like is to know what the hell she's talking about!" But what I said was, "I'll have a Pina Colada."

He ordered my drink, a Tom Collins for himself and orange soda for Frankie. Savannah declined the offer of another beer. "I have to drive back to Tybee in a little while."

While we waited for our drinks, Savannah turned to me. "Georgia, what have you been up to?"

"Oh, just the usual things: walking on the beach; taking bike rides; getting to know more about this beautiful island."

"That sounds wonderful. I keep promising myself I'll spend more time exploring Hilton Head, but I never get around to doing it. I guess I'm a Tybee girl through and through."

Our drinks arrived, and I sipped the frozen concoction, which was just one more tactic at trying to keep from probing deeper into what Jon and her uncle had been discussing, and what Savannah really knew about it all. My reward was, once again, an achy head as the drink froze my brain. I pressed my hand against my forehead and grimaced.

Savannah looked at me sympathetically. "Brain freeze again. That's why I steer clear of their frozen drinks." She took a sip of beer and looked at Frankie. "How old are you, young man?"

He looked at her beneath lowered lashes. "I not a man. I jes this many." He held up three fingers.

"Ooh. That old! Well, you certainly are a handsome boy. You look just like your daddy." She smiled flirtatiously at Jon.

My gut responded predictably. I liked Savannah, at least I thought I did, but I'd had about enough of this conversation full of hidden meanings and unspoken truths.

"Jon, I just remembered I promised Julie I'd call her. Maybe we can take the rest of our drinks to go."

His eyes narrowed as he studied me. I knew he saw through my diversion tactic, but I hoped he'd go along with it. "Okay. Let me go to the bar and pay the bill. I'll ask the bartender for some paper cups."

While he was away from the table, Savannah leaned closer to me and whispered. "I don't care what he said. My uncle thinks he's going to be the answer to a prayer."

I smiled at her politely. "Jon's extremely good at what he does. I'm sure if he decides to work with your uncle, everything will go well."

"I'm sure it will." She replied.

Jon was silent for most of the walk home until we reached the stone steps marking the way to our backyard. Finally, I couldn't hold my tongue any longer. "You want to tell me what that was all about?"

He opened the back door. "Frankie, why don't you go inside? You can watch a little TV until mommy and I come in." Frankie rushed inside, and Jon closed the door behind him. "Let's sit outside for a while. I think I owe you an explanation."

"Gee. Yuh think?" I pulled a chair out from the patio table and sat.

"Her uncle, whose name is Robert Quinn, is part of the group of investors Harry mentioned who are attempting to buy out the Sea Pines Company. Harry said in the beginning of the recession we're in, Fraser turned the operating responsibilities of the company over to someone else to fend off bankruptcy. So far, they've been successful. But Quinn is determined to dig up enough dirt on the company to push things in the opposite direction.

"Where I come in is that Quinn and his group are looking for a realtor based on Hilton Head to help poke around behind the scenes. The person they hoped would fill that role moved away. It became clear to me right off the bat what they were up to, even before Harry shared what he learned at the meeting. I pretended I was interested in what they were asking, although I didn't commit to anything specific. I guess you could say we're in the talking stage of things. I told Harry about our conversation, and he felt it would be wise to play dumb and see what I could learn.

When we met with Henry, he told us about a conversation he overheard in his store between two men who seemed to be discussing some big buyout they were trying to pull off. Henry was standing nearby, but as he put it: "De wite men don' notice de colored eben wen de unduh de nose". Henry told me because he was hoping I would be able to find out through the realtors' association exactly what's going on."

I smiled at his imitation of Henry's accent. "I wonder what Henry would think if he knew the company they're targeting manages the entire Sea Pines Resort? It's my impression that a lot of the local Gullah descendants have been less than thrilled with the way the Sea Pines Company has managed to shift money and services away from the original settlers, in favor of funneling funds into developments that would mostly benefit the rich whites who have been taking over the island businesses."

"True. But, as he explained it, Charles Fraser has endeared himself to the Gullah because of his fair business practices, and efforts to retain the natural beauty of the island. There are still things Henry and his friends would like to see done differently, like improvements in affordable housing; adequate water and waste disposal; better paying jobs on the island so a long-distance commute isn't necessary; better schools and health care; public utilities. I take it they believe Fraser is their best bet to help them make some headway in these issues. The way Henry explained it, Fraser is considered somewhat of a crusader among the Gullah. Besides, a buyout by Quinn's company wouldn't change the racial configuration of the ownership. If anything, it would strengthen the disparity that already exists on the island."

"Okay. That all makes sense. But why wouldn't you share any of this with me? Why do I have to nag you into telling me what's going on? I thought we were beyond that after you kept your plans for buying a house here secret until you blurted it out when we had dinner with your father." I could feel the heat from my anger rise inside of me in tune with the throbbing of the amulet.

He winced at my rebuke. "You're absolutely right to be upset with me. In my defense, it all happened so fast that I'm still trying to wrap my head around it. After I spoke to Savannah's uncle, I was trying to get a clear idea of what the investment company is up to before I shared any of this with anyone. But because Harry was visiting and happened to share details about his meeting in Savannah, which was clearly with the same investors Robert Quinn is involved with, things started moving ahead fast. When you add in the conversation Harry and I had with Henry, and our unplanned meeting with Savannah today, I didn't have a chance to process things in my own mind, much less share them with you."

I could feel my anger dissipate as he spoke. "I agree it's a lot to digest, but you need to promise me that from this point forward you won't keep any secrets from me. You don't have to worry about me saying anything about this to anyone. Except maybe Julie. She's probably already heard a lot about it from Harry." Her comments to Mary about Harry holding something back from her popped into my mind. "Or maybe not. Anyway, you need to know you can trust me."

"I do. I realize I may not have been acting like I do recently, and a couple of times in the past, but I trust you more than anyone." He lifted my hand to his mouth and pressed a kiss on the palm. "Trust is still something I'm working on."

I could understand Jon's reluctance to be completely open to anyone, even his wife. He was raised by an iron-fisted father who taught him to trust sparingly and doubt globally. "I know it's hard for you to let down your guard, and I understand some of the reasons why. I'm just asking you to let me in on what you're feeling, and what's going on in that stubborn mind of yours."

"Deal. But remember; you've had your own worries to contend with. Dead birds, and voodoo doctors, and things that go bump in the night."

I rolled my eyes at him. "That's true, except the man Frankie met is not called a Voodoo Doctor. The Gullah don't use that term. He's known as a Root Doctor or Conjure Man. The magic they perform is called Hoodoo, not Voodoo."

"Aren't they the same thing?"

"Not at all. Mary explained this to me once. Voodoo is a religion with branches in Haiti and Louisiana. Hoodoo isn't a religion at all, but a form of folk magic that originated in West Africa. In the U.S., it's mostly practiced in the South, and most people who practice it are Protestant Christians."

He scratched his head. "I guess we're both traveling uncharted territory. Except mine only involves the living."

"As far as you know." I looked at him purposely.

He nodded thoughtfully. "Yes, as far as I know."

CHAPTER ELEVEN

July was probably my least favorite month on the island. For one thing, it was HOT, and I don't mean just summer in the south hot, but hot enough to melt butter on the pavement. It was also undoubtedly the busiest month for tourists. There were the "local" tourists–folks who lived off-island and headed to the beach most weekends. They began flocking in around midday on Friday and departed in a wave by late Sunday afternoon. The rest of the tourists came from farther away and tended to stay for at least a week. Rentals were usually booked from Saturday to Saturday, with check in at 3:00 PM and check out at noon, or earlier. Locals were well versed in the traffic patterns this dictated, studiously avoiding traveling onto the island on Saturday afternoons, or off-island on Saturday mornings. Grocery shopping during tourist season was also avoided on Saturday afternoons, and a trip to Walmart, the local mecca for beach paraphernalia, was taboo on both Saturday and Sunday.

July also marked the arrival of Emily and Ashley's third birthday. Jon and I discussed driving to Nashville for the occasion, but since the influx of tourists onto Hilton Head also meant a peak in prospective real estate sales, he decided it wouldn't be feasible for him to be away. Instead, he generously offered to purchase plane tickets for Frankie and me so we wouldn't have to drive the long distance by ourselves. That was a wise decision given that Frankie's tolerance for sitting in a car for long periods was even worse than mine.

Our plan was to fly to Nashville on Thursday afternoon and return the following Monday. That way, we would avoid the weekend crush of travelers. Julie had returned part-time to her work at the bank after the twins turned two. At first, she had been reluctant to leave them. But, once she saw how excited they were to have other children to play with, she settled happily into her new routine. Her schedule allowed her to leave work every day at 1:00 PM so she could pick up the girls from day care. Since our flight was due into Nashville at 2:00 PM, we agreed that Frankie and I would take a taxi to her home, which would keep her from having to rush across town to pick us up.

Julie and Harry bought a small house across the street from our former high school shortly before the twins were born. The house was typical for the era: two floors, with the bedrooms upstairs and living space below. Since the idea of toddlers careening down the staircase was not an image they were comfortable with, they converted part of the first floor living space into a master bedroom with a sitting room/kids bedroom next door. That meant the upstairs became their living space where the kids could play, and the parents could work or relax while keeping a careful eye on their whereabouts. There was also a daybed with a trundle underneath that could be converted into guest space.

The taxi driver pulled in front of their house and jumped out to lift our luggage from the trunk. I paid him and turned around to find Frankie tugging the smaller of our two bags up their front steps. The door swung open, spilling out Emily who jumped up and down on the porch when she saw Frankie.

"You're here!"

Ashley stood beside her and perfected an attitude that seemed to say, "I couldn't care less that you're here." I had to smile at the girl's sass!

Julie came to the door behind Ashley. "Girls, go help Frankie and Aunt Georgia with their luggage."

Julie embraced me in a hug before pulling back to look at me. "How was your flight? Did you get anything to eat on the plane?"

Julie was well known for her big appetite and what Harry referred to as her hollow leg. No matter how much she ate, she never seemed to gain any weight, except when she'd been pregnant with the twins.

"Not to speak of. They gave us those little packets of peanuts and a drink. Frankie looked so pitiful when he saw the size of the packet, the flight attendant snuck him two more."

"Harry will be home around 5:30. We can have some snacks now, and I've planned a special dinner for later."

We headed into the house and deposited our luggage on the floor just inside the entrance. "The place looks even nicer than the last time I saw it. Is that sofa new?" I gestured to an L-shaped leather sofa against one wall.

"Yeah. We decided we needed a larger place to relax when we're all watching TV. The leather comes in handy, too, because it's easy to wipe up spills." I felt a wet nose press into my hand. "And dog hairs." She looked down affectionately at the yellow lab leaning against my leg.

I bent and rubbed the dog's head. "Hey, Sunny. Where's your sidekick?" Sunny, and a black mutt named Barkster, were Julie's brothers' dogs. When they left for college, the dogs care fell to her dad until Harry came into the family picture. Harry loved spending his free time outdoors, and he gladly included the dogs on his outings whenever possible.

"Barkster's in the backyard; where Sunny's supposed to be." She grabbed the dog by his collar and led him to the back door. "We're keeping them this weekend while my folks are in Cincinnati." Sunny ran outside where she was greeted by the excited yips of Barkster. "Why don't you and Frankie take your things upstairs and get settled while I put some snacks together? Let's sit on the front porch where the dogs won't bother us."

We did as she suggested and returned to find Julie and the girls settled around a small table out front. Julie handed me a glass. "It's so hot today, I thought you might enjoy this." I took a sip from the icy beverage. It was a gin and tonic with extra lime.

"Perfect." I took another sip and looked at her appreciatively.

Julie and I moved to chairs on the other side of the porch, leaving the space at the table for the kids. School was just letting out across the street. We watched the parade of cars exiting the parking lot, and kids piling out the front door. "It feels like such a long time ago we were in high school," she said.

I added up the dates in my mind. "Ten years. Wow! That IS a pretty long time. But look what we have to show for it." I glanced over at the three kids.

Julie smiled. "Pretty amazing, isn't it? If you'd asked me ten years ago, or even five, what I'd be doing now, I don't think I would have described this scene."

"Would you change any of it?"

She answered without hesitation. "Not a thing. How 'bout you?"

I thought for a moment. "Maybe all that business that happened with the newspapers, except that's how I met Jon." I was referring to the time I found myself in the middle of a battle between the two newspapers in Nashville. The end result: one of them was relocated to the campus of Belmont College–a feat engineered by myself, Jon, my dear friend Ida Hood who passed away shortly before the move was accomplished, and Thomas Bookman, the director of the Journalism program at the College. My involvement resulted in being fired from the Nashville News. Luckily, Thomas saved the day by creating a job for me at the College.

"Yeah, that was a trying time."

We grew silent as we resumed our watch over the activities across the street. Soon, our reflective state was interrupted by the three kids who trooped over to us.

"Mommy, we're bored. Can we go inside and play?" Emily looked at us hopefully.

"Of course, sweetie. Why don't you take Frankie upstairs and show him your toys?"

She nodded eagerly, taking Frankie by the hand as they ran inside. Ashley lagged behind, looking as if she wanted to say something. Julie put her hand on Ashley's shoulder. "What is it, Ash? Is something bothering you?"

Ashley stubbed the toe of one shoe into the floor and shrugged her shoulders. "When Frankie's around, Em doesn't want to play with me."

"Oh honey, I don't think that's true. Emily's simply happy to see Frankie. Why don't you show Frankie that book you have with all the different pictures of fish? I'll bet he'd love to see it." Her eyes lit up as she considered the suggestion, then nodded sagely.

"Okay, Mommy." She turned on her heel and went inside.

Julie grinned. "I swear, that child is a little old woman camouflaged as a three-year old."

I laughed in agreement. "Let me ask you something. Did you ever get Harry to tell you what's been weighing on his mind?"

She rolled her eyes. "Yes, but not until after we had a huge argument. On the way back from Hilton Head, I asked him why he was shutting me out, and he got upset, saying I was badgering him, or something like that. I got offended and refused to talk to him for the next hour or so until he finally pulled off at a rest stop so we could hash things out. Turns out, he's been feeling dissatisfied at work, and was afraid to tell me because my dad is his boss. He thought I'd be offended, but I told him that as long as it wasn't something personal against my dad, he shouldn't be worried how I'd react. Or, even if it were personal, he could still talk to me about it."

"What's he going to do? Do you think he'll quit his job?"

"I really don't know. Financially speaking, we depend on his salary, so he'd need to have something else lined up before he could make a change."

"I remember how it felt when Jon's dad sold his company and suddenly Jon was out of work. It was pretty scary for a while, but eventually everything worked out."

"He seems pretty happy with what he's doing now."

"Most of the time, although lately I sense he's itching for a new challenge. I just try to remind myself of Miss Bessie and Mary's advice about trusting my heart, because my heart tells me I can trust Jon. I'm not saying it's easy for me to let go of my worries, but I'm working on it. The amulet helps."

She looked at me curiously. "It's working, again? I remember you saying it had stopped giving you signals."

"True, but that bottle the Root Doctor gave Frankie seems to be helping. The amulet isn't as strong as it was a few years ago, but I've noticed it's starting to heat up when I have some big question weighing on me."

"Cool. Is it talking to you about your pregnancy question?"

I felt a flush of embarrassment. "I haven't really asked it about that."

She turned to me in surprise. "Why not? I thought that was one of the main things weighing on you lately."

"It is, but I guess I'm not sure I'm ready to hear the answer."

She considered my statement. "Well, that's okay. It'll either happen or it won't. Whichever way it goes, you just have to trust it'll be the right one."

I smiled. "Not you, too? Are you telling me to jes trus' de haa't?"

She laughed. "I guess I am." She stood. "Right now, my stomach is drowning out anything my heart could possibly be saying. What d'ya say we go in and get dinner started?"

I looked at the empty tray of appetizers she had prepared. It was true the kids made a big dent in them, but I could have sworn the tray was still half full after they left. "I'd say your appetite never ceases to amaze me."

Julie went all out for dinner that night. She managed to find fresh shrimp in one of the local markets and fried them in a light batter along with some hush puppies that rivaled the ones at Hudson's. A simple green salad and ripe tomatoes with thousand island dressing topped off the meal. Everything was so good I was tempted to go back for seconds until I noticed a homemade peach pie on the counter.

"Dinner was amazing. Where did you find fresh shrimp in this land-locked city?"

"A friend at work told me of a place in Clarksville that's known for its fresh fish and seafood. She was going there yesterday and offered to pick some up for me. She also gave me the recipe for these hush puppies."

"She must be a Low Country girl. The shrimp were as fresh as anything I've had on the island, and the hush puppies were as good as Hudson's." I glanced at the counter. "Is that homemade peach pie I'm looking at?"

She grinned. "Yep. Made it yesterday, only this recipe is all mine. Harry, would you mind serving the pie? I'll get the vanilla ice cream from the freezer to top it off."

Harry had arrived home from work just as Julie was finishing the dinner preparations. He jumped up from the table in response to her request. "Be happy to, Hon!"

When we'd finished with dessert, and cleaned off the table, I took Frankie upstairs to get him ready for bed. By the time I came back downstairs, the twins had also been tucked in, and Harry and Julie were sitting on the front porch, sipping small glasses of gold-colored liquid. Harry offered one to me when I stepped outside.

"Nightcap? We're having a little Drambuie." I accepted the glass from him and took a sip.

"Um. It tastes like honey, with a dash of herbs."

"Good guess. It's a liqueur made from Scotch, honey, herbs, and spices. I usually mix it with straight Scotch and a twist of lemon to make a drink called a Rusty Nail, but I was feeling lazy tonight. I hope you like it."

I took another sip. "Very much. Thanks." I sat next to them. "What's on the agenda for tomorrow?"

"Harry has to work, but I was able to get the day off. I thought we could roam around Nashville a bit; visit some of our old spots. Then I need to pick up some things we need for the twins' birthday party on Saturday. We can order pizza for dinner."

"Sounds good to me. I need to stop by to visit my parents at some point. I think I'll try to arrange to do that on Sunday if I can borrow your car."

"Sure. Unless you want to invite them to the birthday party? It might be a little more relaxing for you to have the distraction of ten three-year old's running around. Oops! Maybe I shouldn't have suggested that a houseful of three-year olds would be less stressful than the company of your parents…"

"No need to apologize. You know as well as I you spoke the truth, but I don't think it would be fair to insert my parents into the party lineup. Not fair to them? Maybe. But, certainly not fair to the kids. I'll just plan on a short visit on Sunday. I'm sure Frankie will provide a good buffer against whatever they have in mind to criticize me about this time around. If not, I'll just cut the visit even shorter." Things became a little more relaxed with my parents after they hosted my wedding reception, and even more after Frankie was born. But they still had a way of making me feel like an inept child when I was around them for very long.

"When are you going back to Hilton Head?" Harry asked.

"We fly out around Noon on Monday. We have to connect with another flight in Atlanta, which will put us on the ground in Savannah around 4:00 PM. Jon will still be at work, so we'll take a taxi home from the airport."

"Wouldn't it be great if there was a direct flight to the Hilton Head airport?" Julie asked.

"It sure would." I agreed. "Rumor has it that Eastern Airlines will start flying prop planes to the island next year. But that would still require a stop in either Atlanta or Charlotte from Nashville."

"Maybe you could hitch a ride with Arnold Palmer. I hear he has his own private plane he uses to fly to Hilton Head to play golf." Harry wiggled his eyebrows at me.

"Oh yeah, I'm sure he wouldn't mind me tagging along. Remember that first time on Hilton Head when you convinced Jon to play golf on the Harbour Town Links because you'd heard Arnold would be there?"

He laughed. "He was so P.O.'d at me when he learned it was nothing more than a rumor. He wouldn't admit it, but we had a lot of fun that day."

We grew silent as the night settled around us. The moon was a crescent in the sky providing the only visible light except for a lone streetlight standing sentinel over the high school. Julie lit two votive candles and placed them on the porch table. We watched their flickering glow dance in the remaining liqueur in our glasses until the flames disappeared along with the liquid light.

I stood and stretched my arms high overhead. "I think it's time for me to turn in. My body clock is on Eastern Standard Time."

"I forgot about that, although as I recall you've never needed an excuse to go to bed early." Julie picked up her glass and added mine to it.

"Jules, I'll be in shortly. I just want to sit here a little while longer." Harry put his arm around her waist, and she bent to kiss the top of his head.

I hugged Julie goodnight and headed up the stairs. Frankie was snoring quietly. I pulled the sheet over his shoulders and headed for my own bed.

CHAPTER TWELVE

The day of the birthday party brought partly cloudy skies, but no chance of rain. The clouds were actually a relief from the harshness of the July heat. Seven children from Emily and Ashley's Daycare Center were due to arrive by 1, and Julie, Harry and I were hustling to make sure everything would be ready. Harry strung colored lanterns in an x-pattern across the back yard with a globe shaped piñata suspended in the middle. The original plan was for the piñata to bear the image of a smiling donkey, but Ashley had protested against the inhumanity of battering the poor burro in order to free the captive candy and toys. I had to admit, I agreed with her sentiment.

The twins chose a Mexican theme for their party. Julie mentioned that the Daycare Center had thrown a fun-filled Cinco de Mayo party two months prior, and she suspected the girls were hoping for a birthday party to rival that event. Julie and Harry didn't seem to mind. Neither of them had any Mexican or even Southwestern heritage in their family history, but it was an easy party to pull off.

After the last child had been picked up and the assorted party trash disposed of, we put Frankie and the twins down for a nap before collapsing on the sofa.

"That was a lot of fun." I remarked. "A lot of work, but still a lot of fun."

"Could you believe it when that little boy, what was his name... Ben something, cheated at Pin the Tail on the Donkey? It was clear he could see beneath the bandana around his eyes." Harry shook his head.

"I know! But I decided it would be best not to say anything. I guess he just needed to win at something." Julie looked sympathetic, but Harry just scoffed at her.

"You ole softie! You just can't bring yourself to hurt anyone's feelings; even if it means allowing a cheater to win."

She looked at him askance. "He's only three years old! He doesn't even know what cheating means!"

Harry looked unconvinced. "Maybe not, but I can remember stealing Tootsie rolls out of a bag in the grocery store when I was around that age, and I sure knew it wasn't right."

Julie attempted to look alarmed. "Harry the thief! I'm shocked!"

I was watching their exchange through half-closed eyes. "You two are crazy!" I yawned wide. "Maybe I should take a nap, too. I can't seem to keep my eyes open."

"I guess I kept you up too late last night talking." Julie looked at me apologetically.

"I thought I heard the two of you yammering away after I went to bed. It's amazing to me that you never run out of things to talk about even though you speak on the phone almost every day." Harry shook his head.

I opened one eye. "It's always been that way with us. That's one of the first things I liked about Julie: we could talk freely with each other about anything, and we never felt at a loss for words. Of course, we're able to just hang out and say nothing sometimes, too, which I find even more rare."

Julie looked at her watch. "The kids will probably sleep for another hour. Anyone interested in taking a walk?"

I shook my head. "You and Harry go on. I'll stay here and listen for them. I may doze a little, too, on this incredibly comfortable sofa." They stood to leave, and I scooted down so I could rest my head on the sofa arm. The next thing I remembered was the feel of warm breath on my face. I opened my eyes expecting to find Frankie, instead I was looking at the fuzzy muzzle of Sunny. I scratched her behind the ears. "How'd you get in here?" I looked around the room but no one else was in sight. "Come on. Let's go look in on the kids." She trotted along beside me as we went to the twins' room then up the stairs to check on Frankie. The girls were sound asleep, but Frankie was nowhere in sight. "Now, where'd that boy disappear to?" I said out loud. Sunny turned her head sideways and uttered a low woof. It suddenly occurred to me how she may have gotten in the house.

I walked to the back door and looked out. As I expected, Frankie was walking along the fence line batting the wooden boards with a stick and talking to himself. Sunny and I went over to him.

"Hi sweetheart. Did you have a good nap?"

He stopped and looked at me curiously. "Yeah, but dis lady told me to come outside." He glanced over his shoulder as if he were looking at someone. My gut clenched.

"What lady? I don't see anyone."

"She's over dere." He pointed at the fence line to my right. "She say I should tell you ebryt'ing gonna be okay."

I looked around frantically, but the yard was empty. "Frankie, can you describe this woman?"

He nodded. "She hab gray hair that look like rolls on the sides of her head, and she's wearing gray clothes and black shoes." He resumed striking the fence.

My mouth dropped as I tried to register what he said. He was describing a person who sounded a lot like my dear friend Ida Hood who died some seven years earlier. "Can you ask this person what her name is?"

He stopped and stared at the fence to my right. "She say her name's Ida."

I nearly fainted at his last disclosure. Could it be possible that he was seeing the spirit of Ida Hood? But that would mean Frankie had the ability to see ghosts…like his mother.

"Frankie, I can't see anybody. Are you sure you're not just imagining it, like the time you pretended you were playing with Scooby-Doo?"

He shook his head emphatically. "Scooby-Doo not real. I make him up 'cos I was lonely. Dis lady real." He paused as if he was listening to something. Or someone. "She say, tell you she glad you 'n Daddy got married and hab me. Dat she always knew Daddy was uh good man."

I shook my head in disbelief. "Okay. Ask her what she meant when she said you should tell me everything's going to be alright."

He stopped and stared to my right again. "She say, what you worrying 'bout be okay. Jes need tuh gib it more time." He picked up his stick and started hitting the fence again. "Mommy, kin you wake up Emily? I want tuh play wid her some more."

I reached over and gently removed the stick from his hand. "Let's go inside and see if she's awake, but please don't hit the fence anymore. You might damage it, which would make Uncle Harry very sad."

He dropped the stick and wiped his hands on his shirt. "Okay, Mommy." He took my hand as we walked into the house.

That evening, we decided to have a simple dinner of leftover pizza and salad, along with the remains of the birthday cake. Everyone seemed subdued in the aftermath of the day's activities. Even the kids were relatively quiet as they lay on the living room floor and built a lego house. I had been preoccupied with my conversation with Frankie all afternoon and evening, and I was really hoping to have a chance to talk with Julie and Harry about it without little ears close by. When the kids were finally tucked away in bed, I was practically vibrating with the need to unburden my mind. Julie's radar must have been working, because she took me by the arm and led me to the porch.

"Okay, spill it. You've been distracted all night. What's going on in that head of yours?" Harry walked out to join us.

I looked at the two of them and took a deep breath. "Frankie saw Ida today; at least her ghost."

Julie leaned forward in her chair as Harry shook his head. "Ida Hood? You're telling us Frankie saw the ghost of Ida Hood?" Julie asked.

"It would appear so. He was outside in the backyard, and he told me there was a lady there who was talking to him. He described someone who sounded exactly like Ida, and when I asked him what she said, he told me she wanted me to know that what I'd been worrying about would be alright. That I just needed to give it more time."

Julie looked skeptical. "Are you sure he wasn't just imagining it? You know what an active imagination he has."

"I thought of that, but he said the ghost also told him she was glad Jon and I got married and had Frankie, and that she always knew Jon was a good man. I think that's a more elaborate story than even Frankie could cook up."

"Wow. That's pretty amazing," Harry said. "I find it hard to believe, but no more so than when I heard the story about how you met the ghost of Bessie Barnhill in the cemetery on Hilton Head."

We all lapsed into silence; each trying to process this latest twist to the continuing saga of strange happenings in the life of Georgia. Finally, Julie slapped her thighs and stood.

"I don't know about the rest of you, but I'm too wound up to go to sleep. Anyone else want a nightcap?"

Harry and I both raised our hands as she disappeared into the house. Harry turned to face me. "Have you had any communication from Ida before today?"

"No. And I didn't today, either. That's one thing that's very peculiar about this. She appeared to Frankie, not me. And she spoke only to him. Over the years since she's been gone, I've wished I would have some kind of sign from her; something to tell me she's at peace, but there's been nothing. And today, she didn't even address how she was, only seemed to want to let me know that things in my life would be okay.

"I'll say it again. Wow!" Julie returned with our drinks. Harry took his and continued speaking. "What do you make of her message? Is there something that's been worrying you?"

Julie and I looked at each other. "Actually, a few things. Number one, Jon and I have been talking about having another baby, but so far it hasn't happened. I've been wondering whether or not it's even in the cards for us. Number two, a man who, it turns out, is what they call a Root Doctor, gave Frankie a bottle that's supposed to restore power to the amulet Miss Bessie gave me. That was the first time something out of the ordinary, or super-ordinary, I guess you could say, happened that involved Frankie. And number three, there's this business about the potential take-over of the Sea Pines Company you and Jon have been talking about. Any one of them boggles my mind, but the combination has me losing sleep. One thing I've been deliberating is whether there's any connection between the three."

Harry's expression grew serious. "Julie mentioned the first two, and I know Jon spoke to you recently about the third. On the surface, it doesn't seem likely there's any connection between them. At least not between the potential take-over and the other two. On the other hand, I'm learning not to take things at face value. There's definitely more to this than meets the eye. I just haven't been able to put two and two together yet."

Julie giggled. "Sorry. But do you realize you just spouted a string of idioms? I've never known you to do that before."

His expression betrayed his confusion. "A what?"

"Idiom. A commonly used expression whose meaning doesn't relate to the literal meaning of the words." I explained. "Like what I'm doing now, which is putting in my two cents worth. It's a way of prefacing my opinion by suggesting its value is only worth two cents."

He looked from one of us to the other. "Uh huh. All I was saying is I don't think the three things you mentioned are necessarily related."

Julie hid her grin behind her hand. "Georgia, I guess we can let him off the hook. After all, the real elephants in the room are these supernatural things that keep happening to you, or in this case, Frankie. Maybe you should just throw caution to the wind and see this through. Just trust your heart, as Miss Bessie said."

I laughed out loud. "Yeah, I guess we'll cross that bridge when we come to it. But your guess is as good as mine when that will be." We erupted in raucous laughter, causing Harry to shake his head in exasperation.

"Okay, you two. I think it's time to hit the sack before things get out of hand."

And without realizing it, Harry had just hit the nail on the head!

CHAPTER THIRTEEN

Things were fairly uneventful for the next month. Jon's work picked up considerably as more and more tourists clamored to investigate the real estate offerings on the island. He hadn't spoken much about the situation with the Sea Pines Company, but I knew it was still on the table based upon a couple of telephone conversations I overheard. Frankie and Tommy had been spending a lot of time together since the evening the Sanders came to dinner at our house. Jon took Betty and Hal to see four possible houses that fit their budget, and it appeared they were closing in on a decision.

I settled into a routine of early morning walks, afternoons reading or visiting Mary and Henry or Betty Sanders, late afternoons on the beach, followed by a stop at the Tiki Hut to cool off before returning home to get ready for dinner. I had yet to find something that would fill my time in a more professional manner, but I was perfectly satisfied with the way things were for now. After all, it was August in the South: the time when life slowed to a near stop in the unrelenting heat.

One afternoon, just as I was getting ready to walk over to the Red and White market for a few things, I heard a knock on our front door. I opened it to find Betty standing there.

"Betty! How are you?" I held the door open for her to enter.

"I promise I won't stay long, but I just had to share our news with you." She stepped inside, and I motioned for her to take a seat at the kitchen table.

"I'm glad to see you. Can I get you a glass of iced tea or something?"

"No thanks, I'm fine. As I said, I won't be but a minute."

"Okay. What's going on?"

"We bought a house! I know Jon will give you all the details tonight, but I couldn't wait to tell you about it."

"That's fantastic! Is it one of the ones he's been showing you?"

"That's the funny thing. It's a house we never even considered because we thought it was too expensive. Jon called us first thing this morning to tell us the owners lowered the price considerably, and he thought they might be willing to go down even more. Luckily, Hal was home, and we rushed right out to see it. Jon warned us ahead of time not to act too interested and, let me tell you, that was SO difficult! I fell in love with the place the moment I stepped inside.

"It's not far from the beach, but it's on the other side of the island from here. It's off Beach City Road, you know, down from the Hilton Head airport. There's an area they call Mitchelville nearby, and the Fish Haul beach. In between the two is a small cluster of houses. Most of them are in pretty poor condition; run-down, and in need of a lot of work. The one we looked at is one of the rare ones that's been totally renovated, with a modernized kitchen and bathroom, an extension to the porch with one end screened in, new paint and hardwood floors. There's even a little deck off the master bedroom upstairs that has a view of the Port Royal Sound in the distance.

"According to Jon, the owners inherited the house from relatives. They've been living in Philadelphia and planned to move here as soon as the renovations were complete. Unfortunately, for them at least, the husband had a heart attack, and they decided they'd be better off staying put. They listed it for sale a couple of months back, then lowered the price when they failed to have any offers."

"So, you bought it? Today?"

"Just about an hour ago. Hal's with Jon now wrapping up the details. I was so excited, I couldn't wait to tell someone, and frankly, you're the closest friend I have on Hilton Head."

I was touched by her acknowledgement of our growing friendship. "I'm so happy for you! When do you get to move in?"

"Probably by the end of the month. The owners just have to move some of their personal things out, and we have to deal with the bank about the mortgage, but it looks like things will move pretty quickly."

I leaned back in my chair. "That's great. I can't wait to see it. Jon and I will be glad to help you move your things when it's time. Henry has a couple of friends with pickup trucks. I'm sure they'd be willing to let us use them. We might even convince them to lend a hand, especially if there's a chance of free beer and pizza afterwards."

A smile stretched across her face. "That would be great. We don't have that much to move. We sold a lot of our things when we moved down here. Plus, the former owners are leaving a lot of their furnishings in the house."

She stood and began to move toward the door. "I told Hal I'd pick up Tommy and meet him somewhere for dinner. Why don't you, Jon, and Frankie join us? We thought we'd try Fitzgerald's. Have you been there?"

"A couple of times. The décor is a bit dated, but the food is good, and the manager–Hugo–is a real gem. Should we meet you there?"

"That'd be great. How about 6:30? I'll call and make a reservation."

After she left, I thought about the house they were about to purchase. If my estimation was correct, it sat smack dab in the middle of a historic Gullah neighborhood. In that case, the Sanders would probably be the only white faces around. I had to wonder what the neighbors would think about that. I decided to give Mary a call. She picked up the phone after a half dozen rings.

"'Lo. Mary speak'n'."

"Hi Mary, it's Georgia."

"Glad tuh hear fum oonuh. How ebryt'ing?"

"Everything's fine, but I wanted to ask you about a house some of our friends just bought. You remember the Sanders? Their son, Tommy, has been to your house with Frankie."

"Yaas. Fine lil boy."

"Well, his mother, Betty, just told me they bought a house somewhere over near Fish Haul Beach. She said it's the only fully renovated house in the area, and I wonder if you know anything about it?"

The line was quiet for a few seconds. "Dat de Reb'ren' sistuh house. Oonuh 'member Reb'ren' Henderson?" Reverend Henderson was Bessie Barnhill's cousin, and had been instrumental in helping me figure out how her Uncle, Joshua Barnhill, had died. "'E sistuh own de house till 'e pass ober. Leebe 'e uh nephew, but 'e cum down wid sick haa't. Uh hear 'e 'cide tuh stay up Nawth. Spen' lotta money on 'e, but hab hard time fin' someone tuh buy. Say oonuh fren' gonna buy de house?"

"That's right." I hesitated before continuing. "I'm not sure how to ask this, but since they're white, do you think they'll have any trouble being accepted by the neighbors?"

I heard her chuckle over the phone. "W'ite, colored, eb'rybody hab trouble 'cept'in' each udder. No w'ites lib ober dere 'fo'. Likely be liddle uncum'table, but 'ventually folks 'cep' dem. 'Cep'm mek trouble; act uppity like dey better dan de udders. Be nice, 'spectful, t'ings work out. Enry 'n me kin talk tuh sum dem. Prepare dem fo' de news. Mite hep sum. Mite not."

113

"I would appreciate that. The Sanders are good people, but a word or two in their favor from you and Henry would really help. Thank you."

"Glad fuh he'p. Anytime kin mek t'ings easy 'tween folks wu't' w'ile."

I took a deep sigh of relief after I hung up the phone. As I expected, having the Sanders suddenly move into a previously all-black neighborhood would be uncomfortable at best, but having Mary and Henry speak up for them should make things easier. At least, that's what I hoped. I decided to phone Jon to let him know about my conversation with Mary, and our plans to meet the Sanders for dinner that night. Maybe we could find a way to coach them a little about how to make an easy transition into their new neighborhood.

The Sanders moving date was set for the third week of August. Jon was able to recruit the help of two of Henry's friends and their pick-up trucks, and Henry gathered together another half-dozen men to help with the heavy lifting. As Betty indicated, their household goods only managed to fill the trucks and two additional cars, which made the move much easier than anticipated. As a result, the entire move took less than four hours.

Betty just set down the last box when the pizza delivery man arrived with a stack of hot pies. Jon and I placed several six-packs of beer and soft drinks in their refrigerator earlier in the afternoon, which we proceeded to hand out to everyone. Mary and Henry joined us a short time after we arrived at the new house. They suggested that the boys stay with them while the move was in progress. They led them into the house with strict instructions not to run around like "a couple of hound dogs". Of course, they followed that advice for just under two minutes before scampering off to explore the new house. The rest of us took seats on the available chairs or empty spots on the floor.

I looked around for Betty and Hal. Moving to a new home, even under the best of circumstances, was a trying experience. Hal looked relaxed standing with a group of men laughing at some shared joke. But Betty was sitting on the floor by herself. I picked up my pizza and drink and walked over to join her. She scooted sideways to make room for me.

"How're you holding up?" I settled onto the floor next to her.

"Good. The move was a lot easier than I expected, thanks, of course, to all the helping hands you and Jon rounded up."

"You really have Henry and Mary to thank for that."

We both looked around until we spotted them sitting on a couple of folding chairs near the front door. Mary glanced up and gave us a slight wave, which we both returned.

"I don't know them very well, but they seem nice."

"MORE than nice. They're special people."

"Anybody in the mood for some pie?" A woman stepped into the open doorway holding a foil covered pie plate. Two other women and three men followed right behind her, each holding a wrapped dish.

Mary stood and walked over to the group. "Pie alltime welcome!" She ushered in the six visitors and placed a hand on two of the women's shoulders.

"Dese here f'um we chu'ch. Dis sistuh Josephine and Aileen, back dere sistuh Evelyn and bubbas Joseph, Samuel, and Isaiah."

They nodded and looked around at the rest of us. The man Mary identified as Joseph stepped forward. "Mary an' Henry tell us we hab sum new neighbors. Want tuh mek ya'll welcome. De women cook up sum dey special homemade pie."

Betty stood and walked toward the visitors. "Welcome! I'm Betty Sanders, and that's my husband Hal over there by the kitchen door." Hal waved with a grin. "It is so thoughtful of you to stop by."

"Especially with homemade pie!" Hal's booming voice brought a round of laughter from the group.

Betty rolled her eyes at her husband and turned back to the visitors. "Won't you join us? We have plenty of pizza, and there's some beer and soft drinks in the kitchen."

Isaiah glanced around at the others who nodded their agreement. Betty ushered them to where there were still a few empty chairs and instructed Hal to bring more from the back room. She took a seat next to the woman Mary had called Josephine. "Do all of you live in the neighborhood?"

Josephine shook her head. "Samuel and I, dat my husbun', lib down de road uh lil. Us sell fish an' crabs tuh Henry sto'. Swimp, too, we'enebbuh ken. Evelyn an' Joseph lib jes pas' de chu'ch He uh Deke dere, an' she hep wid de chillun. Aileen and Isaiah lib obuh near Mary and Henry house. Aileen uh nuss obuh tuh hospital, an' Isaiah drive de schoolbus obuh een Bluffton."

Tommy appeared at her side with Frankie at his shoulder. "Frankie an' me saw some pie in the kitchen. Can we have some?"

Josephine gave him a big smile and patted him on the arm. "Leh we go tuh de kitchen tugedduh. Eef dat be alright wid yo' momma?" She turned to look at Betty.

Betty stood and took Tommy's hand. "Let me help. I'm sure the rest of this bunch would love some pie, too." The two women led the boys in the direction of the kitchen.

I turned back to Mary and smiled at her warmly. "I'm sure you had a hand in inviting them to stop by today."

She narrowed her eyes as she grinned in response. "Jes mite hab. Pie good way tuh mek fren's. Dese good folks. Hep Betty an' Hal feel welcome."

I looked around at the assortment of people gathered in the Sanders' house. It was quite a mixed group. Some old, some younger. Some white and others various shades of brown. Most people knew each other at least a little bit, and some were obviously long-time friends. Most important, everyone seemed at ease. I was reminded of something I once read: Family and friends make a home. Good neighbors make good neighborhoods.

I glanced over to where Jon was sitting, and we exchanged a satisfied smile. One thing I could say with certainty, in the midst of the uncertainties of my life, was that sometimes the simplest things brought the greatest pleasure.

CHAPTER FOURTEEN

Back when I was pregnant with Frankie, I picked up an old edition of The Readers Digest in my obstetrician's office. When I say old, the magazine was dated January 1957. It was a well-thumbed copy, with torn pages and what I assumed were coffee stains across the front. In other words, it was pretty nasty, but it was the only thing at hand to help me pass the time while waiting for my appointment.

I remember one particular section of the magazine called "Quotable Quotes". It contained a list of nine statements. The one that especially caught my eye was attributed to Allen Saunders, who I later learned wrote a comic strip called Steve Roper. The quotable quote of Mr. Saunders read: *Life is what happens to us while we are making other plans.* It was thought provoking, confusing, and intriguing, but I had to admit I didn't really understand what it meant. Until now.

My life has been preoccupied with trying to figure things out for as long as I can remember. Exactly what I was trying to figure out kept changing as I grew older, and life got both more and less complicated. Most recently, I was puzzling over the strange occurrences of supernatural spirits in my life; that Frankie had been pulled into this circle, and the serendipitous events that seemed intent on linking my past and present with an as-yet undisclosed future.

I didn't plan on getting pregnant with Frankie, but he was a welcome addition to my life. I didn't plan on quitting my job at Belmont College, moving to Hilton Head, and becoming basically unemployed. My life became surprisingly richer when I allowed my mind to open to other interests. I didn't plan on becoming close friends with Mary and Henry Palmer, or the ever-expanding circle of local Gullah descendants I met through them. Their presence in my life opened my eyes to the still-present inequities and disparities of life. I hadn't planned on Jon becoming so immersed in the real estate business on Hilton Head, but his involvement led him to discover a plot that threatened to reverse the long-standing efforts of a few good people determined to keep the natural beauty of our new island paradise relatively intact.

What I did plan on was figuring out whether or not I wanted to have another baby and, more importantly, if it was even in the cards for Jon and me. Ever since Frankie gave me the potion from the Root Doctor that was supposed to restore my amulet's power, I began to notice it throbbed with a growing heat whenever this question occupied my mind. I assumed that meant a second baby was a definite possibility, but I was still puzzled why nothing had happened yet. Perhaps the answer lies in the fact that, while my head was certainly preoccupied with the baby question, the message of my heart was less clear. Was I ready to have another child? Did I want to add to the already full and satisfying state of our family? I hadn't really resolved the issue of my career change either, or that I basically had no career or professional involvement whatsoever. Having a second child would likely take that possibility off the table, for the foreseeable future, and I wasn't sure how I felt about that. I talked all of this over at length with Julie on more than one occasion and sought out Mary's advice. But the voice I really wanted to hear was sadly quiet.

I wanted to talk to Ida. She had been an unexpected gift in my life at a time when I dearly needed motherly, or grandmotherly, advice. When she died unexpectedly in 1972, I would have fallen apart if not for the loving support of Julie and Jon. Since then, Mary occupied an important role for me as an older female voice of wisdom. When I thought of these things, I felt incredibly lucky. But I still couldn't deny the aching absence I felt for Ida.

My mind was full of these thoughts as I watched the news a few days after we helped the Sanders move into their new home. I was flipping through channels hoping to find a pleasant distraction for my worries when I came across the image of a large circular mass of clouds projected across the TV screen. I turned up the volume and learned that what I was seeing was an immense weather system forming over the African coast. I picked up the phone and dialed Julie.

"Are you watching the news?" She asked, before I could say hello.

"Yeah. Pretty scary, huh?"

"I'll say. The local weather forecaster says it's supposed to head for the Dominican Republic. They're not sure yet if it will become a hurricane, but they're betting it will."

"Hang on a minute. The Savannah news is discussing whether or not it poses any threat to Hilton Head and the surrounding area." I leaned closer to the screen and listened intently. "They said it will probably reach the Bahamas by the first of September, then head for Florida. After that, what areas it will impact depends on whether it stays more inland, pushes to the West, or skips up the Eastern coastline." I let out a deep breath. "I don't wish bad luck to anybody, but I sure hope it stays away from us."

"Me, too. I guess you haven't talked to Jon yet?"

"No. Or anybody on the island. I called you as soon as I saw the news."

"Well, don't be foolhardy. Stay on top of this and let me know what your plans are. Maybe you should consider heading for Nashville until it passes. At least hurricanes never make it this far."

"Yeah, there's that. I'll let you know."

I hung up the phone and called Jon.

"Have you heard about the hurricane?"

"They were just talking about it in the office. The best prediction is it won't come anywhere near Hilton Head."

"I sure hope they're right. Julie suggested we might want to come to Nashville for a few days."

"I don't think that's necessary. Besides, we won't even know where it's going to make landfall in the United States for five or six days. The weather forecasters should have a much better idea before then whether it will head this way. I don't think there's any need to worry."

His words did nothing to reassure me. "If you say so. I think I'm going to stock up on some non-perishables just in case."

I could hear him grin over the phone. "Make sure you add some of the liquid kind to your list. I'll be home around 5:30."

I replaced the phone in its cradle and went to the back deck to see how things looked. The sky was a brilliant blue with only a trace of wispy clouds. Ebie mewed at the back screen, and I let her out. She'd become rather good at staying close to home even when we allowed her to venture into the yard. A couple of run-ins with a blue heron who'd strayed too far from shore had cured her of the desire to explore further. I scooped her up and settled her against my chest.

"What do you think, sweet girl? Do you sense a hurricane in our future?"

She sniffed the air and mewed quietly. I couldn't tell if her reaction was to the far-off scent of fish or my weather worries, but I decided it was better to be safe than sorry. "Come on Eb. I think it's time to head to the store for some things that can carry us through whatever's coming." I headed inside the house where I placed her on the living room carpet before grabbing my purse to leave.

For the next four days, every radio and television on the island seemed to be tuned to the weather. It was impossible to go into any store without hearing an update on the storm, which had become an official hurricane upon reaching Dominica.

The reports indicated that the small island of Dominica had taken a hard hit on August 29th with wind speeds reaching up to 150 miles an hour. At least 37 people died, and over 60,000 lost their homes. One report said that amounted to nearly 75 percent of the entire population of Dominica. Both the banana and citrus crops, which were essential to the island's economy, were wiped out, as well.

Early on the morning of August 30th, the hurricane turned towards the Dominican Republic, pummeling the island with 175 mph winds and gusts over 200 mph. Waves were reported to be as high as 20 to 30 feet. Mudslides were particularly deadly to the island, contributing to the death of nearly 1,200 people. One particularly scary incident occurred in Padre Las Casas where more than 400 people had tied themselves together as they attempted to climb to higher ground. Unfortunately, they were washed away when a dike broke, releasing a flood of water in their direction. No one survived.

I had taken to asking everyone I came across what they planned to do in the event the hurricane headed our way. Everybody had a ready answer, although there were as many different opinions as there were people to offer them. Most of the long-term residents were fond of quoting the statistic stating that Hilton Head hadn't been hit by a major hurricane for nearly 50 years. I found that reassuring, in a vague sort of way, but my skeptical side said that only means we're overdue for a big one. When I visited Mary and Henry, they showed me the plywood they stored in the barn in case they needed to cover their windows. Henry had a similar stock of boards at the store, and he offered to give some of his extra to Jon and me.

Betty was probably the only person I spoke to who felt a similar level of concern as I did. Perhaps it was because we were both relatively new to coastal living and feared the risk of becoming trapped on an island in a major storm. We spoke to each other almost daily; comparing weather reports and thoughts about what we should do.

During one of our recent phone conversations, she mentioned a visit from Evelyn and Joseph. Joseph was a Deacon at the First African Baptist Church located on Beach City Road, a short distance from Betty and Hal's house. Joseph and Evelyn stopped by to invite them to an evening prayer service at the church. They decided to attend, and Betty described what she experienced.

"Everyone was so kind and welcoming to us. I think we were the only white faces in the room. In fact, I'm sure we were. But after a while, I stopped noticing our differences, and began to feel we were all the same. There was talk of the storm, and what we should all prepare ourselves for, but instead of alarming me further, it gave me a sense of relief to realize we weren't alone. There was a strong sense of community in the church. Even strangers went out of their way to say hello and welcome us. I'll tell you, Georgia. I don't think I've experienced anything like it before."

"I'm really glad to hear that. It's nice that Evelyn and Joseph have continued to reach out to you since your moving day." I thought about what else she said. "What sort of suggestions were they offering about the storm?"

"Everyone seemed to agree that we should be prepared to board up our houses as well as possible and bring in things from outside that might fly around in a strong wind. One lady suggested filling buckets and jugs with fresh water and stocking up on candles and matches in case of a power outage. Several people mentioned having made arrangements to stay with friends or family members inland if the storm turned in our direction. Others seemed determined to stay put even if it becomes a hurricane. I guess it left me feeling like I'm straddling a fence. I don't know whether it's best to be prepared to leave, or to be as prepared as possible to stay. What do you think you and Jon will do?"

"I'm just as confused as you. I'm leaning in the direction of leaving, but Jon is balking at the idea. Our friends in Nashville invited us to come stay with them." Something suddenly occurred to me. "I bet they would welcome you and Hal to join us if we go. They don't have a lot of room, but we could make it work."

She smiled gratefully. "That's sweet of you to think of us. Hal has a cousin who moved to Charlotte a couple of years ago. He mentioned she invited us to come there, should we have to evacuate."

We lapsed into silence for a few moments, finally broken by Ebie jumping onto my lap. "I just had a very pointed reminder from our cat, Ebie, that wherever we go, she goes, too. I guess I'd better prepare myself for that possibility." My mind started ticking off a list of things we would need for her.

"Well, I can tell you've got a lot on your mind. Let's promise each other to stay in touch as things progress. Let me know if you hear anything more definitive about the storm, and I'll do the same."

After I hung up the phone, I cradled my arms around Ebie's neck and looked at her closely. "What do you think we should do?" She looked directly into my eyes before curling up on my lap. She looked at me through half closed eyes and began purring. I stroked her head. "It seems that at least one of us has made up her mind."

CHAPTER FIFTEEN

We didn't have to wait much longer for news of the hurricane's likely path. After ravaging the Dominican Republic, the hurricane lost strength as it moved toward the Bahamas. It was still fierce enough to uproot countless trees and wreak havoc on numerous houses when it reached the Bahamas on September 1st. After that, it continued to head toward Florida, coming ashore on September 3rd at West Palm Beach before moving out into the ocean.

I was told by a few locals that the weather service didn't begin to give hurricanes or tropical storms serious attention until they reached the U.S. This seemed to be the case for Hurricane David. Once it arrived in Florida, the airways were lit up with constant status reports of its projected path in the United States. I was doing a little last-minute shopping in the Red and White when I ran into our own David.

"I guess you heard the news about my namesake?" He asked.

"You know, I didn't think about that coincidence until I saw you. It must feel strange to have a hurricane share your name."

"This is the first time they've used a man's name for an Atlantic hurricane. I'm not sure what that says about me." He grinned as he continued to place a fresh batch of trout in the display case.

"So, what have you heard? Is it coming our way?"

"It could. Last report said it's sliding up the Florida coast, but they've downgraded it to a Cat 1. They're expecting it to weaken some more as it moves northward, but it could still pack quite a punch."

I looked at his full display case. "I'm surprised you're putting out more fish. Won't you have a lot to throw out when people start leaving the island?"

He shrugged his shoulders. "IF they leave. Some will. Some already have. Most will ride it through. We've never closed the market as long as I can remember when there's been the threat of a hurricane. Folks have come to count on picking up groceries and gossip here during a storm. People look out for one another; make sure everyone's accounted for." He lifted his cap and scratched his head. "I don't know if that makes us crazy or wise. It's just the way things are done around here." He studied me for a moment. "Are you staying or leaving?"

My hand went automatically to rest on top of the amulet. I realized it had been heating up while I was listening to David, and I wondered what that meant. I decided to try to plant one thought in my mind and see if that elicited a reaction. Finally, I looked up at David with a slight smile. "I guess we're staying."

He looked confused. "You decided that right now? Why?"

"Just a feeling I had. A feeling that everything's going to be alright." As I said the words, I remembered the message Frankie relayed from Ida, or at least, from her ghost.

He stared at me a moment longer before continuing to fill the seafood case. "I hope you're right. In any event, you know where to find some fresh fish if you need any."

I left the store and headed home. I told myself I went to the Red and White to stock up on some things that might tide us over in case we lost electricity because of the storm, but the truth was I just wanted to be out among people. The irony of running into David and hearing the store would remain open through his namesake weather system, gave me a sense of peace. That feeling was magnified when I felt the amulet's response to my unspoken question. Will it be okay if Jon, Frankie, and I remain on the island through the storm? The heat it had been emitting before I posed the question intensified noticeably, giving me a clear answer. I was also aware of a voice in my head that said: *trust your heart and all will be fine.* It wasn't so much that I could hear the words. I could feel them.

When I first began getting messages from Miss Bessie to trust my heart, I was puzzled exactly how to go about doing that. It didn't really begin to make sense to me until something Julie said one day. We were walking in Centennial Park in Nashville, and I kept fingering the amulet pinned beneath my blouse. At one point, she stopped walking and turned in my direction. "You know, that amulet is right over your heart. I wonder if that's intentional?"

Her question shook me. Of course, it was! How best to read what my heart feels and listen to what it's telling me than to place the charm directly on top of it. I also suspected it was more than coincidental the amulet was contained in a red sack. Red was typically thought of as the color that represents love, which is the emotion of the heart. Miss Bessie told me more than once to trust my heart, which was a message Ida also gave me through Frankie. I assumed they meant I should look deep into my heart to hear what was there, but now I realized they may have simply meant I should pay attention to the amulet. It was over my heart, and it reacted to what was in my heart. If that was the case, it was clearly telling me that staying on the island was the right choice.

I arrived home to find Jon resting on the couch with the television on. He looked up as I arrived and waved me over.

"Come sit. I dropped Frankie over at the Sanders on my way home. They said they'd bring him home after dinner. The Daycare Center has decided to close until the storm has passed. I've just been listening to the news, and it seems the hurricane has weakened some, but they're still predicting it will head our way. I'm thinking we should pack the car and head to Nashville."

I sat next to him and thought about what he'd said. "I guess you'll find this surprising because I'm still a little surprised myself. I think we should stay."

His eyebrows rose as he turned to look at me. "You do? I thought for sure you'd be dead set on leaving. What changed your mind?"

My hand automatically moved to cover the amulet. "Just a feeling, really. But a pretty intense one."

He looked where my hand rested. "A feeling, huh? I guess that little red sack has been sending you messages again."

"I was over in the Red and White talking to David. When he asked me what we were going to do, I decided to plant a question firmly in my mind and see how the amulet responded. It heated up significantly when I asked if we would be okay staying here. I also heard a voice in my head say everything will be fine, if I just trust my heart." I tried to gauge his reaction. "I guess that sounds crazy to you?"

"A little, although I've come to accept that you have some sort of strange connection to the supernatural. To tell the truth, I've been feeling surprisingly calm through this whole thing. I'm good with the idea of staying put."

Ebie hopped up and settled on his lap. "I think someone else likes that idea, too." I remembered my conversation with Betty. "Betty was at a gathering over at the church Mary and Henry go to, and some of the people there had some good suggestions on how to ride out the storm. Things like filling buckets with water and bringing things inside that could be dislodged by the wind."

Jon gently lifted Ebie and placed her on the sofa before standing. "Why don't you work on the indoor things, and I'll go outside? I want to get those boards that Henry gave us ready to put on the windows. Then I'll bring the patio furniture in."

"Sounds good. I'll start filling everything I can find with water, and make sure we have a good supply of candles and matches. I'm going to phone Betty and Julie first and let them know our plans."

Later that evening, we were in the kitchen clearing the dinner dishes when Hal Sanders arrived with Frankie and Tommy. Jon shook his hand and offered him a drink, which he declined. "Thanks, but we'd better get back home. Betty and I still need to storm proof the house, since we've decided to stay." He looked at me. "After talking to you, she announced she didn't want to go to Charlotte. I could tell she'd made her mind up, so there was no point in arguing. I just hope we're not making a mistake."

It hadn't occurred to me that sharing my decision with Betty would sway her in the same direction. "Me, too, Hal. Maybe I shouldn't have said anything."

He waved off my suggestion. "Don't worry about it. She's been talking to those ladies over at the church, too. They're all of the same mind as you. If anyone is crazy, it's me for listening to a bunch of women." He grinned to let me know he was teasing.

Jon spoke up. "I laid out the boards we'll need to cover our windows, and there's a few left over. I can get them for you if you'd like."

"Thanks, but I think we're all set. You remember that guy Samuel who was part of the group who stopped by the house on our moving day? He and another couple of men brought us a stack of boards this afternoon. I guess his wife heard of our plans from Betty. They even helped me nail them together, so they'd be ready to put over the windows. Nice fellows."

Frankie and Tommy ran back in from wherever they'd disappeared. "Mommy! Daddy! Can Tommy stay here tonight?

Miss Browne said the Center will be closed till the her-cane is gone."

I caressed his head. "Not tonight, sweetheart. Tommy's mommy and daddy will want him to stay close to them until the storm has passed."

Hal nodded. "That's right, young man. You should stay here and help your dad. He'll need a big strong fellow like yourself to protect the house."

Frankie clenched his fists and took a stance like a boxer. "Dat her-cane can't get past me! I'll beat it back!"

We all laughed as Hal and Tommy headed for their car. Before they drove off, Hal rolled down the window and leaned out. "We'll stay in touch the best we can. When things settle down, let's plan on getting together."

Jon and I nodded our agreement as we waved goodbye.

It was hard to wait for the storm to arrive. The hours ticked by as we listened to the redundant television and radio reports that seemed to repeat what we already knew. When it felt as though we couldn't stand being housebound one second longer, Jon, Frankie and I decided to take a walk along the beach to the Tiki Hut at the Holiday Inn. We arrived to find a large crowd gathered, filling almost every spot along the bar and the tables, and spilling over onto the sand. The beach chairs which normally surrounded the hotel swimming pool had been stored away, and the pool was drained of water. Workers were busily wrapping wire netting around the top of the thatched roof of the Hut, and a sign stated that all service would be discontinued at 5 PM in order to allow the tables and chairs to be put away, and the staff to get home safely.

The atmosphere was jovial when we walked onto the deck of the Hut, which I assumed was mostly due to the alcohol being consumed in an effort to thwart concern over the pending arrival of David. Jon went to the bar to order our drinks, while Frankie and I claimed the last available lawn chair on the sand next to the volleyball court. The nets had already been removed in anticipation of the winds, and the concrete-footed poles had been turned over onto their sides.

Jon returned with the drinks and handed me two t-shirts. I held one up to read what was lettered on it. "I survived Hurricane David. September 1979. I'd say someone's getting a little ahead of themselves."

"I agree, but I thought they'd make good souvenirs."

"Where's my t-shirt?" Frankie frowned at his dad.

"I got something else for you." Jon reached behind his chair and pulled out a plastic kite emblazoned with the image of a smiling dolphin. "I thought we could try this out before the wind gets too strong."

Frankie jumped up in excitement. "Wow! Can we fly it now?"

Jon looked at me and smiled.

"Just as soon as I finish my drink. In the meantime, let's see if we can put it together." They laid the kite down on the sand and attached a tail to one end and a cord to the back. Frankie grabbed it and started to dash off. "Wait a minute, son. The wind is a little too strong for you to handle that by yourself." He swallowed the last of his drink and handed his glass to me. "I guess you'd better hang onto this for me. I might want a refill after our kite flying expedition." He took Frankie by the hand and led him down to the water's edge where the sand was firmer. I watched with pleasure as Jon showed Frankie how to hold the kite in the air until the breeze lifted it upwards. Jon kept a tight hold on the cord to keep it from flying away, while Frankie ran under the kite laughing and jumping in an effort to catch the tail. Eventually, I could see Frankie growing tired, and the two headed back to where I still sat.

"Mommy, dat was so much FUN!"

I brushed the sand off his shorts and pushed the hair from his face. "I'm so glad, sweetheart. Are you thirsty?"

"Um hum. Kin I hab some more Orange drink?"

Jon gestured for me to stay put. "I'll get it. I'm going to get a refill for myself. Can I bring you another one?"

I eyed my gin and tonic. "No thanks. This one made me sleepy."

He smiled. "Must be the extra lime."

While I waited for Jon and Frankie to finish their drinks, I wandered over to the Holiday Inn to visit the restroom. When I entered through the back door, I heard the sound of voices. I quickly walked to the lobby where I found a small group of people gathered around a radio. I moved closer to try and hear what they were listening to. A woman saw me walk up and turned to speak to me.

"It's heading for Savannah. They're telling everyone who hasn't already evacuated to move to higher ground. They've already opened up shelters for anyone who doesn't have a safe place to stay."

"What are they saying about Hilton Head?" I asked.

"Nothing much. All of the reports are directed at Savannah. I guess that's because we're listening to a radio station from there. They did mention there's a good chance the storm will head further inland once it reaches Savannah."

I hurried back to Jon and Frankie. Jon's expression looked grim. "The wind has picked up. I think we ought to head home soon," he said.

We both looked at Frankie. Luckily, the dolphin kite was still absorbing his attention. I tried to act nonchalant. "Hey, sweetheart? Why don't we head back home? I'll bet Ebie is getting lonely for us."

"'K. Kin I fly my kite again when we get there?"

I gathered our glasses and took them to the bar while Jon collected the kite. "I'm afraid the wind's too strong for your kite now, buddy. We wouldn't want it to get torn apart."

Frankie looked at the kite and nodded. "Yeah. We better wait."

We walked out to the edge of the surf and looked in the direction of Savannah and Tybee Island. Dark clouds were gathering along the horizon, and the ocean appeared choppy as the waves grew higher and lapped the shore with increasing intensity.

"Where are the dolfs?" Frankie asked. "Kin the storm hurt dem?"

I stroked his head. "The dolphins are really smart. They know sooner than we do when a storm is coming, and they swim to a safe place. I'll bet that's why we haven't seen any around here for a few days."

Jon glanced at me across Frankie's head. "Your mom's right. I heard someone talking about this on TV the other day. He said dolphins can sense changes in the ocean water several days before a big storm even gets close. They head out to deeper waters where they know they'll be safe."

When we arrived back home, I warmed up a chicken stew I cooked earlier in the day and tossed a salad to go with it. The stew was the epitome of comfort food: savory, warm, and delicious. The increase in wind brought cooler temperatures, so Jon decided to start a fire. I opened a bottle of Chardonnay, and laid placemats out on the cocktail table in front of the sofa so we could enjoy the fire while keeping an eye on the television. Frankie fell asleep on the floor in front of the fireplace around 7, and we decided to cover him with a blanket and leave him there so we would all be together. Jon covered the windows with boards earlier in the day, and the fire helped warm up the darkness they imposed on the house.

We lost the TV broadcast just before 8 PM, which is when the radio stations reported David reached Savannah. Ninety mph winds and torrential rains were described as it came ashore, which quickly died down to around 58 mph with wind gusts of 68. Soon, even the radio broadcasts ended as the city of Savannah lost power. It took until the next day before we received more detailed news of the storm's effects.

The reports indicated that the storm lingered over the city for approximately two hours before moving northward toward Columbia. The winds and high water caused scattered damage to buildings across Chatham County, but the greatest impact of the storm was on trees and power lines. Hundreds of trees fell, and tree trunks and limbs were reportedly littering roofs, lawns, and roads, causing widespread power outages. Streets in the historic downtown were said to be impassable due to the remains of stately trees and other debris. One large oak was split from the top to its base due to a lamp post the storm hurled into it. The city lost power, and fresh water was being brought in on tanker trucks. The greatest damage reportedly occurred offshore as numerous ships were pummeled by the wind and waves.

The only mention of Hilton Head was a report that the Causeway used to travel between Savannah and the low country of South Carolina was flooded, preventing anyone from leaving or returning to Hilton Head by that route. We lost power shortly before 10 PM, which reportedly coincided with the time of peak wind gusts on the island.

Jon and I carried Frankie to bed after the wind died down, then decided to try to sleep ourselves. I had a restless night, filled with dreams of flying objects and tall waves that reached the roof of the house. Luckily, my dreams were not prophetic.

When I finally gave up the attempt to sleep, Jon was already up and standing at the kitchen counter. The smell of fresh coffee greeted me.

"Oh, coffee!" I closed my eyes and inhaled the welcome aroma, opening them to accept the mug he handed to me.

"The Electric Coop put our power on about an hour ago. I've been listening to the radio, and they said the edge of the storm moved up through the Charleston area and then continued to the Northeast. Lots of wind and water damage and some people are still without power. I'm anxious to see how things look around here. The radio commentator made a point of scolding the residents of Tybee, Hilton Head, and other nearby islands who chose to ignore the voluntary evacuation orders." He looked at me with a smirk. "I guess he doesn't understand the meaning of voluntary."

I yawned and rubbed my eyes. "I hope you slept better than I did. My mind was full of worrisome dreams."

"I slept for a couple of hours. I wanted to check the windows and make sure there weren't any leaks. Everything seems to have held up well. I took the boards off in a couple of places so I could look outside. I'm waiting for things to brighten up a bit more before continuing."

I moved to one of the uncovered windows in the kitchen and looked out over the front yard. There appeared to be quite a lot of tree debris scattered across the yard, and what looked like a child's bike was laying on its side in the middle of Dune Street. Pools of water were evident in several locations, especially in our driveway, which now looked like a small pond.

Jon walked up to peer over my shoulder. "It doesn't look too bad, at least, not as bad as I expected." He placed his coffee mug on the kitchen counter. "The sun should be up soon. I'm going to go out onto the deck to see how things look. Would you mind checking on Frankie? I thought I heard his voice a minute ago."

Jon walked toward our bedroom and I headed across the hall to Frankie's room. The room was still dark from the boarded-up windows, but I could make out his shape on the bed. The covers had been tossed aside, and he was sitting up and talking to himself. I walked closer and sat on the edge of his bed, resting my hand on his back.

"Good morning, sweetheart. Did you sleep well?"

His smile warmed my heart. "It was cool! The wind made the boards rattle, and I pretended I was on a raft heading into the ocean with the dolfs. Dey was leading me."

I shook my head with a grin. "You certainly have a good imagination."

He frowned. "Dat's what de lady say. She tol' me I smart, an' gonna grow up to be sumt'ing 'portant."

His mention of a lady caused my breath to catch. "What lady, Frankie?"

"De same one was in Aunt Julie's backyard. I didn't know she libbed here, too. I like her. She's nice tuh me."

My heart was pounding in my chest. "Did she say anything else?"

He scrunched up his face as if he was thinking hard. "Oh! She say not tuh worry 'bout de dolfs. Dat dey be okay. She say dey be back to de island soon."

I shifted around on the mattress so I could scan the room. "Is she here now?"

He pointed to a chair next to the bed. I squinted in the still dim light, but I only saw an empty chair. I sighed and stood. "Come to the kitchen and I'll make you something to eat." He hopped from the bed and scurried down the hall. I started to follow him, then decided to look once more at the chair. As I continued to stare at it, I began to see the wispy image of a woman. Her shape began to fill in the longer I looked until finally her face came into focus. "Ida?"

She nodded and smiled.

"Is it really you? I've missed you so much." I started to walk closer to the chair, but the image began to fade as quickly as it appeared. When I stood next to the empty chair, I noticed a small piece of paper on the seat. I picked it up and examined it. The light in the room was too dim to make out many details, but I could tell it was a photograph of Ida and me that Thomas took on the day we first visited him at Belmont. "Ida," I whispered. "It really is you." I tucked the photo into the pocket of my robe and left the room.

CHAPTER SIXTEEN

The storm continued to pummel a wide area across the Eastern highlands and coastline for three more days, downing numerous trees and power lines, and causing flooding from Virginia to New York before finally heading out to sea. The Battery district of Charleston was hard hit by huge waves that flooded East Bay Street, reaching the porches of the area's historic old homes. Tornado-like winds caused major power failures along the Grand Strand area of Myrtle Beach, but the most damage occurred on the small barrier islands off the coast of Savannah.

Tybee had been the first island to be hit by the storm. One report stated that only 500 of the 3,000 inhabitants left Tybee before the hurricane arrived. Luckily, most people rode out the storm unscathed. There was even one tale about five men and a woman who holed up in the 70-year-old lighthouse located on the island. They armed themselves with beer and sandwiches to wait out the storm, only abandoning their plan when the lighthouse door showed signs of crashing in.

On Folly Beach, an island just south of Charleston, one house was thrown wholly into the sea, and numerous others suffered extensive wind and water damage. Five-foot sea walls, built to stop erosion, were torn down, and large areas of beach were swept away. Luckily, Hilton Head fared much better than most of its island neighbors. The assault on Tybee and Savannah deflected a direct attack on Hilton Head, causing the storm to veer off to the Northwest instead. As a result, David was only able to strike a glancing blow to Hilton Head.

Once it became light enough to venture out, Jon, Frankie and I set out to take a look at what impact the storm had on our neighborhood and Coligny Beach. We started on Dune street and walked in the direction of the Sea Crest Motel. There were several other people out and about. We all greeted each other warmly and shared stories about how we spent the night, and what damage, if any, had occurred to our homes. Most people reported only minor damage from debris and wind, with the exception of one couple who neglected to bring their patio furniture inside, waking in the middle of the night to the sound of it crashing through their living room window. Unprotected cars consistently suffered from flying debris, and many bicycles ended up with the same fate as the one I spotted in the street outside our house.

We made our way over to Coligny Plaza, stopping along the way to survey the businesses located there. Shop owners were sweeping up assorted trash from the drive outside their entrances or uncovering boarded up windows. We waved hello as we passed, receiving a hearty "at least we're all safe" in return. When we reached the Red and White, I was surprised to see the doors open and several people moving around inside.

"David told me the store would stay open through the storm because the neighborhood people count on it for picking up necessities. From the looks of things, he was absolutely right," I remarked.

"Let's go inside and say hello." Jon steered Frankie through the door.

I immediately spotted David wearing his customary baseball cap standing just inside the entrance, welcoming everyone as they walked by. He looked up and stuck an arm up in greeting. "Hey, y'all. Everything alright at your house?"

Jon nodded as we walked in his direction. "We fared well, thanks to the advice we received to board up the windows and bring in anything that wasn't nailed down. How about you?"

David smiled and shrugged. "We're good. Spent the night in the store keeping an eye on things. Had to run the generator for a while when the power went out, but, luckily, it came back on pretty quickly." He reached behind him and produced a napkin-covered doughnut that he held out to Frankie. "Everyone who comes by gets one of these." He looked at Jon and me and gestured behind him. "Help yourselves to a doughnut and some coffee. I've got to head out back and make sure everything's running smoothly. Most of my workers made it in today, but we're a little short on stockers."

Jon and I helped ourselves to a cup of coffee and shared a doughnut between us, giving our second one to Frankie. We headed back outside and began walking in the direction of the beach past the Holiday Inn Hotel and the Tiki Hut. We were pleased to see that it was relatively unscathed with the exception of several fronds of the dried wheat straw that came loose from the roof of the Hut. When we reached the beach, we gazed as far as we could see. There were several people walking along the shoreline, stopping periodically to pick up a treasure from the sea. That turned out to be one of the pluses of a wave surge: it left behind a delightful assortment of shells and driftwood.

Frankie began to fill his pockets as we walked in the direction of our house. I glanced over at the dunes in front of the Sea Crest Motel, noticing they were flatter than before the storm.

"It looks like the tide level came up much further than usual," I said.

Jon glanced in the direction I was looking before pointing a little further down the beach. "There are a couple of boats down there that appear to have been washed ashore. At least, I don't remember seeing them before the storm."

"What are dem birds doing?" Frankie pointed to our right, where we saw a flock of seagulls hovering above the shore, occasionally diving close to the sand.

"I don't know, sweetheart. Let's go see."

We walked to where the birds were gathered, also noticing a group of people lingering close by. As we got closer, I could make out the shape of something large lying on top of the sand. I put my hand on Jon's arm to get his attention. "Maybe Frankie and I should wait here while you go check it out."

He nodded and began walking toward the group, stopping to talk to one of the men before returning to where we waited. "It's a loggerhead. From the looks of things, she must have gotten caught up in a fishing net. I suspect she was dead before she drifted ashore. The Beach Patrol has been contacted, and they're on their way. The man I spoke to said he and his friends are staying close by to keep the birds from doing more damage."

Frankie looked up at his dad in alarm. "Duh turtle is dead? How'd she die?"

"I think she drowned, son. I'm sorry you had to see that."

Frankie stared at where the turtle lay then shook his head. "It's okay, Daddy. I jes sorry for duh turtle."

I looked down at my son and felt a surge of love. He was such a kind soul, and at that moment, seemed much older than his three-plus years. Suddenly Frankie started hopping up and down and pointing. "Dat's de 'Fuskie man! De one gave me duh bottle tuh give you, Mommy!"

His words startled me, and I looked in the direction he was pointing. "Are you sure, Frankie?"

He nodded vigorously. "Uh, huh. Dat's him." He began to tug on my hand. "Let's go say Hi."

I looked at Jon with alarm but allowed Frankie to pull me down the beach. When we reached the man, Frankie stopped and addressed him. "Dis my Mommy. She duh one you say I should give duh bottle to."

The man slowly turned in our direction, smiling as he recognized Frankie. "Why, hello young man. It's nice to see you again." He looked up at me and Jon and tipped his chin in greeting. "I'm Benjamin Scott. I hope I didn't alarm your son when I saw him on Daufuskie a while back."

"It alarmed me a lot more than it did him," I said.

"I suspect it did." He offered his hand to Jon to shake. "And how are you, sir?"

Jon shook his hand and looked him directly in the eyes. "I'd be better if you'd explain to me why you approached my son during a private trip. If you had something to say to him, you should have gone to his teacher first."

Benjamin's eyes narrowed as he took in Jon's angry countenance. "I agree that would have been a better approach. Please forgive my insensitivity." He leaned down towards Frankie. "Young man, would you do me a big favor? Would you take this shell down to that woman carrying the big blue bag?" He produced a shell I recognized as a lightning whelk.

"Cool!" Frankie took it from him, carefully cradling it in his hand before running off in the direction of the woman.

"I thought it would be best if we talked in private. That morning on Daufuskie, I received a vision telling me I needed to seek out your son and deliver the potion. I was to give it to him and tell him to make sure to give it to you. He was also supposed to let you know it would restore power to your amulet. That was one of the few times I received a message of that type. Especially one that used a small child as an intermediary. I'm afraid my mind was so focused on fulfilling the directive, it didn't occur to me there might be any misunderstanding about my intentions."

"You say you received a vision?" I asked.

He turned his gaze to me. His eyes were kind, as Frankie had described them, and seemed to look deep into my heart. "A visitor from the Spirit world. A woman. Said her name was Bessie. She told me you needed help from the potion, and I should seek out your son on Daufuskie that day. She said his name was Frankie. When I went over to the yard where the kids were playing, I heard one of the children address your boy by that name. I didn't want to draw attention to myself, so I waited until he ran into the woods to approach him."

"I still don't understand why all the secrecy. If you had a message for Frankie, why didn't you just go to his teacher?" Jon asked.

"Let's just say some folks don't believe in the spirit world. Miss Browne is one of those. I've known her family for a while. She used to believe in what I do quite strongly, but her attitude changed at some point. I didn't want to take a chance she would get in the way of me delivering the potion. The spirit who appeared to me made it clear how important it was. I was just the messenger following through on her request." His gaze turned to me. "She said you helped her once, now she wanted to do the same for you."

"Then why not come to me directly with the message? Why involve my son?" I asked.

He looked behind him to where Frankie was walking up the beach with the woman carrying the big blue bag. "Sometimes young children are better vessels for receiving messages from spirit guides. Their hearts are purer, and their minds free of preconceptions. The spirit told me your son has a special gift that allows him to communicate with those who have passed on."

I remembered his sightings of Ida, and wondered if he had any other experiences I wasn't aware of. The image of the dead sparrows popped into my mind. "Did you have anything to do with placing two dead sparrows at the front and back of our house?"

"Yes. The spirit guide also instructed me to do that. It's supposed to help you transition from the past and open the door to the future. Sparrows are believed to represent our throat and heart chakras. Opening those helps us voice our dreams and fears, hear the truth in our hearts, and have the courage to act on what we believe is right."

I shook my head in bewilderment. Ghost sightings. Messages from the dead. A Root Doctor handing me potions. The symbolic placement of dead birds in our yard. It was getting to be too much for me to comprehend! Something else occurred to me. "Why are you here today?"

He nodded his understanding. "I didn't come here to see you. Or your son. That was purely coincidental. My sister lives on Hilton Head. I came over from my home on Daufuskie a couple of days ago so I could stay with her through the storm. Her husband is a fisherman, and he was down in Florida when the storm first came ashore. He hasn't been able to get back yet, and I didn't want her to be alone. Her house is over near Fish Haul Beach. She collects shells that she uses to make jewelry, and we knew there would be quite a collection of them after the storm passed. She wanted me to drive her around to some of the other beaches on the island this morning." He looked up as the woman approached with Frankie. "Here she is now."

There was something vaguely familiar about the woman that I couldn't quite put my finger on. As she moved closer, I realized she was one of the visitors I'd met at the moving in pizza party at the Sanders new home. She smiled at me warmly as she reached us.

"I remember you. We met at Betty's house over near Fish Haul Beach. I'm Georgia Barnett, and this is my husband, Jon, and that's our son Frankie."

She nodded at each of us. "Your son's been keeping me cump'ny. He's quite an expert on dolphins!" She smiled down at him before addressing her brother. "How you know dese folks, Benjie?"

He motioned to Frankie. "This is the young man I told you about, and Georgia here is his mother."

Her eyes grew wide as what he was saying sunk in. "He gib yuh de potion! Well, dat sumpt'ing, fin' ya here 'n all."

I was curious why her accent was clearly influenced by her Gullah roots, while her brother's bore no traces of his ancestry. Jon must have been thinking the same thing because he chose that moment to intervene.

"Where did you live before Daufuskie, Benjamin? You don't seem to share the same accent as your sister."

"We both grew up here, but I left for college up North right after high school. Studied medicine at Howard University in D.C."

Jon's head jerked up at his announcement. "You lived in D.C.? That's where I'm from originally. Howard University's School of Medicine has a good reputation." He looked at Benjamin curiously. "Do you practice medicine around here?"

Benjamin nodded thoughtfully. "Yes, but not strictly in the traditional sense. While I was still in medical school, I became fascinated with the use of ancient potions and practices for healing and sustaining health. Once my interest became known, I was regarded as somewhat of a kook by both my fellow students and professors. I had to keep my studies in those areas on the downlow until I graduated. Since then, I've mostly taught myself, except for a period of time I spent living around a healer I met over on St. Helena Island. He's the one who introduced me to the use of potions like the one I gave your wife.

"I became an apprentice of his while we were on St. Helena, and eventually followed him to Daufuskie. I've been living there for some ten years now. I provide regular medical care for the island residents, often accepting payment in the form of food or services. Once my mentor passed on, people began to come to me for potions; things they were used to getting from him." He grinned at his sister. "Josie's always telling me I should just be a 'real' doctor and stop all this root nonsense, but I can't ignore the messages of help I get from the living, as well as those beyond the grave." He turned his attention back to me. "Like the one I received from Bessie."

I felt like my head was ready to explode from the abundance of information he had shared. All I could do was stare at him with what I suspected was a dumbfounded expression. Luckily, Jon came to my rescue.

"Well, it's certainly been an interesting coincidence to run into both of you today."

Benjamin looked at his sister who responded with a raised eyebrow. "I don't believe in coincidences. Maybe our paths were meant to cross today for some unknown reason." He held out his hand to Jon. "It's been a pleasure to meet you, Jon. I wish you and your family a wonderful rest of the day."

Benjamin and Josephine started to walk away.

"Wait!" I called. "I need to ask you one more thing."

They turned back to face me.

"Frankie has been telling me about conversations he's had with a woman. The way he described her appearance, it sounds like a dear friend of mine who passed away several years ago. Earlier today, he told me she was sitting in a chair in his room, and when I started to leave, I was able to see her faintly. I'm wondering why she never appeared before, and why Frankie is the one she's communicating with?"

Benjamin's eyes narrowed as he considered what I was saying. "I've seen your friend once myself. She appeared to me in a dream shortly after Bessie told me I should give you the potion. She said she hadn't been able to come before, because she was waiting for the young boy to get old enough to understand. Like I said, sometimes young children are better vessels for this type of communication. In the dream, she said she is always watching over you, and she would appear to you when the time was right. I got the impression she didn't want me to say anything to you before then."

His explanation was oddly comforting. "Do you think I'll be able to see her again?"

"I can't say for sure, but I think that's highly likely."

My heart soared with hope. "Thank you, Benjamin. I really appreciate your honesty today."

He nodded and took his sister's arm as they continued walking up the beach.

After they left, Jon put an arm around me and pulled me close. "Living with you is a constant adventure." He squeezed me gently.

"I don't know if that's a good or a bad thing," I replied.

"It's all good. Even the bad. Because without adventure, we're not really living."

And as he said it, I realized he was right.

CHAPTER SEVENTEEN

By September 7th, Hurricane David had moved completely out to sea, leaving behind a wide swath of damage and destruction from Florida all the way up to New York. The damage to my beloved island had been minimal, except for a few homes that took a more direct hit from the storm. Most of them were located in the Singleton Beach area, which lay about six miles North of Coligny. Beaches all over the island were also impacted by the hurricane, causing dunes to be flattened and huge amounts of sand to be washed away. There were still remnants of the storm visible along roadsides and in neighborhoods, mostly in the form of uprooted trees, and broken branches and palm fronds. The hurricane continued to be a favorite topic of discussion for quite some time. But for Jon and me, our focus was forced to shift to more immediate concerns.

Jon returned to work two days after the storm passed to find chaos in his office. Two of the realtors had pending contracts on houses that were cancelled when the buyers panicked out of fear of future hurricanes. Since the cancellations occurred prior to a home inspection, there was nothing the realtors could do to stop them. Three homes listed for sale prior to the hurricane suffered extensive damage, forcing the sellers to take them off the market until repairs could be made. Two more sellers, who happened to be working with Jon, got cold feet, and decided not to sell at all.

Jon's reaction to these events was to hustle even more than he normally did; contacting potential buyers with tempting offers and reaching out to prospective sellers with the carrot of a lowered brokerage fee. His success in these endeavors was noticed by the owner of the company, who approached him with a compelling offer. Jon came home that night full of an equal amount of excitement and concern.

I was sitting on the back deck watching the light change in the sky when he arrived. The sunset was getting earlier each day as we headed into Fall, causing it to be almost dark by 6 PM.

I smiled when he stepped onto the deck. "Somebody looks happy."

He pulled out a chair and sat. "It was a good day. I signed a pending contract on a house just off Palmetto Bay Road, and the boss asked me if I wanted to become a partner in the business."

"Wow! What did you say?"

"I told him I'd have to think about it."

"You did? I thought you would have jumped at the chance."

"That's just it. He attached a pretty hefty price tag to his offer. It's true I'd be earning more, since I would not only get commission on my own sales, but everyone else's, too. But it would take a while to replace what I'd have to spend to buy into the business. I don't know if we're in the position to do that right now."

I frowned at his disclosure. "I thought our financial situation was good. At least, I assumed so. I guess I should have paid more attention or asked you to explain it to me in more detail."

"You're not wrong. I've been making more than enough for us to live comfortably. I just don't know how the impact of this storm is going to affect things. We've already been seeing a lot of fear-based reactions from both buyers and sellers. People who were excited about the idea of living on the coast are suddenly afraid they'll be swept away by a hurricane. I can't say I blame them. I'm glad we made the decision to ride this last one out, but I wouldn't welcome having to deal with this same scenario every year."

"Me either. Why do you think your boss is interested in bringing you on as a partner?"

"A lot of the other realtors I work with seem to have lost heart in the aftermath of the storm's impact. My response has been to bust my butt even more and the boss has noticed. If I were in his position, I'd want to capitalize on my energy and enthusiasm, too. Sort of make me an example of what could be in store for the other realtors if they put in an equal amount of effort."

I nodded. "Sounds like a no-brainer on his part. When does he expect an answer?"

"He told me to think about it for a couple of days. He wants to meet with me again on Friday."

I slapped my hands on my thighs. "Well, whatever you decide to do, I think this calls for a celebration! What do you say we collect Frankie, and walk over to the Tiki Hut? They've started selling burgers, and I hear they're some of the best on the island."

He chuckled at my suggestion. "Leave it to you to find an excuse to go to the Hut. That seems to have become your favorite go-to place for celebrating, commiserating, or doing nothing at all."

"You're not wrong."

He stood and grinned at me. "Okay. Let's do it. Just let me change, and I'll meet you and Frankie back out here in a few."

The Hut was booming with business even more than usual. We scanned the crowd for an available table, finally spotting one at the far edge of the deck. Once we were settled, Jon signaled for a waitress.

"You want the usual?"

I shook my head. "Those frozen concoctions give me too much of a headache. I'll just settle for a glass of white wine and some ice water."

Frankie hopped up and down on his seat. "Kin I hab sum Coca Cola? Tommy give me a taste of his, and I like it better dan Orange Soda."

I wasn't happy to hear he'd been allowed to have Coke at Tommy's house. It surprised me Betty would allow it without asking me first. "Did Tommy's mommy give you the Coke?"

He stared at his feet as he swung them back and forth. "She weren't dere. She hab tuh go next store. Tommy say it was okay for us to hab some."

I could tell by his sheepish expression that he suspected it wasn't okay; with Tommy's mother, or with me. "You know we have a rule in our family about you drinking Coke. What have we told you about it?"

He thought for a moment. "Dat it hab too much sugar and caff-beans. Dey mek me too jumpy." He swung his legs rapidly from side to side.

"That's right. Sugar and caffeine are not a good combination for little boys. I'm surprised Tommy's mother lets him drink Coke."

He looked uncomfortable. "Tommy maybe drinks it when she not dere."

The scenario suddenly became crystal clear. Betty stepped out for a short time to go to a neighbor's house. Tommy decided to take that opportunity to sneak a drink he wasn't normally allowed to have. He offered to share the forbidden elixir with Frankie. It was a situation any normal three-year old boy would have a hard time passing up. "I think you know that what you and Tommy did was not right. I want you to promise me you won't do things you know would make your dad and me unhappy. Can you promise me that?"

His face grew serious. "I try, Mommy. But sometimes being good is so hard!"

I glanced at Jon as I stifled a laugh.

Jon winked at me as he addressed Frankie. "Being good is always hard, no matter how old you get. But if you grow up to be a good man, one day you may be lucky enough to find a wonderful woman to marry, like I did."

Frankie looked at me with a grin. "When I grow up, I kin marry Mommy, too!"

Jon shook his head at me with a sigh. "I see I'm going to have to step up my game if I want to beat this competition." He held out his hand to Frankie. "Come on, young man. Let's you and I go to the bar. It's time you learned how to order a drink."

I smiled. My two men, or at least my man and the boy who would hopefully grow up to be as good a man as his father.

"Georgia!" A familiar voice grabbed my attention.

"Hi, Savannah. It's nice to see you again." It wasn't totally a lie. I liked her when we first met. It was just her uncle's involvement in the attempt to buy out the Sea Pines Company that made me regard her cautiously. "How are things over on Tybee? I heard it was hit pretty hard by the hurricane."

She pulled out a chair and sat. "Yeah. David made landfall on Tybee before it moved on to Savannah. The beach is pretty torn up, and there's still a lot of debris scattered everywhere. Luckily, no one died or was even hurt very badly. My house lost some shingles, and a screen door was wrenched off its hinges, but that's all. How are things at your place?"

"Good. We battened down the hatches, as they say, so the house didn't suffer any damage."

"You and your family didn't evacuate? I'm surprised."

"Why? I take it you didn't either?"

"No, but I've been a beach bum for a pretty long time. Well, at least for a few years longer than you. I've gotten used to the variances in the weather. It's been a long time since anything major hit Tybee, or Hilton Head either, for that matter." She looked up as Jon and Frankie returned with our drinks.

"Hey, guys. Georgia and I were just comparing notes from the hurricane."

Jon set the glasses on the table and regarded her with a smirk. "I take it you didn't leave either. Pretty crazy of all of us, in retrospect. Can I get you something from the bar?"

She looked over her shoulder. "No, thanks. I believe that's my drink heading this way now." A waiter placed a bottle of beer and a frosty mug in front of her. She poured the beer into the mug, causing foam to spill over the edge. Frankie burst out in a fit of giggles, and she looked at him with a pretense of horror. "Are you laughing at me? Did I do something funny?"

Frankie started to hiccup he was laughing so hard. "It's all fluffy. Like clouds." He pointed at the sky where fluffy, cumulus clouds were visible.

Savannah looked where he was pointing and nodded. "Right you are, but I bet those clouds don't taste as good as this beer." She took a sip, intentionally causing a foamy mustache to appear on her upper lip. Frankie's giggles returned with a vengeance.

"Look at dat, Mommy. She hab a white mustache!"

Savannah smiled, using her napkin to dab at the foam, restoring the table to normalcy. She glanced at Jon. "Have you had any more conversations with my uncle?"

"No, I haven't."

"I heard the storm has put quite a damper on things."

He looked at her curiously. "What do you mean?"

"Some of the investors have been getting cold feet since the hurricane hit. There's talk of foregoing the whole idea of buying out the Sea Pines Company."

Jon swirled the ice in his glass. "Interesting. I've been experiencing some similar reactions in my real estate business. I guess it makes sense that people would get nervous about what the future holds for property on an island that has just been visited by a hurricane." He took a drink before continuing. "Did your uncle give you any idea when a decision will be made?"

"He mentioned a meeting that's supposed to take place in the next few days. I imagine he'll be in touch with you about it."

Jon looked thoughtful before he resumed his poker face expression. "He probably will. Georgia, are you ready to order some food? I'll bet Frankie is hungry."

Frankie rolled his eyes. "Starving, Daddy!"

Jon smiled at Frankie's woeful expression before addressing Savannah. "We heard they have some pretty good burgers on the menu now. Would you like to join us in trying one?"

"Sounds good, but I can't stay. I'm meeting some friends in the parking lot of the hotel, and then we're going to carpool it into Sea Pines. One of them is staying at the Adventure Inn, and a gate pass into Sea Pines was included in the rental rate."

We chatted about inconsequential things until Savannah left. Jon and I ordered the burgers, then watched as Frankie batted around a volleyball in the sand just off the deck. "What did you make of what she said?" I finally asked.

"I'm not sure. I'll admit I'm a little surprised that Quinn hasn't called me, but maybe he's just waiting until the dust settles. He impressed me as a cagey sort of guy. I don't imagine he'd be too quick to show his hand until he knows exactly what he's been dealt."

"Do you think this could be a good thing for the island? I mean if the investors decide to call off the potential buyout?"

"Possibly. It certainly opens the door for other options to be considered."

Our burgers arrived, and we called Frankie to return to the table. After taking a few bites, we declared them to be as good as promised: juicy and flavorful, and surrounded by a generous number of crispy fries. We ate in silence, only broken by our moans of pleasure. When our plates were cleared of everything except crumbs, Jon leaned back in his chair and looked around the deck. "I really like this place. I can see why it has become one of your favorite spots."

"That it's so close to home is a big selling point, but I mostly like that it's one of the only beachfront bars in the area."

"It's the only beachfront bar, at least in the proximity of Coligny." He leaned over to wipe a spot of ketchup from Frankie's chin. "Looks like someone enjoyed his burger."

Frankie smiled at his dad. "Um hum! De fries was really good, too!"

We paid the bill, then decided to stroll along the beach for a while, digesting our food, and looking for more shells to add to our growing collection. When we returned home, I noticed a light flashing on the telephone answering machine. I pressed the button to listen to the message.

"Hi Jon, It's Robert Quinn. There's going to be a meeting of the investors tomorrow at 10 AM, and I'm hoping you can join us. We'll be in the old house at Rose Hill Plantation in Bluffton, just over the bridge from Hilton Head. I'll plan on seeing you there unless I hear differently."

"Well, I guess that answers my earlier question," I said. "It looks like you won't have to wait very long to find out what's happening."

He nodded solemnly. "If you don't mind, I'm going to give Harry a call. I want to bring him up to date on what Savannah told us and see if he's heard anything on his end."

"Sure. Tell him to let Julie know everything's fine here, and I'll call her soon."

Jon left by 9 AM the next morning so he would be sure to arrive in plenty of time. We didn't have a chance to talk about his discussion with Harry, but I noticed his face wore a pensive expression when he kissed me goodbye. I had read about Rose Hill Plantation. It was supposed to be the sight of a wonderful old house that dated back to the 1800s. The plantation itself originally consisted of 1,880 acres, used to grow cotton, rice and indigo. Salt was also harvested from the nearby brackish creeks. The Plantation suffered in the aftermath of the Civil War, never recovering the wealth and prosperity of the pre-war years. The main house sat hidden in the woods for many years, until it was purchased in 1946 by a couple who restored it to its original style with elegant additions. It remained a private home until 1978, following the death of both the husband and wife. Since then, it has been empty except for the assorted creatures who had likely taken residence.

I couldn't help but wonder if Robert Quinn had an ulterior motive for picking that house as his meeting site. I really wanted to know what he was up to, and how he planned to involve Jon. I decided to distract myself from worrying about things I had no control over by making a visit to the Palmers. I woke Frankie and got him dressed and fed.

When I pulled into the Palmers' driveway, I spotted Henry around the corner of the house. He turned at the sound of the car and waved. Frankie and I walked toward him before being accosted by Beau who stood on his hind legs and placed his paws on Frankie's shoulders. From that angle, he was a good three inches taller than Frankie.

"Git 'way ole dog! Leabe dat boy 'lone!" Henry shooed Beau away and put his hand on Frankie's head. "Hope 'e di'n't hurt you none?" He peered down at Frankie.

"I'm okay, Uncle Henry. Kin I go play wid Beau now?"

Henry chuckled and waved him toward the house where Beau had taken refuge on the porch.

"Uh luk wen dat boy caw me Uncle. Mek 'em feel luk fambly."

Jon and I taught Frankie to refer to any adult male friend of ours as Uncle, and every adult female friend as Aunt. Since he didn't have any actual aunts and uncles, except for Jon's sister and brother-in-law, who we rarely saw, we hoped it would give him a sense of belonging to a larger family.

"You are family, Henry. Both you and Mary." I could tell by his smile he was pleased by what I said.

"Uh jes been nailing sum boa'ds dat cum loose in de sto'm. Oonuh house okay?"

"Fine, thanks to your advice. We didn't have any damage at all."

He turned toward the house. "Mary out back heng'n clothes. Go on see huh."

I walked around to the back of the house where I found Mary hanging clothes out to dry on lines strung between two trees. She stopped what she was doing when she saw me.

"Geo'gia. Uh hope oonuh stop by tuhday. Weh Frankie?" She looked past me.

"He's out front with Beau. That boy loves dogs. I'd get him one of his own, but Ebie would never forgive me."

She laughed. "Naw, don' reckon 'e like dat much. Cum. Sit een de shade wid me."

We settled onto a bench located under a large oak tree. There was a gentle breeze blowing that brought the scent of fish and greenery.

Mary sniffed appreciatively. "De win' fetch de smell ub de maa'sh. Mek me t'ink ub summuh, 'do' Fall on us now. Us lucky dat sto'm pass on ober. Don' leabe too much mis'ry behime."

"How many storms like that have you lived through here on the island?"

She thought for a moment. "T'ree, maybe fo' dis bad. Mos' time, don' cum 'fo' Octobuh. Wen uh lib obuh neah Fish Haul, seem tuh do mo' debblement." She glanced at me sideways. "Weh Jon tuhday?"

"He went to a meeting over at Rose Hill Plantation."

She nodded knowingly. "Um hum. 'Enry know 'bout dat meet'n."

"He did? What did he hear?"

She called for Henry, and in a couple of minutes he appeared around the corner of the house with Frankie and Beau on his heels. "Wha' oonuh tell me 'bout dat meet'n obuh Rose Hill?"

He sat on an overturned bucket in front of the bench. "Hear man een de sto' say sto'm mek change ub plans. Say need tuh ret'ink ebryt'ing. Don' know wha' 'e mean, but seem 'paw'tun'."

"Jon thinks it may have something to do with the plans to buy out the Sea Pines Company. We ran into a relative of one of the main investors, and she hinted that the plans to take over the company may be dropped."

"Dat so? Reckon dey t'ink 'e mo' a risk attuh de sto'm," Henry said.

"Say Henry? What do you know about Rose Hill? I mean, I'm wondering if there's some special reason why the investors would want to meet there?"

"De big house jes need leetle wu'k tuh set 'e right 'gen, but de lan' gone tuh 'gleck. Tek many han' set 'e straight. Could be dey hab uh min' tuh tek 'e on."

"Jon seemed to think so, too. He didn't say much before he left this morning, but his face looked serious."

Mary chuckled. "Yo' husbun' uh serious man. Tek 'e time study t'ings. Nutt'n' wrong wid dat!"

Henry nodded his agreement. "Mary say de trute." He stood to leave. "Gots tuh go finish de wu'k. Tell Jon call wen 'e done meet'n. Wan' ask him sump'n."

I stayed and visited with Mary a while longer before collecting Frankie to head home. I decided to stop by the Sanders on the way since they didn't live far from the Palmers. Betty was happy to see me. We decided to take the boys for a walk on Fish Haul Beach to take advantage of the good weather. It was a mild day with plenty of sunshine and the warmth felt good on the bare skin of my arms and face. When we returned to the house, Betty offered to bring Frankie home later if I wanted to leave him to play with Tommy. I decided to accept her offer, which was reinforced by Frankie's begging to stay. I was glad he had a good friend to play with, and it would free my mind to mull over the things that had been occupying it since we ran into Savannah.

Jon's car was in the driveway when I arrived home, causing my heartbeat to accelerate. I hurried in the front door and looked for him, spotting him sitting outside on the deck. He turned around at the sound of my footsteps.

"Hi, Georgia. I wondered where you were."

"Frankie and I went over to the Palmers, then I stopped by to see Betty. She invited Frankie to stay, and said she'd bring him home later." I sat next to him. "How'd the meeting go?"

"Okay, I guess. There were about a dozen men, all of whom seemed to be somehow associated with Quinn. The discussion was mainly about the plan to buy out the Sea Pines Company, and whether or not that was still a good idea. The room was split pretty much down the middle, with Quinn casting the deciding vote."

I held my breath as I waited for him to tell me the outcome.

"They decided not to move forward with the buy-out."

I let out my breath in a whoosh of air. "Wow. I was guessing that might happen, but it's still a surprise."

"There were a lot of unhappy people at the end of the meeting. I overheard a couple of guys talking outside about taking legal action against Quinn. I don't think they have any grounds to make that happen, but it gives you a measure of just how upset they were."

"What was Quinn's main argument against the buyout?"

"Financial, which always seems to be the bottom line with him. He's just not convinced that buying out the Sea Pines Company will be a good move in the long run. He pulled me aside after the meeting and asked me to wait around. There were some others lagging behind, too. Mostly the same ones who had voted on his side. Eventually, we reconvened in another room. The main topic of discussion was the Rose Hill Plantation. Quinn was proposing that the investors shift their interest into developing the original plantation into a multi-use residential community, much like Sea Pines, but on a smaller scale. He brought out some blueprints showing how the land could be separated into 950 home sites, a golf course, Equestrian Center, a community center, and other amenities for the residents. The original plantation house would be preserved as a showplace and focal point for tours and various social events."

I had to admit the idea had merit. "Where does that leave the Sea Pines Company?"

"When I spoke to Harry, he said the homeowners' association has been rallying the residents to recapture control of Sea Pines. Apparently, along with the help of several local banks and savings and loan institutions, they've already come up with $3 million. Harry said that's enough to tide things over until April, which is when the Heritage Golf Classic opens. That tournament brings more people and money to Hilton Head than any other event. They're hopeful it will put the Resort back in the black."

"Where would that leave Charles Fraser and the other members of the Sea Pines Company?"

"As I understand it, Charles has been in on this from the get-go. He's in favor of the Resort becoming more under the control of the local citizens, and if the current plan is successful, he intends to step down as President of the Company, and just serve as a consultant to the homeowners' board."

"That's very big of him. It sounds like he cares more about the community than his own pocket."

He rolled his head from side to side. "I believe that's true in part, but Fraser is also an astute businessman. The Sea Pines Company is on the verge of bankruptcy. I think he saw the writing on the wall and decided it would take some drastic action to keep that from happening. You also have to remember that Sea Pines was Fraser's dream. I doubt he would want to see it dashed on the rocks of complacency."

What he was saying made sense. If the homeowners were correct in banking on the Heritage to bail the Resort out of the red, then the dream Fraser hatched of an environmentally sound community would be preserved. Fraser would be able to keep his fingers in the pie without burning them, and the island would avoid a take-over motivated by greed. It sounded like a win-win situation to me. I suddenly had another thought. "What did Quinn want from you today?"

He looked thoughtful. "He still wants me involved. He indicated he'd like me to be his point person on the island; see to it that the plans for development move forward without a hitch. Then when the residences are ready for occupancy, he suggested I'd be first in line to arrange the sales."

"Wouldn't that mean you'd have to leave your current position?"

"Yes. He wants me on-board immediately."

"I'm sure you'd need some time to wrap up the sales you've been working on. What will you tell your boss about his offer of a partnership?"

"I'll tell him how much I appreciate it, but I've decided to go in another direction." He studied my face. "Are you okay with this? I know unexpected change can be hard for you."

"Honestly, I think I'm getting used to it. I've begun to realize there's very little I actually have control over; at least when it comes to predicting the future." I noticed he was staring at my chest. "What?"

"I was wondering if that amulet has anything to say about what I've been telling you?"

I placed my hand on top of it in a protective motion. "It's definitely been heating up. I didn't notice it until you started talking about leaving your current position and joining Quinn. Do you trust this man? You seemed to have some reservations in the beginning."

"It's like that gut instinct you and Julie are always talking about. Something tells me Quinn is genuine. I even find myself liking the man. I don't doubt for a minute he'd put money in front of friendship at the drop of a hat, but I think that's a good trait to have in a business relationship."

"Then, I think you should do it; wrap up what you have to and move on to the next stage of your career. You've been looking for something new to sink your teeth into." The amulet began to throb more noticeably. "I just remembered. Henry wants to talk with you."

He grinned. "When has Henry NOT had something to say? Did he give you any hint what it was about?"

I shook my head. "He mentioned he overheard a man in his store talking about how taking over the Sea Pines Company might not be a good idea, but I got the impression it wasn't about that. Why don't you give him a call?"

He stood and stretched. "I will. But first…" He held out his hand to me. "What do you say we take advantage of having a little time alone before Frankie storms through the door?"

I grinned at him as I took his hand. "Great idea, Mr. Barnett."

CHAPTER EIGHTEEN

Jon called Henry later that evening. He didn't say much about their conversation. Just that Henry had an idea he wanted Jon to consider, and they arranged to talk face-to-face later in the week. We had a quiet dinner and put Frankie to bed before relaxing on the sofa. I rested my head upon Jon's shoulder, and he shifted so he could pull me onto his chest. I suddenly remembered I meant to phone Julie earlier in the day. In fact, it had been almost two full days since we spoke, which was some kind of record for us. I glanced at the time and decided it was too late to disturb her, but made a mental note to call first thing in the morning

"What did Harry say when you spoke to him? Has he heard anything about the plans to buy out the Sea Pines Company?"

"Surprisingly, no. Well, maybe it shouldn't be a surprise. Quinn and his group seem pretty good about keeping things close to the chest."

"Except when they're talking in Henry's store. Henry suggested the reason the man he overheard spoke so freely in his presence was because they didn't regard him as significant. You know, like maybe he wasn't capable of understanding what they were saying because of his color."

"Huh. I'm ashamed to have to admit it, but he's probably right. There wasn't a single black face around the table when I met with the investors group, except for a waiter who kept the water glasses and coffee pot filled."

"It's a shame prejudice is still so prevalent. I would have thought the Civil Rights Movement would have made a greater impact on that."

"People are afraid of what they don't understand. Racial differences, as well as differences in culture, creed, and sexual orientation, fall into that category for a great many individuals." He shifted slightly so my head rested more firmly against his chest. "Say. Have you heard of a place called Mitchelville?"

The name seemed to stir something in my memory, but I couldn't pull it up to the surface. "Maybe, but I'm not sure. Why do you ask?"

"It's just something Henry said. Or at least something I think he said. You know how difficult it is to understand him sometimes. He was explaining he wanted to talk with me about something, and I believe he said it had to do with Mitchelville. Only he said it more like Mi'chebill. I guess I'll find out what he meant when we meet." He shifted again, causing me to have to lift my head to avoid it falling. "I'm sorry. I guess I'm a little restless tonight."

I sat straight. "That's okay. I'm feeling sleepy anyway. I think I'll go on to bed."

He leaned forward and kissed me gently. "Sleep tight. I'm going to stay up a while."

I caressed the dark stubble of his beard. "I guess you've got a lot on your mind. I hope you can get some sleep eventually." He answered with a nod of his head.

Over the next two days, Jon accepted Robert Quinn's offer to join his development company in hopes of capitalizing on their plans to purchase the Rose Hill Plantation. He gave his current boss notice he would be leaving as soon as he was able to wrap up some pending real estate transactions, suggesting he wanted to retain his commission, and reserve the right to decide to whom he would turn over any unfinished business. The boss wasn't thrilled with Jon's decision, but he reluctantly agreed to the terms Jon proposed.

Work suddenly became very hectic for Jon, causing him to leave early in the morning and return later than usual at night. I was left with more time on my hands than I was used to, and I began to feel restless for something to do. I talked over my feelings with Julie, who wisely suggested I begin to think seriously about revamping my career in journalism in some way, shape, or form. I hadn't really missed the work since Frankie was born, but I knew there was a place deep inside me that felt unfulfilled–at least when it came to professional matters. I loved my life with Jon and Frankie, although I still harbored thoughts of adding to that number one day. I treasured the wealth of friendships I had developed over the years. Julie was the greatest friend anyone could ask for, and I had come to love the time I spent with Mary, Henry, and Betty.

It suddenly occurred to me there was another name that should be on that list. Before we moved from Nashville, I began to develop a friendship with Susan Bentley. I met her at a journalism conference hosted by Thomas Bookman at Belmont College. Her work in microbiology helped me solve the mystery of Bessie Barnhill's grandfather's death. She and her husband, Stan, visited us on Hilton Head twice since our relocation, but it had been several months since I had seen or spoken to her. The old adage *out of sight, out of mind* seemed to apply in this situation. I certainly liked her and valued her friendship. I had just fallen out of the habit of staying in touch.

I picked up the little book where I kept a list of phone numbers and dialed hers.

"Hello?" She answered.

"Susan? It's Georgia."

"Georgia! How nice to hear from you! Stan and I were just talking about you and Jon the other night. We were remembering what a wonderful time we had when we visited you on Hilton Head this past Summer. I can't believe it's been that long since we've spoken."

"I was just thinking the same thing. It's certainly no reflection on how much I value your friendship. Life just has a way of rolling along."

"Well, I'm sure you've had plenty of things to occupy your time, including a very active little one. How is Frankie?"

"He's fine. Just as rambunctious and curious as ever. He's made a new friend on the island, and that's been really good for him."

"That's wonderful. I remember what a relief it was when our two kids finally had a group of friends to get together with. It takes some of the pressure off the parents to entertain them."

Susan and Stan were a good bit older than Jon and me, so their kids were already teenagers. "We also had a bit of excitement with the recent hurricane."

"Oh, right! I meant to call and see how you all managed with that. Did you have to evacuate the island?"

"There was a voluntary evacuation, but we decided to stay. Luckily, everything turned out fine, but I'm not sure I'd make the same choice if one comes our way again. It was pretty scary watching and wondering what was going to happen. How about you? Anything new in your life?"

"Not really. My work at the Ellington Agricultural Center is winding down, so things have been a little calmer. Stan still works at the Methodist Publishing House, but he's been spending more and more time over at Belmont. He and Thomas are cooking up some project involving New Journalism that he seems terribly excited about. How's Jon?"

"Actually, he's about to change jobs. He's been meeting with a group of investors who he thought were going to buy out a large Company on the island, but after the hurricane, they decided to switch gears. That is, half of them did. There was a split vote, and a slim majority decided to shift their funds and attention toward another project. Jon was invited to join them. He's been looking for something new to get involved in, so he made the decision to leave his real estate company. The new project will entail buying up a historic plantation just off island and overseeing its development into a planned residential and multi-use community."

"That does sound exciting." There was a pause on the line. "And what about you? I got the impression the last time we spoke that you were getting a little restless, too. Do you have any irons in the proverbial fire?"

I had to laugh as my amulet started heating up at her last question. "Not really, although I have been considering some options." I started to mention the possibility of a second child but decided that was not a conversation I was ready to have. Especially over the phone. "It's really good to talk with you again. I hope you and Stan can plan a visit here again in the near future."

"I'd like nothing more. And if you and Jon get to Nashville, please let us know. We'd love to have you over for dinner."

I hung up the phone, expecting to feel a sense of satisfaction at reconnecting with Susan, but instead I just felt a nagging sense of edginess. Susan had nailed it when she asked if I was getting restless. I needed something to do. Something that defined me as more than a wife, mother, and friend.

The question Jon asked me earlier in the week popped into my mind, and I walked to the bookshelf. I began collecting books on the history of Hilton Head during our first trip to the island, and I now had a sizable compilation." I began thumbing through them to see if I could locate any mention of Mitchelville. It was listed in the index of one of the books, so I settled onto the sofa to do a little reading.

The chapter I came across was titled *The Civil War, Hilton Head Island, and the Evolution of Mitchelville*. It described how in 1861, a Union fleet of about 60 ships and 20,000 men sailed from Virginia to the coast of Port Royal, South Carolina to launch an attack on the Confederate forces. By the afternoon, the Confederate forces had retreated, leaving the Port Royal area to Union forces.

Within two days, Sea Island blacks, who were part of the 20,000 enslaved Africans brought to South Carolina in the 1700s, flocked to the newly established Union camps by the hundreds, escaping slavery for the hope of freedom. Hilton Head Island was used as the Union's southern headquarters and military supply. The Union Army considered these escaped slaves to be "contraband of war" rather than free men. The former slaves were housed in ill-constructed shacks and hired by the Army to perform a wide variety of jobs for paltry pay.

In February of 1862, Edward L. Pierce, an attorney, and strong abolitionist member of the Lincoln cabinet, was sent to Hilton Head to look into the "contraband negro" situation. He discovered 16 plantations on the island and at least 600 blacks scattered across Hilton Head, Pinckney, St. Helena, Port Royal, Spring, and Daufuskie islands. He took his observations back to Washington where they helped launch what became known as "The Port Royal Experiment".

The Port Royal Experiment, initiated by the Philadelphia Freedom Society, involved the creation of the Penn School on St. Helena Island. It provided the means for former slaves to receive education in wheelwrighting, carpentry, cobbling, blacksmithing, and the agricultural sciences. The school also provided regular educational classes and teacher training. On January 1, 1863, the Emancipation Proclamation was signed by President Abraham Lincoln, officially making the "contraband of war slaves" freedmen. In the aftermath of the signing, a military order was issued freeing the blacks on the Sea Islands.

According to the report, things finally began to change for the better for freed slaves on Hilton Head Island when General

Ormsby Mitchel assumed command of the Union Army Post. He selected a location near what was then called Drayton Plantation for a "Negro village", then commandeered building supplies to allow the freedmen to construct their own houses. A teacher was brought in to instruct the children, and the residents were encouraged to establish their own governing body. In March of 1863, the township of Mitchelville was established.

The list of things the government of Mitchelville was responsible for was mind-boggling. The town was divided into districts with elected councilmen charged with establishing police and sanitary regulations, schools, preventing and punishing vagrancy, idleness and crime, licentious-ness, drunkenness, offenses against public decency and good order, and petty violation of the rights of property and person. The governing body was also responsible for collecting fines and penalties, punishing offences against the village ordinances, settling disputes over wages, personal property, and controversies between debtor and creditor.

The list went on. The councilmen were accountable for levying and collecting taxes, laying out, regulating, and cleaning the streets, establishing sanitary regulations to prevent disease, appointing officers, and regulating all other matters affecting the well-being of its citizens. The article made it clear that the governing body of Mitchelville was as well-developed as any modern-day government, and more comprehensive than some. The town was also unique in that it created the first compulsory education law in South Carolina, requiring every child, between the ages of six and fifteen years residing within Mitchelville, to attend school.

I flipped a few pages ahead and read that by 1865 there were around 1500 people living in Mitchelville. Houses were surrounded by quarter acre lots used for growing food and raising animals. Religious practices were a mainstay of life in Mitchelville, and by 1866 there were three different churches in the town. In the aftermath of the Emancipation Proclamation, Mitchelville became a template for the creation of future freedmen towns. Unfortunately, the U.S. government didn't plan for the protection and preservation of Mitchelville. Many of the freedmen worked for the Union army, while others worked for wages on the plantations where they once provided slave labor. Nearly all of the wage jobs ceased when the Union military left Hilton Head Island in 1868. At that point, the residents switched to a subsistence farming-based economy, with many forming farming collectives, joining together to rent large tracts of land from the government.

The town remained relatively intact until the early 1870s but was mostly abandoned by 1890 in the aftermath of laws that called for the return of lands confiscated by the U.S. government to the Southern landowners. Most of the remaining residents of Mitchelville took apart their homes and moved inland toward the areas of Squire Pope, Baynard and Chaplain. Money was scarce, and the islanders bartered for goods and services. In 1890, the number of negros living on Hilton Head totaled approximately 3,000, but by 1930 that number was reduced to only about 300.

I closed the book and leaned my head against the sofa. Everything I just read suggested that Hilton Head was the site of a robust movement intended to provide a better life for former slaves. My mind was filled with images of what that life must have been like, and I was curious to view the actual site of this freedmen's township. From what I could gather, it must have been near to the Sanders home. I picked up the phone to call Mary.

"'Lo."

"Hi, Mary. It's Georgia."

"Uh jes t'ink 'bout oonuh!"

I smiled at the warmth of her words which rolled over me like sunshine. "I wanted to ask what you know about a place called Mitchelville. I've just been reading about it."

"Unh, unh, unh. Not much dere now, but Mi'chebill was fus' freedmens town on dis I'lun'. Fus' anywhere, uh t'ink. Why oonuh ask 'bout 'e?"

"Jon said Henry mentioned it to him, which made me want to learn more about it. From what I could tell, it was located near where the Sanders live now."

169

"Yaas, dat 'bout right, 'do' jes dirt, trees, an' scrub brush dese days. Henry say sump'n 'fo' 'e leabe dis mawnin'. T'ink 'e an' Jon gone head-off dat wey attuhw'ile. Uh don' know wha' 'e hab een min'. Sumtime 'e keep t'ings een 'e head."

"Jon can be the same way. It looks like I'm going to have to do some investigating on my own if I want to find out anything. Thanks Mary."

My next phone call was to Betty Sanders. We arranged to meet at the corner of Dillon and Beach City Roads, in the parking lot of the old Cherry Hill School. While I was waiting for Betty, I read a wooden sign nailed to the front of the building. It described how the one-room frame and weatherboard-sided school was built in 1937 to replace an earlier school held in the parsonage of St. James Baptist Church. The original school was built and maintained by descendants of Mitchelville until it was closed in the 1950s. At that time, it was purchased by the St. James Church and preserved as a reminder of the role Mitchelville and Hilton Head played in bringing education to Southern blacks.

The crunch of tires brought my attention away from the building. Betty waved from the window of her station wagon. I walked to where she parked and waited for her to step out of the car.

"Good morning, Georgia."

I checked my watch. "By golly, it is still morning. It feels much later than that."

"You must have been up with the birds today."

I nodded. "I have to get up early most days to get Frankie ready, and I like to take a walk on the beach before that. I've been doing some reading this morning, and I guess I lost track of time."

She closed the car door and pulled her sweater snugly around her chest. "It's still a little chilly. I'm glad I thought to bring a sweater." She glanced around her. "Where are we headed? You mentioned something about a hidden village?"

"It's really just the site where an old town used to be. It was called Mitchelville, and it was the first freedmen's township in the entire United States."

Her expression showed her puzzlement. "Okay. I'm not going to try and figure out what that means. I'm sure you'll explain when we get there."

"It's just down the road a couple of blocks. I thought we could walk there, and I'll tell you about it on the way."

We began the trek down the roadside toward the area where Mitchelville once stood. As we walked, I described what I read about the history of the town, and its significance to the Gullah descendants of Hilton Head.

Betty shook her head in amazement. "That's impressive. To think there was an entire town created and governed by freed slaves."

We arrived at the entrance to Mitchelville, marked only by a small wooden sign, and turned down the dirt path. As we walked, I was struck by the realization that there were no buildings or any other indicators that a thriving town once existed. I heard a rustling in some nearby bushes and turned in that direction, expecting to see a squirrel or bird. Instead, I was surprised to see Jon and Henry emerge from the undergrowth. They looked at us with equal amounts of surprise and alarm.

Jon frowned when he spotted us. "What are you two doing here?"

I wasn't pleased at his gruffness. "I could ask you the same thing."

His expression softened somewhat. "I'm sorry. You just took me by surprise. Henry and I were just taking a look at where the town of Mitchelville once stood. There's not much to see nowadays, but Henry was helping me get an idea of how things used to be."

Henry removed his straw hat and smiled in greeting. "'Mawnin' Georgia. Miss Betty."

"Please just call me Betty. How are you today, Henry?"

"Ebry day uh on dis side ub de groun' uh doin' fine." His smile stretched into a grin.

Jon placed a hand on Henry's shoulder. "Why don't you tell the ladies what you told me? About how things used to look around here."

Henry nodded and looked around. "Ebyt'ing uh know was passed down f'um my granpappy and his pappy fo' him." He pointed in the direction of the Port Royal Sound. "Mi'chebill cover sum hund'ud fitty acres f'um de watuh edge obuh cross tuh de ole Drayton Plantation, an' back tuh weh Fort Howell sat. Stretched 'cross bofe sides Beach City Road. Houses all lined up in rows wid leetle yard 'roun' dem. 'Nuff tuh grow food an' maybe hab chicken pen. 'Ventually hab t'ree chu'ch een middle ub de houses. Use tuh hab sum sto' fo' buyin' t'ings, but dey close up attuh de aa'my leabe. Folks hab tuh scratch hard tuh mek nuff tuh libe, but was happy 'cos dey free."

The description he painted of the town encompassed a lot more land than I imagined. I looked over my shoulder in the direction we had walked from. "You mentioned a Fort. Is it still here?"

Henry shook his head. "Can't see much ub 'e dese times. Fort Howell built tuh protect Mi'chebill. Built by colored soldiers fum up nawth. Build 'e een middle ub cotton field. Wen not need 'e no mo', sat fo'got. Couple harricane tore down de wall. Leebe nuttin' tuh see but big mounds ub dirt cover wid leaves 'n trees. Nice place tuh walk, but hard tuh 'magine uh fort sat dere."

Jon had been walking around the area while Henry spoke. "Why hasn't there been any effort to restore any part of Mitchelville? I would think the governing body of Hilton Head would be interested in preserving such a significant piece of history."

"Ask dem one time een uh meet'n'. De say 'Dat lan' ent wu't' nuttin'.'Mek clear dey don' 'tend tuh t'row money on 'e." His face grew serious as he looked at Jon. "Dat why uh ask oonuh cum here. T'ink maybe oonuh hab influence obbuh sum dem folks wid deep pockets. Spread sum dat money here 'stead ub jes off-island. Uh know dis not hep mek money. Not at fus'. But eef could gib back sum ub what was, be rich een hist'ry."

Jon looked thoughtful as he listened to Henry. "I don't disagree with you. I think it would be a wise decision to restore enough of Mitchelville to give folks an idea what it was all about. I also think it would draw more tourism to the island, especially if advertisements were created to emphasize its early role in bringing about reconstruction and civil rights."

Betty had been listing to the two men talk without comment. "I don't mean to intrude. But it seems to me that what both of you are suggesting would be a huge undertaking. You would have to convince the people who control the purse strings of some fairly sizable corporations they should invest time and money in a project that has little chance of proving profitable. At least not in the beginning. I realize I'm fairly new to the island, but I can't imagine that would go over very well."

"I have to agree with Betty," I said. "Unless you can make a case that investing in such a project would generate a return on their investment over time, I think you'd be fighting a losing battle." I turned to Jon. "Why don't you talk to Harry about it? I remember when Julie's dad was working with all those men from the entertainment and music industries, he was successful in convincing them to commit funds to several projects that stood a good chance to lose money. Harry could run this by him and see if they can come up with a way to present it in a financially attractive manner."

"Good idea. Henry, give me some time to mull this over, and I'll get back to you."

Henry nodded. "Dat's all uh ask."

CHAPTER NINETEEN

I awoke the next morning to heavy rain. The weather in September on Hilton Head was always unpredictable, fluctuating between Summer and Fall in the blink of an eye. I walked to the back and opened the screen door to look out. A warm breeze greeted me, carrying with it droplets of rain from the deluge that battered the deck. The scent of fish was evident, as it was most days on the shore. We were lucky to live so close to the beach, but the downside was the inevitable presence of sand, dampness, and sea smells. I didn't mind it most of the time, but today I longed for sunshine and the scent of flowers and freshly mowed grass. As that image filled my mind, I thought of Nashville, and the home Jon and I had shared. We spent many wonderful evenings sitting on the patio, sipping drinks, or sharing dinner with friends. The patio had been surrounded by an assortment of potted plants overflowing with flowers and fresh herbs. It pained me to leave them behind when we moved to Hilton Head. Luckily, Julie was able to take several, and the folks who rented the house were grateful to have the rest.

We decided not to sell the Nashville house when we moved to Hilton Head. It may have been overly sentimental on my part, but since it was left to me by Ida Hood, selling it seemed disrespectful. Luckily, Julie and Harry agreed to oversee the property and deal with any issues that arose from the renters.

The rain lessened slightly, so I decided to brave the weather and walk over to the beach. I pulled on a raincoat and cap and slipped into waterproof boots before unfurling an oversized umbrella. It was almost 8AM when I left the house, which would normally mean the sunrise had peaked at least an hour earlier. However, the horizon was darkened by heavy gray clouds that occluded the sunrise, making it feel like it was much earlier than it was.

There were only a few other people on the beach. We glanced at one another with a grin, shaking our heads at our craziness in being out in such weather. The waves were higher than usual and lapped the shore close to my feet, sending me scampering for dryer ground. By my estimation, it was close to high tide, which meant the longer I walked, the less shore I would have available. I traipsed on a few more minutes before turning around to head for home, stopping at the entrance to the path to look once more at the scene in front of me.

Jon was awake when I returned. I hung up my coat and cap and placed my boots below them before going inside. He turned around from where he stood at the kitchen sink and looked at me askance. "Don't tell me you've been outside in this weather?"

"Okay, I won't tell you, but I was. It wouldn't have been too bad except it's high tide. I didn't have much room to walk, so I decided to come back." I looked around the room. "Isn't Frankie up yet?"

He nodded. "I already got him dressed and gave him some cereal. He's in the living room watching cartoons now. I told him if he were quiet, he could hang out there until it's time to leave." He held out a steaming cup of coffee and raised an eyebrow in question. I accepted it without hesitation.

"By the looks of the sky, there's a good chance this rain is going to continue most of the day."

I closed my eyes as I sniffed the aroma wafting up from the cup. "Why is it that coffee always smells much better than it tastes?" I took a hesitant sip, and then another when I realized it wasn't going to burn my tongue.

He poured a cup for himself and leaned against the counter. "Oh, I don't know. I think the smell and taste are about equal. Except when you make a pot of that perfumed stuff."

I laughed. I sometimes liked to perk up a batch of hazelnut flavored coffee, which Jon felt was blasphemous.

"What are you doing today?" I asked.

He reached under the counter and pulled out the toaster. "I still have a couple of pending real estate transactions I need to look into. After that, I want to talk with Harry about my conversation with Henry yesterday. I also need to touch base with Quinn and see what the plans are for proceeding with the Rose Hill project. How about you?" He placed two slices of bread in the toaster and pressed the lever, then opened the cabinet to take out some peanut butter and jam.

"I thought I'd take a drive over to the library and see if I can find anything more about Mitchelville. There's a pretty good description in one of the books we have here, but it stops short of describing what's happened to the town in more recent years."

He studied my expression. "It seems you've taken quite an interest in this issue."

I nodded. "I have. The way it came about. What it stands for. What it could be. I find all of that intriguing."

The toast popped up and he laid the slices on plates before carrying them to the kitchen table. I collected the peanut butter and jam and placed them on the table, then added utensils and glasses of milk.

Jon looked at me thoughtfully. "If this idea of Henry's turns into anything more than a pipe dream, it might be something you'd want to get involved in."

I frowned at his statement. "What do you mean?"

He chewed as he considered my question. "It could become a professional opportunity for you. Not in the same way as your job at Belmont, but I was thinking about what we discussed regarding the need to promote tourism by emphasizing the historical importance of the Mitchelville site. That might be something you could really sink your teeth into."

I felt a rush of excitement as he spoke, combined with an increase in heat from the amulet. "You really think Henry's idea could work?"

"The issue of funding is still a huge question mark, but I think it's worth exploring." He downed the remainder of his milk and started collecting his dishes. "I'd better get a move on if I want to have time to do everything on my list today." He placed the dishes in the sink and bent to kiss the top of my head. "I'll call you later and let you know what I find out from Harry."

I lingered at the table a while longer after he left. His comment about how the Mitchelville project could be a way for me to use my journalism training again was intriguing. The amulet kept throbbing insistently in a way that was impossible to ignore. I laid my hand on top of it, closing my eyes to try to sense its message.

"Mommy, what are you doing?"

I opened my eyes to find Frankie standing next to me. "Just relaxing a bit, sweetheart. Do you need to go potty?" Potty-training was a fairly recent accomplishment in our household, and I still felt the need to check in with Frankie about it.

"Nuh-uh. I went." He held up his stuffed Dolphin. "When are we going to see the dolfs again? I miss 'em."

I caressed his head. "Maybe this weekend, if the weather is good." I looked up at the kitchen clock. "We need to leave pretty soon so I can drop you off at the Daycare Center. Why don't you put Dolf away and get your jacket? It's still a little cool outside."

"'K, Mommy." He rushed off down the hall.

I washed our dishes then walked down the hall toward our bedroom, making a stop in the bathroom before grabbing a sweater from the chest of drawers. When I returned to the kitchen, Frankie was waiting by the front door.

Frankie's teacher was standing at the curb in front of the Center when I pulled up. She waved slightly and stood back so Frankie could step out of the car. I leaned across the seat and rolled down the window. "Hi Vanessa. How are things today?"

She smiled at Frankie before answering. "So far, so good. Big plans for the day?"

"I'm heading over to the library to do a little research."

Frankie stuck his head back inside the car window. "Kin Tommy come to our house today?"

"Not today, sweetheart. But I promise I'll arrange something with his Mommy soon." I rolled up the window and waved goodbye.

The Hilton Head library was a short drive from the Daycare Center on William Hilton Parkway. There were a few cars already in the parking lot when I arrived. I pulled into one of the vacant spots, and headed inside the building, making my way to the head librarian's desk. I met her a couple of times before when I visited the library, and she gave me a friendly smile as I approached.

"Hello, Georgia. Can I help you find something?"

"Hi, Hillary. I'm hoping you have some information on the recent history of Mitchelville."

She looked at me curiously. "Mitchelville? I don't often get queries about that. There used to be a library at the Penn Center over on St. Helena Island that carried several accounts of the founding of Mitchelville. The library closed in 1973, at which time a lot of the books were relocated to the main Beaufort County library." She began walking around her desk, gesturing for me to follow. "A couple of boxes were sent here. Most of the books are about the discovery of Hilton Head and the early inhabitants, but I think I recall one or two that mention the Civil War period. They might have some of the information you're looking for." She stopped in front of a bookcase with four shelves, pulling out two books located near the bottom. "Here. Feel free to look these over. We don't allow them out of the building because, as you can see, they're rather fragile. But you can take a seat at one of the tables and look at them as long as you like."

I thanked her and made my way to the reading area. I leafed through the first book but couldn't find any mention of Mitchelville. I opened the second book and scanned the table of contents. Eureka! I hurriedly flipped to the chapter titled *Mitchelville After the Civil War*. Most of what I read was a repeat of the information I already knew.

It described how the Union forces left Hilton Head in 1868, taking with them the jobs that sustained the Gullah descendants living in the town of Mitchelville. The townspeople were forced to form farming collectives, joining together to rent large plots of land from the U.S. government with hopes of eventually purchasing that property. Unfortunately, Congress passed laws calling for the restoration of confiscated lands to Southern owners, as long as they paid taxes, costs, and interests. As a result, much of the land purchased by the freedmen in good faith was taken from them. That included the Drayton plantation on which part of Mitchelville was located. However, the Drayton heirs weren't interested in using the land, and began selling it off to anyone interested. Some of the purchasers included freedmen.

During the last quarter of the nineteenth century, most of Mitchelville was purchased by a black man, March Gardner. March placed his son, Gabriel, in charge of the town, which at the time included a store, cotton gin, and grist mill. Apparently, that's where things began to rapidly go downhill. March trusted his son to have a proper deed made. But Gabriel obtained a deed in his own name and then transferred the property to his wife and daughter.

In the early twentieth century, the heirs of March Gardner took the heirs of Gabriel's wife to court, claiming they owned what was left of Mitchelville, and that Gabriel had stolen the property. The book continued to describe how, as part of the court mandated hearings, testimonies were taken from several people living in the town at the time. The daughter of March Gardner, Emmeline Washington, testified that a number of families were living in Mitchelville and farming three to four-acre plots next to their houses. She stated the money collected for rent went to pay taxes on the property.

The chapter contained copies of court papers listing by name several Mitchelville residents in the late nineteenth and early twentieth centuries. What was apparent in the account, was that the Draytons' heirs sold Mitchelville twice; first to March Gardner, then again to his son Gabriel Gardner. The court directed a survey be made and the property of Mitchelville be divided among the heirs after each paid their share of the costs associated with the case. It stated that Eugenia Heyward redeemed a tract of 35 acres on June 7, 1923. Celia and Gabriel Boston obtained the adjacent tract on September 2, 1921. Linda Perry, Emmeline Washington, and Clara Wigfall also obtained parcels in 1921.

In 1927, a wealthy New Yorker named Roy A. Rainey purchased the Honey Horn Plantation and the entire south end of Hilton Head. Rainey also purchased the Heywood tract after it was put up for sale by the Sheriff. The tract sold for $31.00 to pay a defaulted tax bill of $15.00.

I set the book aside and picked up another titled *Hunting on Hilton Head Island.* I scanned the appendix searching for the name Roy A. Rainey, and was rewarded by a reference to several pages. I read through the first few and was surprised to see the name Rainey cross-referenced with another man named W.P. Clyde. Clyde was described as a New England shipping magnate who partnered with Roy Rainey for the purchase of large plots of land on Hilton Head. In 1930, the two sold their Hilton Head land for $6 an acre to two men named Landon Thorne and Alfred Loomis.

Thorne and Loomis spent winter seasons on the island, using the land primarily for hunting for 20 years before selling out to Georgia timbermen. In 1950 and 1951, the timbermen eventually sold the land in two transactions totalling $1,080,000. This began the period of development on Hilton Head Island that took place under the guidance of a few men known locally as "benevolent dictators". The names associated with that title included Fred C. Hack, Olin T. McIntosh, and Charles E. Fraser. Mention of this last name jogged my memory. One of the timbermen mentioned must have been Joe Fraser, Charles Fraser's father.

I scanned the appendix for the name Joe Fraser and turned to the page cited. I read that in 1949, a group of lumber associates from Hinesville, Georgia bought 20,000 acres of pine forest on the South end of Sea Pines for $60 an acre. They formed the Hilton Head Company to handle the timber operation. So, it was indeed true that Joe Fraser and associates were the timbermen mentioned as having purchased the Hilton Head property from Thorne and Loomis. I read further and discovered that in 1956, Joe Fraser and his sons Charles and Joe Jr founded a real estate company called The Sea Pines Company.

I closed the book and leaned back in my chair. My head was beginning to spin with the various names and dates referenced in the chapters. From what I could gather, the inhabitants of Mitchelville who remained after the War had been robbed, first by the government, and later by greedy landowners. The more recent land transactions involving wealthy Northerners, followed by the timbering and then real estate businesses generated by the Frasers, brought the story up to date, or at least as close to current times as anything I had been able to find so far.

I started my reading search to answer the question of what happened to the town of Mitchelville, and why no one had tried to restore it, or at least to retain a little of its historical significance. I wasn't sure I had been successful in my search. There was still a lot I didn't understand, but at least I had a better idea of what led to its abandonment.

I returned the books to the shelf and walked back to the librarian's desk.

"Did you find what you were looking for?"

"Partly. I was hoping to find more information about Mitchelville in modern times, or at least during the time period between the 1950s and now."

"I doubt there's much of a written record of that time period for the town of Mitchelville. Most of the accounts of the island I've read during the years you're interested in skip right over Mitchelville and focus on the actions of a handful of wealthy businessmen. If you want any information on what was happening to the lives of the descendants of Mitchelville, I'm afraid you're going to have to track some of them down for a face-to-face talk. I have to warn you, most of them are going to be wary of a white woman asking questions about their ancestors, and the ones who're willing to talk may be a little difficult to understand."

My thoughts went immediately to Mary and Henry, and I realized how lucky I was to have met them. "I know what you mean. Thanks again, Hillary."

CHAPTER TWENTY

It would be several days before I looked any further into the Mitchelville story. Jon became extremely busy wrapping up his former real estate activities and beginning his involvement in the Rose Hill redevelopment. When I asked him about Mitchelville and his conversation with Henry, he only looked thoughtful and said he was still working on it. Julie and I spoke a few times since Betty and I ran into Jon and Henry on the land where Mitchelville once stood. When I asked her if Harry mentioned anything about a conversation with Jon regarding the former freedmen's town, she replied that she knew they had spoken about it but didn't have any details.

The things I read about the history of the town kept nagging at me. Especially the part describing the government's role in bringing about its demise. I decided I needed to visit the site once again.

I picked up Frankie from the Daycare Center Friday afternoon, and headed for the Cherry Hill School. The day started out partly cloudy, but we were rewarded with bright sunshine as we pulled into the parking lot of the school. Remembering what Henry said about Fort Howell, I led Frankie in the opposite direction from the route Betty and I had taken. The site of the former fort lay just south of Cherry Hill. Luckily, its location was marked by a sign displaying a drawing of the original fort. Frankie and I stopped to gaze at it as I tried to decipher exactly where the main parts of the fortification lay.

"Is dis where the soldiers were, Mommy?"

I told Frankie we were going to see a fort and gave him a brief description of what that meant.

"Yes, sweetheart. A long time ago, there was a fort here that allowed the soldiers to protect a town that used to sit all over this area." I moved my arm in a wide sweep back in the direction of the Sound.

Frankie gave me a puzzled look. "But dere's just grass and dirt here now!"

He was correct. The area identified as a fort was nothing more than ditches and grass-covered mounds in circular patterns. Pine trees grew throughout the area, further obscuring the connecting shapes of the fortress. I led him to the drawing of the original fort and pointed out the various parts it displayed. "This picture shows what the fort used to look like. There was a main enclosed area with high walls. Piles of dirt, like these we can see, allowed the soldiers to see over the walls. The parts of the walls sticking out above the roof were called parapets. And see this ledge? It ran all the way across the parapet so soldiers could stand there and shoot over the top."

"Where was the guns?"

I pointed to the diagram. "The cannons were here, and rifles could shoot through these holes. The ammunition for those weapons was stored in the middle of the fort in an area called a magazine."

He giggled. "Dat not a magazine, Mommy."

I smiled. "You're right. It's not the type of magazine you're familiar with. The ones like Mommy reads at home sometimes. This is a different kind of magazine that stores things, like guns and food."

He frowned at the picture before nodding his head. "Cool. Kin we go see?"

I took his hand and led him into the enclosure so we could walk along the raised mounds of earth and peer down into the ditches. When he seemed satisfied with what he saw, I suggested we walk back down the road in the direction we had come. After about fifteen minutes, I spotted the same small wooden sign that led to the dirt path Betty and I had taken. I let go of Frankie's hand, admonishing him to stay within sight, then sat on a large rock that looked across the land toward the Port Royal Sound. I squinted and tried to imagine the town as it had been described in the books I'd read: the rows of wooden homes surrounded by small plots of land; a church placed in the center of each cluster of homes; women hanging clothes out to dry while small, brown-skinned children played nearby; men plowing fields behind mules or hammering on metal chunks of machinery; the smell of collards or shrimp wafting from large iron kettles. I closed my eyes and allowed the images to form in my mind.

"Are you resting again, Mommy?"

"In a way. I'm trying to imagine what the town that used to be here looked like."

"Duh lady say tuh tell you tuh jes look in here." He reached and patted me on my chest above the amulet.

His words startled me. "The lady? What lady?"

"You know, duh lady dat was in my room."

Ida! My heart started hammering in my chest, matched by the rapid throbbing of the amulet. "You saw here again? Where?"

He pointed over his shoulder. "Over dere. She was sitting on a tree dat had fell down. I weren't scared of her. She was nice. Like duh man I saw on 'Fuskie, only she not look like him. Uh think dey friends."

"What makes you think they're friends?"

"She say dat bottle de man gib me working good. Dat de thing you wear gonna help."

I felt light-headed as I tried to make sense of what he was saying. "What is it going to help, Frankie? What exactly did she say?"

He scrunched up his face. "Dat all she say. She go 'way after dat."

I thought to myself, Oh Ida. Where are you, and why can't I see you? I sighed and rested my face in my hands until I felt his little hand patting my shoulder.

"Don't be sad, Mommy. De lady say she be back when you need her."

His words gave me hope. "She did?" I pulled him close for a hug. "Oh, thank you, sweetheart. That's wonderful news." I squeezed him tightly until I felt him squirming to free himself from my embrace.

"You squeeze me too tight, Mommy!" His lower lip trembled.

I released my hold on him and stood. "I'm so sorry, sweetheart. What do you say we stop on the way home and pick up some pizza?"

"Yah! Pizza!"

I wish every difficulty in life was so easy to resolve!

When we arrived home with the pizza, there was a message from Jon on the answering machine saying he would be home a little earlier than usual. Apparently, he was able to wrap up the sale of one of his remaining real estate listings. His message also said he had news to share with me about our discussion with Henry.

I sighed. More waiting and wondering. It seemed lately my life had become a series of unknowns, or at least of puzzles with missing pieces. I placed the pizza in the oven to stay warm, and ushered Frankie to the bathroom to wash up.

While I was waiting for Jon to arrive, I tried to keep myself busy by trimming the shrubs that grew beside our deck.

The shrubs bore bell-shaped flowers called azaleas that normally bloomed from late March until late April, sometimes lasting until early Summer. I knew the best time to prune the shrubs was soon after the flowers disappeared, whereas, cutting them back this time of year could prevent them from blooming at all. However, the recent hurricane had broken several of the branches, and I wanted to remove them and give the plants a healthy dose of water and fertilizer to aid their return to health. Our azaleas produced a glorious spread of flame pink flowers, with a few white and purple varieties mixed in. Not only were they strikingly beautiful, but they smelled wonderful. A neighbor once explained to me that our azaleas were of the native variety, which were much more aromatic than the evergreen type. Whatever the cause, their scent was almost intoxicating.

I picked up a pair of hand clippers to remove the smaller broken limbs, and loppers for reaching down into the center of the shrubs to trim the thicker branches. I stood looking at my work with a feeling of satisfaction that helped erase my uneasiness at the uncertainties in my life. Ebie sauntered up and stood beside me. She sat on her haunches and looked at me with what I could swear was a smirk.

"What?"

I didn't have a chance to see her reaction because I heard the phone ringing and hurried inside.

"Hello?"

"Hey, Georgia."

I smiled at the sound of Julie's voice. "Hey, you. I'm so glad you called."

"What are you up to?"

"I just finished trimming some dead branches off the azalea shrubs. The hurricane did quite a number on them."

"I'm glad they weren't destroyed. Your azaleas are beautiful!"

"I agree. What's new with you?"

"I was wondering if Jon told you about his conversation with Harry?"

I frowned at her question. "No. What do you know about it?"

There was a moment of silence on the line.

"Come on, Jules, spill."

"I'm just not sure if I should say anything or wait for Jon to talk with you."

I started to say something about how she couldn't just throw her question out there and leave me hanging, but she continued to speak.

"Okay. I guess I've already let the cat out of the bag by bringing it up at all. I overheard them talking the other night. Of course, I don't know what Jon was saying, but Harry was describing some kind of business arrangement whereby a grant can be obtained from the government for the purpose of historical preservation."

"Really? Did you hear him say anything else?"

"Umm, only that he could help Jon find out how to apply for one of the grants if he were interested. After that, he just 'uh huh-ed, and um hum-ed' a few times and then said goodbye. I asked him what they were talking about, but he said he couldn't really say anything about it yet."

"It must have something to do with Mitchelville. You remember me mentioning the freedmen's town that used to be on Hilton Head?"

"Yeah. But didn't you say it wasn't there any longer?"

"That's right. But Henry was talking with Jon the other day about how someone ought to try to restore it, or at least enough of it to give people a sense of what it stood for. I'll bet that's what he and Harry were talking about."

"You could be right. Maybe you can ask Jon."

I remembered his phone message. "He left a message on our answering machine earlier saying he had some news to share with me about what we were discussing with Henry. Hopefully, he'll explain what he meant when he gets home."

"Well, keep me posted."

I hung up the phone after promising to call Julie A.S.A.P with any update.

I decided to set up the outdoor table for dinner and called Frankie to help. He came running and grabbed a handful of napkins before following me outside. Outdoor eating called for paper plates and cups, and I placed these on top of the napkins so they wouldn't blow away in the light breeze. I was just filling a pitcher with water when I heard Jon pull in.

Frankie skipped into the kitchen. "Sweetheart, would you mind filling Ebie's bowl with water from the faucet, then put some dry food in the other one?"

He nodded enthusiastically.

"Be very careful not to spill anything." I knew I was taking a chance of a gigantic mess, but it would also buy me a little private time to talk to Jon. I walked out the front door and down the steps to where the car was parked. "Welcome home."

"He turned to me with a smile. "Thanks. It's good to be home." He put his arm around me and started walking toward the house. I tugged on his arm to stop him.

"Let's sit on the steps. I asked Frankie to fill Ebie's bowls, so we can talk privately out here for a few minutes."

He raised his eyebrows. "You really think that's a good idea? The last time we ended up with kibble all over the floor."

"I know, but I thought it was worth the risk. Julie called. She overheard a conversation you and Harry were having. Something about grants to restore historical sights. I was wondering if you were talking about Mitchelville?"

He laughed. "She stole my thunder. I was planning to surprise you with my news. Harry was telling me the government provides nonprofit organizations grants for projects that contribute to the preservation or recapture of what they call an authentic sense of place. I checked into it and, from what I could understand, Mitchelville would likely qualify. Of course, that means a nonprofit would need to be established before a grant request could be made. I plan to talk to Henry to see what he has up his sleeve, but I also think I could interest Quinn in being one of the organizers."

His news filled me with hope. "That sounds wonderful, but I'm trying to envision what it would look like. Would the plan be to rebuild the original town?"

"I don't think that would be possible. I envision a small-scale replica of some of the houses, a church, a store or two. Something that will give people a feel of what life was like for the original townspeople."

Images of what the town might look like began to fill my mind.

"I can see the wheels turning in your brain. What are you thinking about?"

"Mitchelville. Or, at least how I imagine it once looked."

His eyes narrowed in thought. "I still think this could be a career opportunity for you. Let's say, for example, we manage to get a grant to build a model of the original town. Someone would need to take the reins on reporting what we're doing; contacting the media; writing articles; keeping a running record of the progress."

What he was suggesting intrigued me. "I have to admit that sounds exciting, but let's not get ahead of ourselves. Once you have a better idea about whether this is going anywhere, we can talk about it more."

The sound of the front door opening caused us to swivel in that direction. Frankie stood at the top frowning at us. "Why are you sitting down dere? Ebie and me is lonely."

Jon winked at me. "Did Ebie tell you that?"

"No. But she doing dat thing she does when she wants someone to hold her."

Jon stood and offered to help me up.

"We're coming inside now. Why don't you and Ebie go out on the back deck, and Daddy and I will bring the pizza in a little while?"

He rushed inside with a big smile while yelling out "Come on Ebie. We're gonna hab pizza and I kin gib you some of mine!"

I linked my arm through Jon's. "I hope something works out with the grant."

He nodded. "Me, too. I'm going to give Henry a call a little later before I run any of this by Quinn. Let me change, and I'll join you shortly."

CHAPTER TWENTY-ONE

I always thought of Jon as being a deliberate, methodical type of person. I learned that about him when we first started dating. Since then, I witnessed the same characteristics, whether he was planning a change in his career or our move to Hilton Head from Nashville. It came as no surprise when he approached the idea of the restoration of Mitchelville with unhurried, measured steps.

A week passed since we first spoke of the possibility of the grant to fund the project. I resisted the urge to prod him daily for an update, although I could hardly contain my curiosity. With Jon, it worked best if I could just bide my time until he was ready to disclose what he knew. I wasn't always successful at doing that, but this time I was determined to try.

The opportunity finally came on a Sunday afternoon. We were sitting on the sofa sharing the newspaper, when he looked at me over the top of the section he was reading. "Let's invite Henry and Mary over for dinner this evening."

His suggestion surprised me. "Okay. What brought that on?"

"I need to talk a few things over with Henry, and I thought it would be nice to invite them here. It's been a while since we've had them over."

My mind started running down a list of what we would need to do to prepare for company. "I guess I could make some sort of spaghetti dish."

He folded the paper and stood. "Let me take care of dinner. I'll run over to the Red and White and pick up something to grill. Why don't you just straighten up the house a little, and when I get back, I'll clean off the deck? The weather is supposed to be nice all day.

"Shouldn't we call them first? They may not be available."

He looked at me sheepishly. "I may have already mentioned something about it to Henry when I spoke to him a couple of days ago. I'm sorry I forgot to tell you."

"You already invited them? And what time did you forget to tell me they're coming over?"

He gave me an apologetic look. "Around 6. As you may remember, they go to church services in the morning, after which there's usually some sort of food. I thought 6 PM would be a good time, and they agreed. Oh. Mary said to tell you she'd bring a couple of pies."

I shook my head in exasperation. "I still can't believe you didn't mention anything about this to me." I pushed up from the sofa. "I'd better get started on the house. Just make sure you get everything we'll need for dinner. That is, everything YOU'LL need since that's your job."

His face twisted into a crooked smile. "Got it. I'll be back in a little while."

After he left, I sighed and looked around the room to gauge how much work would need to be done to make things tidy. Both Jon and I were relatively neat, but there was no way to avoid some mess since we lived with a three-year old. Three and a half, I quickly corrected myself. Frankie had become quite adamant at insisting we attach the latter part of that statement whenever his age was mentioned. Thinking of Frankie made me wonder what he was up to. I hadn't seen him since breakfast, and the house had been unusually quiet. I walked down the hall and peeked into his room. He was sitting on the floor with an assortment of plastic toys spread around him.

"Hi, sweetheart. What are you up to?"

"Jes playing. This is gonna be dat town we visited."

I looked at the plastic pieces more carefully. There were several houses, a few buildings topped by a steeple that I guessed were meant to be churches, and an assortment of animals and human figures. They were laid out in a way that bore a surprising resemblance to the black and white photographs I saw of Mitchelville in some of the articles I read at the library.

"That looks really interesting. How did you know what the town looked like?"

"Duh lady tol' me." He pointed at a cluster of houses surrounding a church. "She say everyone live around a church. Dat way, dey kin go whenever dey want to."

His mention of a lady caused my heart to beat rapidly in tune with the throbbing of the amulet. "Are you talking about the same lady you saw in your room? The one you also saw when we were visiting the Mitchelville site the other day?"

He shook his head. "Dis lady dark like Aunt Mary."

I looked around cautiously. "Is she here now?"

He glanced up before shaking his head. "She leabe. Say she come back 'nudder time."

I let out the breath I'd been holding. "Frankie, can you do me a favor? The next time you see her, or the other lady will you come let me know right away?"

"Okay, Mommy." He returned to playing with the plastic figures.

"Uncle Henry and Aunt Mary are coming to dinner tonight, so I need you to straighten up your room before then."

"Kin I show Uncle Henry duh town?" He looked up hopefully.

"I guess that would be alright, as long as you put away the rest of your toys."

I left his bedroom and headed back to the living room, plopping down on the sofa with my head resting against the back. Ebie's lap radar must have been working because she appeared beside me a few seconds later and draped herself across my legs. I stroked her soft fur from the top of her head to her tail, eliciting a contented purr as she settled more firmly. I caressed her ears and allowed my eyes to close for a few moments, opening them just as quickly. My head was spinning with thoughts that would not let me rest. I gently shifted Ebie onto the sofa, receiving a disgruntled *unh* in reply, and busied myself with getting the house ready for company.

The last time Mary and Henry were in our house was shortly after the hurricane. On that evening, we invited them and the Sanders to join us for a pot-luck dinner. All of us had food that needed to be cooked in the aftermath of the power outage on the island, so we decided to make a party out of it. I was pleased the four of them seemed to genuinely enjoy one another's company. Things had begun to change between blacks and whites in the aftermath of the Civil Rights Movement, but that didn't mean there wasn't still a lot of prejudice and discrimination in both directions. Betty told me once that being around Mary was like being swaddled in a warm blanket, and that Henry was the father she always wished she'd had. That pretty much summed it up for me, too.

Jon returned from the store loaded down with four bags of groceries. "David insisted I buy some pork ribs. He said if I marinate them in some of this special sauce, they'd be 'fall off the bone delicious'." He began to empty the bags on the kitchen table. "He also suggested some sweet potatoes and corn to go with them. The good news is everything can be cooked on the grill, so there's no need to heat up the kitchen." He stopped and looked at me.

"You're awfully quiet. I hope you're not still mad that I forgot to tell you I invited the Palmers for dinner."

I shook my head. "Something else pushed that out of my mind. Frankie saw Ida again when he and I visited the Mitchelville site, and today he told me he saw the ghost of another woman in his bedroom. He said she was dark like Mary, and that he knew what the town looked like because she told him."

Jon looked alarmed. "It was hard enough to get used to the idea that you met the ghost of Bessie Barnhill back when we first visited Hilton Head, but the thought that our son is seeing her and Ida's ghost is more than I can fathom. Are you sure he's not imagining it?"

"I don't think so. I saw black and white photos of what Mitchelville looked like in a couple of books at the library, and he was creating a fairly good replica on the floor of his room. The way he described the other woman - what she looks like, and things she said – I've no doubt it's Ida. I saw her once, too."

"When?"

"In his room, the second time he saw her. He told me where she was sitting, and after he left the room, I looked where he mentioned, and her image began to appear. It was faint, but I could tell it was her. I spoke to her, but she just smiled at me and disappeared. I found something, though. Something that left me with no doubt it was her. It was a photograph of the two of us on the Belmont campus. I remember the day it was taken."

"Why haven't you mentioned this to me before?"

"I did. Remember? I told you about Frankie seeing her in Nashville when we stayed with Julie and Harry. It's true, I forgot to mention the second time. I guess I still wasn't sure it really happened. Then I meant to tell you about him seeing her at Mitchelville, but after you told me about the possibility of a grant to bring some semblance of the town back to life, it slipped my mind. Until today. For him to have four sightings in such a short period of time makes it clear they're both trying to communicate something important. I just don't know what, or why they're mostly communicating through Frankie."

He ran his hand through his hair, combing it backwards. "Was he frightened? It must have been scary for him to see ghosts."

"I don't think he thought of them as ghosts. He just referred to each of them as the lady. He didn't seem nervous or frightened at all. I asked him to let me know right away the next time he saw one of them."

Jon shook his head in disbelief. "Like mother, like son? Although I seem to recall you weren't as cavalier about your ghostly sightings as he seems to be. I suggest we table this topic for now and get things ready for tonight. It might be worth bringing it up with Mary at some point. She always seems to have a good way of explaining these kinds of occurrences."

The Palmers arrived right on time. Mary came in with a broad grin on her face. She was holding a pie in each hand that radiated warm deliciousness. "Jes tek dem out 'fo' we cum. One's pecan and tuh odduh apple. Can't hab none myself 'cos ub de di'betes, but mek some pumpkin cornbread dat taste sweet eben widout sugar." She nodded over her shoulder at Henry who held a foil wrapped loaf in one hand.

I took one of the pies from her before giving her a quick hug, then showed her where to place the pies and bread. "That's so thoughtful of you! The pies sound delicious, and the cornbread will be perfect with the dinner Jon planned."

Her eyes grew wide as she registered what I said. "Yo' hus'bun' mek dinnuh? How you get 'e do dat?"

I laughed at her surprise. "Let's just say he owed it to me."

Jon rolled his eyes and turned his attention to Henry. "How are you Henry?"

"Hab uh tetch ub rheumatism 'w'ile back, but 'e allright now." He looked around the room. "Weh Frankie?"

I pointed down the hall. "He's in his room. The last time I saw him he was deeply involved in building an imitation of

Mitchelville with some plastic pieces. He said he wanted to show it to you when you arrived."

He chuckled. "Dat uh fact? T'ink uh go dere now." He began to walk in the direction of Frankie's room. I noticed his gait seemed slower than usual, and he was favoring his right leg.

Mary noticed me watching him. "'Enry hurt'n uh leetle, but 'e don' wan' tuh worry oonuh none. 'E bettuh den 'e wus 'w'ile back. Mek 'e happy we cum' see all ub oonuh."

"Why don't we sit out on the deck a while before dinner?" Jon suggested. "What can I bring you to drink, Mary?"

She smiled and patted him on the arm. "Oonuh know Mary only hab one t'ing uh drink no mattuh time ub dey year."

"Unsweetened iced tea, coming right up!" He headed for the refrigerator and pulled out an icy pitcher I hadn't noticed before.

"When did you make that?" I asked.

"Earlier this morning. I guess you didn't notice it when you took out the milk for breakfast."

I shook my head in wonder. The man could still surprise me, although not all of his surprises were as welcome. I decided to forgive him for his earlier slip in not telling me he'd invited Mary and Henry for dinner. After all, I forgot to tell him about all of Frankie's ghost sightings, as he referred to them.

He was still standing in front of the refrigerator looking at me questioningly. "I'm sorry, did you say something?" I asked.

"I just asked what you wanted to drink. I know Gin and Tonic or white wine are your go-to summer choices, but I thought maybe you'd prefer red wine this time of the year."

His thoughtfulness touched me. "Red wine would be great. I'll take the pitcher of tea and some water to the deck while you get our drinks."

Mary and I settled onto a couple of the metal chairs on the deck. I had covered them with thick cushions, which made for a softer seat than the bare, hard metal. I poured her a glass of tea and filled three glasses with water for the rest of us. Jon returned with a goblet of red wine for me, and two cocktail glasses filled with amber-colored liquid over ice. He set them down just as Henry stepped onto the deck.

"Dat boy sump'n'. 'E build uh town look jes like Mi'chebill. Least f'um stories uh tol'. 'E hab big 'magination!"

Jon placed one of the cocktail glasses in front of him. "Try this, Henry. It's called a Rob Roy."

Henry lifted his glass and took a sip, smacking his mouth with satisfaction. "Dat uh good drink. What 'e hab?"

"It's made with Scotch and sweet vermouth, with a dash of bitters."

Henry took another drink and smiled with pleasure.

Mary shook her head. "Don' gib 'e mo' dan one, Jon. 'E got tuh dribe us home attuhw'ile,"

Henry scowled at her with a pretense of anger. "T'ink uh kin 'cide wha' uh kin drink, ole woman."

"'Spect oonuh kin, ole man. 'Cept w'en hab too much." She looked at me with a wink. "Hab tuh ask 'e 'bout de time 'e an' 'e fren's share uh boddle w'iskey. 'E sleep on de po'ch dat night." She laughed heartily while Henry shook his head.

"Dat uh mistake, fo' trute. Hab bad head next mo'nin'." He lifted his glass and looked at it appreciatively. "Uh jes sip dis. Uh like duh taste."

I looked across the table at Jon and raised my eyebrows in question. He shrugged and nodded.

"I wanted to talk with you both about something that's happened to Frankie a few times."

Mary looked concerned. "Uh hope 'e awright?"

"Yes, he's fine. I'm the one who's a little shaken up. On four different occasions, he told me he saw a ghost. Three of the times, he described someone who sounded like an old friend of mine named Ida Hood who passed away several years ago. The other time, the person he saw resembled Bessie Barnhill. I was only able to see the ghost of Ida briefly on one of those times, but I didn't see Miss Bessie at all."

Mary and Henry looked at each other intently for a few seconds before Mary spoke. "Oonuh 'membuh uh say Frankie got uh gift? Uh t'ink 'e see t'ings udders don', like 'e murruh. Oonuh hab de gift, too. Eben eef 'e not clear dis time, dat don' go 'way fo' long. Wha' 'e say dese sperrits wan'?"

I thought back to the four instances he described. "The first time the ghost told him everything would be alright if I listened to my heart. She also said the potion the root doctor gave me was working, and what I was worried about would be okay if I just gave it more time. I asked him to describe how she looked, and it was exactly as I remembered my friend Ida."

The conversation I had with Benjamin Scott came to mind. "We ran into the root doctor one day when we were walking on Coligny beach after the hurricane. Just like you and Henry suggested a while back, he told me Miss Bessie appeared to him and told him to give Frankie the potion to restore power to my amulet. He said Miss Bessie told him I had helped her once, and now she wanted to do the same for me. She also instructed him to place the dead sparrows at our front and back doors. He said they're supposed to help make the transition from the past and open the door to the future. He said sparrows represent the throat and heart chakras. They help with voicing dreams and fears, hearing the truth in the heart, and giving courage to act on what we believe.

"The root doctors' name is Benjamin Scott. He's the brother of Josephine, one of the women we met at the Sanders moving in party. Benjamin also told me he saw Ida in a dream, and she said she's always watching over me. She told him she'd appear to me when the time is right.

"The second-time Frankie saw Ida's ghost in his bedroom. I was able to see her briefly on that occasion before she faded from sight. She left a photo on the chair where she'd been sitting. It was a picture of the two of us on the campus of Belmont College shortly after we met. That's how I knew for certain it was her.

"Frankie saw Ida again when he and I visited the Mitchelville site. On that day, she told him the potion the root doctor gave me was working and it was going to help.

Unfortunately, she didn't say what it was supposed to help. Then today, he told me he saw another lady, and his description fit that of Bessie Barnhill."

Mary leaned forward in her chair as I spoke. When I finished, she leaned back heavily. "Eef dat don' beat all. Duh boy hab berry special gift. 'E not bodduh wid wha' 'e see?"

"He seems unaffected by it all. He just says the ladies are nice; like the root doctor." I looked at Henry. "What do you make of it all, Henry?"

He scratched his chin and sipped from his glass. "Seem tuh me, Frankie be gett'n' sum strong messages f'um dem sperrits. Messages 'e s'posed tuh gib tuh oonuh. Don' know why dey not show demse'fes tuhreckly tuh oonuh, but sperrits hab dere reasons us on dis side kin't always undu'stan'."

"It seems to me the messages have something to do with Mitchelville." Jon offered. "Benjamin was told to put the sparrows in our yard, and they're supposed to help us make the transition from the past to the future. It can't be a coincidence that one of Frankie's sightings occurred where Mitchelville used to be. What I don't understand is what Ida Hood has to do with any of this? I can see why Bessie Barnhill might show herself again. She and Georgia have an obvious bond because of their past exchanges." He directed his next question to Mary. "Do you think there's a connection between Ida and Bessie, or is it just a coincidence they've both appeared to Frankie?"

She drank deeply from her glass of tea before answering. "Dis cumpuhsayshun mek mout' dry." She looked at Georgia. "Wha' Ida do wen oonuh met?"

"Do you mean what kind of work did she do?" Mary nodded. "She worked for the Metropolitan Historical Commission in Nashville. Their job was to document the history of old buildings and make the public more aware of the need to preserve them. The commission also reviewed and approved requests for new construction, alterations, additions, repair and demolition of buildings and areas considered historically significant." As I spoke, I became aware of the amulet growing red hot and throbbing rapidly. I placed my hand over it and lifted it away from my skin. I noticed Henry watching me carefully.

"Dat chaa'm gib oonuh message?"

I nodded. "I don't know why it didn't occur to me before, but the work Ida did is exactly what you and Jon have been investigating to help bring back Mitchelville; or at least part of it. Do you think that's why she's been appearing to Frankie?"

Jon spoke up. "I think you may be on to something, Georgia. I mean, I can't say I buy into the idea that a ghost, or in this case ghosts, are using our son to communicate a message about Mitchelville, or anything else, for that matter. But if I did believe that was possible, I would have to say it's no coincidence. Just consider the facts: Bessie Barnhill would have a vested interest in seeing the memory of Mitchelville preserved because of her close ties to it; Ida understands the significance of preserving, not only the memory, but the place; she's likely been watching over you closely, as has Bessie. If the two of them are capable of joining forces, I imagine they would make quite a formidable team." He shook his head. "I can't believe I said any of that as if it could be true."

Mary chuckled. "Kin be trute an' still hard tuh bleebe." She looked at me. "Didn' oonuh say dat root doctor see bofe Ida an' Bessie?" I nodded. "Well den, dat say uh lot 'bout wha' we wond'rin'."

I waited for her to say more, but she remained silent. I glanced at Jon who was staring intently at Mary. Finally, he stood and walked toward the grill. "The vegetables should be about ready. I'd better put the meat on the grill if we're going to eat anytime soon. Henry, would you like to help me?"

Henry stood slowly and smiled. "Cook'n' on de grill sumt'in' uh kin manage."

"Good. I'll bring out the ribs."

"Ribs? Um-hum. Me mout' staa't tuh watuh awready!"

"I got them started cooking in the oven so all we have to do is finish them off on the grill."

While the men headed off to work on dinner, I scooted my chair closer to Mary. "Do you really think Ida and Bessie are trying to tell me something about Mitchelville?"

"Uh 'spec' so. 'Membuh sumt'in' similar 'w'ile back."

I waited for her to continue.

"Ooman hab fren' dat done cross obuh. Didn't heah f'um 'e long time. One day, 'e hab vision ub de fren'. 'E wid nudduh ooman. Tuhgedduh dey gib 'e metsage 'bout 'e daa'tuh. Say 'e een dainjuh. Fin' out, daa'tuh spos' tuh wed uh man awready marri'd. Hep huh mek track f'um dat man. 'Ventually, fin' out udduh sperrit niece ub de man wife. 'E know 'e bad man, an' wan' tuh hep stop 'e mischeef. 'E tell 'bout 'e tuh ooman's fren' sperrit. Wu'k tuhgedduh."

"Interesting. So, it's completely possible that the spirit of Ida and the spirit of Bessie are teaming up somehow to help us make something happen with the Mitchelville site. I still don't understand why they involved Frankie."

"Frankie may be leetle pitcher, but hol' mo' dan sum. Got uh pure haa't. Sperrits see dat. Draw dem tuh 'e."

I shook my head in disbelief. "Speaking of Frankie, I'd better go see what he's up to. Would you like to join me?"

"Uh t'ink uh jes sit an' 'joy de wawm breeze. Wintuh be here soon 'nuff."

I stood and touched her briefly on her shoulder. "I'll bring him back with me." She nodded peacefully.

CHAPTER TWENTY-TWO

We spent the rest of the evening talking about Mitchelville and the possibilities of the grant to aid its restoration. From the loving comfort of Mary's lap, Frankie kept us entertained with his input about the town, including a description of how the cows were kept in the same fenced-in area as the chickens, making for some near-misses as feet became entangled, and wings made contact with heads. I was still flabbergasted over how he seemed to know anything at all about Mitchelville, but the way Mary and Henry nodded their agreement of his description of life in the town, I had no choice but to accept the reality: my son saw dead people, and not only saw them, but spoke to them.

After dinner, Henry and Jon went into his study to continue their discussion about exactly how a non-profit business could be formed to allow submission of the grant application. After Mary helped me clear up the dinner dishes, I suggested we move into the living room. The temperature had grown cooler after sunset, and I lit the fireplace before settling on the sofa. We sat in silence for a while until Frankie came running into the room.

"Mommy, dat lady is back. You told me tuh tell yuh if I saw her again."

His announcement startled me, and I looked at Mary to gauge her reaction. Her eyes were wide with astonishment.

"Which lady, sweetheart? The last one you saw, or the one before that?"

"Um, the one wid the gray hair and white face. The other one not here now."

He grabbed my hand and pulled me in the direction of his bedroom. Mary followed close behind. When we stepped into his room, I looked in all directions to see if I could spot his apparition. A motion near the window caught my eye, and I peered closely to see what I could make out. "Frankie, can you point to the lady for me?" He indicated the area where I had detected movement, and then skipped from the room while announcing he was going to find his daddy. I walked in the direction he indicated. As I got closer, an image began to appear. It was still hazy, but there was no doubt I was seeing Ida. I looked back over my shoulder at Mary. "Can you see anything?" I whispered.

"Uh t'ink so, but 'e hazy. Dat oonuh fren'?"

I nodded. "It's Ida." I walked even closer, stopping when I was a couple of feet away from where the image appeared. "Ida? Is that you?"

The image became more distinct. "Hello, dear girl. I'm so happy to see you."

My heart skipped a beat at her greeting. "It's really you! Frankie told me he's seen you a few times, and I thought I did once. Did you leave a photo for me?"

"I did. I wanted you to know it was me."

"But why didn't you talk to me?"

"It was important to choose the right time so I wouldn't frighten you away. It isn't exactly commonplace to see a spirit. I know I never did when I was on the other side."

"I suppose it is rather unusual. I wouldn't have believed it was possible until I saw Bessie Barnhill."

She smiled. "What a fine lady she is. I've enjoyed our communication."

"You've met Miss Bessie?"

"A few times. She's been looking out for you, too. When she heard about the hurricane, she managed to reach out to someone they call a root doctor. He lives near you, I believe. She told him to prepare a potion that would help you stay safe. I didn't meet her until after that. She told me about the amulet she gave you that you wear under your blouse. I thought it was a wonderful thing. She said it would not only provide protection, but help you make important decisions. The only thing was it had grown weak over the years. She felt bad she didn't instruct you how to keep it strong. That's why she involved the root doctor; to give you something to restore its vitality. I trust it worked?"

I lay my hand over the throbbing pouch. "All I can say is it has grown more insistent since I started putting the potion on it." Her image started to waver, and I searched for something to say to keep her with me. "Why are you here, Ida? Do you have something important to tell me?"

Her image grew more distinct again. "Not so much to tell you, as to remind you. It's a message Bessie has been giving you, as well."

"What is it?"

"To trust your heart. Listen to it. Believe in its truth. It won't lead you wrong if you are open to its message."

She started to fade away again. "Ida? I don't understand. Is there something I'm supposed to do?"

Just before she disappeared, I heard her say: *Remember what you know to be true and remember how we met.*

The room grew eerily silent after that. I felt as if I could hear each beat of my heart, and the throbbing of the amulet only accentuated that impression. I felt a hand on my arm, and remembered Mary was also in the room.

"How oonuh feel'n, chile?"

I shook my head. "I'm not sure. It helps that you saw her, too. What did you make of the things she said?"

"Oonuh fren' say sum wisdom. Bleebe 'e looks attuh all ub fambly. Fin' 'e curious 'we know Bessie. Bofe dem look out fo' oonuh tuhgedduh. Wha' oonuh t'ink 'e mean 'bout de last?"

"We met because she worked for the Metropolitan Housing Commission and I went there to find out what she knew about Jon. I didn't trust him in the beginning, and she helped me see what he was really up to. I suppose she was reminding me to look inside myself and believe what I saw. Does that make sense?"

"Not ebryt'ing dat true come clear right 'way. Ef mek sense tuh oonuh, den 'e wu't'w'ile tuh 'vestigate." She patted me on the arm. "Bes' tuh gib 'e leetle time. T'ings mo' clear en de mawnin'."

We walked into the living room to find Jon and Henry sprawled out on the sofa. Henry's eyes were closed, and Jon was caressing Ebie while Frankie lay against his side. Mary walked over to Henry and jiggled him awake. "'E time fuh gone, 'Enry."

He looked up in surprise. "Jes rest us eyes."

"Um hum. Ef dat wha' wan' call 'e." She helped him to his feet.

Jon gently shifted Frankie to lie flat on the sofa before placing Ebie next to him. "I guess the fire was too relaxing. How'd things go in the bedroom? Frankie said you were talking to one of the ghosts." His face twisted into a half smile/half smirk.

"Okay. I'll tell you about it later. Let's help Mary and Henry to the car."

The four of us trooped down the front steps to where their car was parked. Jon tried to convince them to let him take them home, stating he would bring their car to them in the morning, but Henry insisted on driving. We watched until they pulled out of the driveway and headed in the direction of North Forest Beach Drive. "I hope they'll be okay," I said.

Jon nodded. "They should be fine. Henry didn't even finish one drink. I imagine the little nap he took on the sofa will revive him some."

We entered the house. Jon picked Frankie up and carried him to his bed. I removed his shoes and pants and tucked him under the covers. We returned to the living room, stoking the fire to restore its flame. Jon sat and patted the seat next to him. "That was an interesting evening."

"Yes. In more ways than one. What did you and Henry figure out about the grant?"

"I can't say we figured anything out with certainty. But it's clear we're going to need to recruit somebody with deep pockets if we have any chance of establishing a nonprofit."

"Do you mean Robert Quinn?"

"Hopefully. If he's willing to get involved, I imagine he'll be able to persuade some others to join him." He yawned widely. "To tell you the truth, it's a rather daunting task we have ahead of us."

"I can imagine." My mind was jumping back and forth between what he was saying and the experience I encountered in Frankie's room. Jon must have noticed my preoccupation because he nudged me with a smile.

"The wheels are turning again. Are you thinking about Mitchelville, or whatever happened in Frankie's room?"

I considered his question. "Both, in fact. I believe they're connected in some way."

He looked interested. "Tell me what happened."

I summarized the encounter with Ida's ghost: what she told me about Bessie and the root doctor; how she looked; her parting comments. When I finished, he looked at me with disbelief.

"How do you do it? How do you manage to attract these spirits, and not only see them, but have conversations? Has it ever occurred to you how unusual that is?"

"Of course. Sometimes I'm not sure if what I think I see and hear is really happening. Except this time, Mary was right there with me to see and hear the same things. It's hard to deny the facts when they're confirmed by someone else."

"What do you think Ida wanted you to understand? What was the point of her message?"

I thought about his question. What DID she mean exactly, by telling me to listen to my heart and remember where I met her? "I'm afraid I'm still trying to figure that out. Mary suggested I sleep on it, and maybe things would be clearer in the morning."

He yawned again. "That sounds like good advice. Why don't you go on to bed, and I'll join you as soon as I put out the fire? A good nights' sleep can only help."

Yeah, I thought. But would I be able to get a good night's sleep with everything that was weighing on my mind?

I awoke a little later than usual the next morning. Whether it was the late night, or the things that troubled my mind, something made me toss and turn most of the night. I looked out the back door to check the weather. Once again, the sky was heavy with gray clouds and a steady rain was falling. I stood staring at it for a few moments before deciding that even a rainy walk was better than remaining inside. I grabbed my raincoat and cap off the coat rack and headed out the door.

The rain was heavier than it appeared from inside the house and my shoes slipped on the wet surface of the stones placed along the path leading to the beach. I picked my way along the path until I felt firm sand beneath my steps. I pulled my cap more firmly on my head and turned up the collar of my coat. There was a slight breeze from the North that blew the rain into my face as I walked against it. I trudged along for a good half hour before turning around to head in the other direction. I only encountered a few other walkers. I imagined most people had chosen the dry warmth of their homes instead of braving the chilly dampness of the outdoors.

My pace quickened when I thought of the hot coffee and warm fire I hoped would be waiting for me at home. I opened the back door and hung up my damp items, removing my soaked shoes before stepping inside. My wish was granted as the smell of coffee and the sound of popping cedar greeted me. I found Jon in the living room sipping from a cup with the newspaper open in front of him. He looked up as I entered.

"Wet out there? The news says we're in for a change in the weather. I guess Fall is here to stay."

I stood with my back to the fireplace, allowing its warmth to penetrate my skin. "Yeah, it's definitely chillier than yesterday, but I kind of like walking in the rain. Thanks for making a fire."

"You're welcome." He folded the paper and placed it on the sofa beside him. "I heard from Quinn after you went to bed last night. We're going to meet later this morning. I told him I had an idea I wanted to run by him, but I didn't give him any more details. He probably thinks I want to talk about the Rose Hill project."

"How's that going, by the way?"

"Pretty good. Construction has begun on the home sites, and we were able to locate letters and records from the family that originally owned the plantation house that will help with its restoration. It's a beautiful old mansion. I should take you to see it one day"

"I'd like that." My legs were beginning to feel scorched by the fire, so I moved to one of the overstuffed chairs located on either side of the sofa. "I hope you won't have too much to handle if you end up juggling both Rose Hill and the Mitchelville project."

"I can only hope to have that problem. I really don't know if Quinn will be open to involving himself and his corporation in starting a non-profit."

"Do you have any other ideas in case he isn't?"

He frowned. "I spoke to Harry about it again. He said he might know someone who'd be interested. He didn't give me any details, but said he'd look into it and get back to me."

His mention of Harry brought Julie to mind. "I miss them. Harry and Julie. I wish they lived closer."

"Me, too. He's become a good friend, and I appreciate having someone with whom I can bounce business ideas around." He glanced at his watch. "I'd better get moving. I need to stop by the real estate office to wrap up some paperwork on the last sale I made, then get out to Rose Hill. I'll probably try to catch Henry at the store afterward, too, depending on how things go."

I stood and stretched. "I'm going to have some breakfast before I wake Frankie. Then I think I'll drop in on Betty after I leave him at the DayCare Center."

He grinned. "Busy day, huh?"

I waggled my head at his obvious sarcasm. "Not busy enough, if I'm being truthful. I'm getting more and more restless to find some sort of work to get involved in."

He raised an eyebrow as he looked at me. "You know what I think on that matter."

"I know. And I've been giving it some thought. I'm just waiting to see if anything will really materialize."

He pulled me into a hug and kissed the top of my head. "I should know more about that today. I'll give you a call."

Betty wasn't home when I stopped by. I didn't think to call first, assuming incorrectly that she'd be as free as I was. I was sitting in my car in front of her house deciding what I wanted to do next when I became aware of a figure approaching from the rear. I turned to see who it was, recognizing Josephine–one of the women I met at the Sanders' moving in party, and the root doctor, Benjamin Scott's, sister. I rolled down the car window.

"Hello, Josephine!"

"Uh t'ink dat was you. How you doin', Georgia?"

"Fine. I was hoping to visit with Betty, but, apparently, she's not home."

She nodded. "Saw huh an' Hal drive off 'w'ile ago. Uh gwine tuh de chu'ch. De hab cawn and maters fuh sale tuhday. Brought dem up f'um Flor'da. You wanna cum 'long?"

Josephine's accent wasn't as strong as Henry or Mary's, but I still had to listen closely to make out every word. "That would be nice. Thank you. I didn't know it was possible to get fresh corn or tomatoes this time of the year."

"Not 'roun' dese parts, but t'ree men bring sum f'um down de coast. Sumtime hab swimp, too. My husbun, Samuel, go down dere dis time ub yeah fo' de sweet w'ite swimp. Um, dey taste good!"

I smiled at her enthusiasm. "That sounds great. Do you want to ride with me?"

She seemed to hesitate before answering. "Dat be nice." She walked around to the other side of the car and got in.

There were a few other cars in the parking lot of the Cherry Hill School when we arrived. Several folks were milling around a few tables on one side, and more were sitting on wooden chairs placed along the edge of the yard. I scanned the crowd and was pleased to spot Mary standing in front of one of the tables. I pointed her out to Josephine. "Mary's here."

She smiled. "She a'ways weh dere good food!" She greeted us with a broad smile.

"Look who 'e is!" She moved quickly to embrace both of us warmly. "Lots ub good t'ings tuhday." She held up an overfilled shopping bag that had been resting on the ground next to her. "Got tuh git sum swimp next. 'Enry mek me promise bring sum back. Got 'e min' set on swimp fo' dinnuh."

"That sounds good to me, too. I think I'll pick up some corn and tomatoes, then hunt up that shrimp." I left the two women talking while I walked to the produce table. After I purchased what I needed, I turned to look for them again, spotting them standing by a large cooler I assumed held the shrimp. Mary was talking to a man standing behind the cooler, while Josephine looked on.

Josephine turned to me when I walked up and whispered behind her hand. "Mary gib 'em what fo' cos 'e try 'n weigh de swimp wid de head on. She tell 'em 'cos' mo' dan s'pose tuh dat wey! By de look on 'e face, uh t'ink she gon' win dis argument."

We shared a chuckle as we waited to see what would happen. Soon, Mary turned away from the table clutching three large plastic bags holding shrimp and ice. She held one out to each of us. "Dat man try an' chaa'ge too much! Mek 'e cut off dem heads fo' 'e weigh dem."

I accepted my bag from Mary and reached into my purse for some money. She placed a hand on top of mine to stop me.

"Uh gib oonuh dis swimp. Mek me happy." I started to protest but I could tell by the look she gave me it was pointless.

"Thank you, Mary. That's extremely generous of you."

She waved off my thanks. "Psst. Nutt'n' but sum swimp. Kin mek uh nice dinnuh fo' yo' fambly." She handed Josephine her bag and again refused to take any money. "Well, uh got tuh get back home. One ub my granbabies comin' obuh attuhw'ile. Ax me special tuh mek 'e fab'rite cookies." She waved overhead as she walked away.

Josephine shook her head. "Dat ooman hab mo' get up an' go dan anyone uh know!"

"She sure does!" I looked down at the bags in my hands. "I think we'd better get these shrimp home before the ice melts. I'll drop you at your house if you'll tell me how to get there."

She looked pleased with my offer. "It's jes down de road from Betty's. De yellow house on de corner wid de blue do'."

I drove in the direction she indicated and pulled up in front of her house. The house looked freshly painted and there was a row of white azaleas growing on either side of the door. "What a pretty place! And I love the color of your front door."

"We caw dat haint blue cos it s'posed tuh keep 'way ebil sperrits. Least, dat wha' de ole folks b'leebe. Dese days, we use it tuh keep way spiders an' wasps. Don' know ef it wuk, but uh like how it look."

Her explanation prodded a memory from one of my first trips to Hilton Head. "I heard about something they call a blue bottle tree. In fact, I saw one a few years ago. Is it supposed to work the same way as painting a door blue?"

"Not 'zackly. Blue boddles 'posed tuh catch ebil sperrits cos dey drawn tuh de blue. Get stuck en de boddle till mawnin' so de sun kin kill dem. Brother Benjamin, 'e bleebe strongly en blue on de house. Dat why we hab 'e on de do'. Sum folks paint dey po'ch ceiling an' winduh frame blue, too."

I was hesitant to voice my next question but decided to take a chance. "Do you believe in ghosts? I mean, do you think some people can see the spirits of people who've died?"

She turned her face away from me. "Benji tell me wha' happen. Say sperrit ub ooman show herself tuh him an ax fo' help tuh guide you. Say he should gib sumt'ing tuh yo' boy." She cut her eyes in my direction.

"Yes. He gave my son, Frankie, a bottle containing a potion that was supposed to restore strength to an amulet I wear." I unbuttoned my blouse and unpinned the pouch, holding it in my hand for her to see. "The spirit of that same woman who appeared to your brother gave me this a few years ago. Apparently, it has been losing strength since then, and the potion is supposed to help restore it."

She studied it curiously. "De potion wu'k?"

"I think so. The amulet has been giving me more signals since I've been applying the potion."

"Dat good, den. Glad Benji hep. Dat de only time you see uh sperrit?"

"It was until recently. Frankie has been seeing the spirit of a dear friend of mine who passed away several years ago. Her name was Ida. He's seen her four times, but I've only been able to see her twice. The first time, she left a photo for me, and the second time she spoke to me. Frankie also saw the spirit of the woman who gave me the amulet, Bessie, but she hasn't appeared to me again."

"Wha' yo' fren say wen she talk tuh you?"

I thought back to that day. "She told me to remember how she and I first met, and to trust what my heart was telling me. It's funny, but when I first saw Bessie, she kept telling me the same thing: to just trust my heart."

She nodded solemnly. "Must be uh reason de bofe say dat." She began collecting her bags. "Uh best be going. Ice staa't tuh melt." She stepped out of the car and waved goodbye before closing the door. "T'anks fo' de ride."

As I drove away, my mind was full of thoughts about the strange occurrences, coincidences really, that had been happening lately. Running into Benjamin Scott on the beach. Finding out he and Josephine were related. Hearing that Miss Bessie had

214

appeared to him and asked him to help me. Ida's spirit appearing to Frankie, telling me she had been in communication with Bessie. Running into Josephine today.

It suddenly occurred to me that Josephine hadn't answered my question when I asked her if she believed in ghosts. At least not directly. The fact that she brought up Benjamin suggested she was more than a little familiar with spirit sightings.

I shook my head to clear it of the thoughts that were muddling my mind and turned the car in the direction of home.

CHAPTER TWENTY-THREE

When I arrived home, there was a message on the answering machine from Jon saying he could pick up Frankie from Daycare on his way home. I put the shrimp in the refrigerator and lay the fresh vegetables on the counter. Jon's offer meant an unexpected free afternoon for me, and I spent a few minutes considering my options. A walk on the beach was always nice. A bike ride would be even better. But I was having trouble letting go of the worries that had been hampering my peace for several days. I decided to put off any form of activity, and call Julie instead.

"Hey, Georgia! I've been thinking of you."

"Stop that! How is it you always know when it's me calling?"

She giggled. "I don't. It's just that there are only a handful of other people who call regularly, which ups my chances of guessing correctly. Besides. It's fun to hear how surprised you always sound."

"That must tick off the others when you answer as if it's me."

"Nah. It's usually some member of my family, and they know why I answer that way. How are you?".

"Feeling a little overwhelmed."

"Tell me…"

I spent the next several minutes rehashing the oddities of my recent life: ghost sightings times two; Frankie's propensity for seeing the dead; meeting Benjamin Scott and finding out his sister is someone who lives near Betty; running into her today; the messages from both Ida and Bessie telling me to trust my heart; Jon's new involvement with the Rose Hill project; the possibility of a grant to restore the town of Mitchelville. I ended with the news that I'd been toying with the idea of getting involved on some level if a grant could actually be obtained.

"Whew! Your life is never dull. Tell me more about the last thing you mentioned. How exactly do you envision yourself involved in restoring Mitchelville?"

"Not the actual restoration, but helping to promote it, write articles, chronicle the steps along the way. Of course, all of this hinges on Jon's ability to set up a nonprofit in order to file for a grant." I remembered something he told me. "Say, has Harry said anything to you about this? Jon mentioned they'd spoken, and that Harry might have an idea."

"Now that you bring it up, he did mention something about an idea he was working on that he'd spoken to Jon about. He didn't seem inclined to want to say anything more about it yet, so I didn't pursue the subject further."

I smiled to myself. "That doesn't sound like you."

"I know. I'm trying to loosen up a bit."

"You'll have to tell me your secret. I still have difficulty letting go when something's nagging at me. Like now."

"Believe me, I understand. On a happier subject, Harry and I have been kicking around the idea of coming to see you all."

"Really? That would be wonderful! When are you thinking of coming?"

"He has another meeting in Savannah next week. We thought we could come a few days earlier and stay a few days after he finishes. Of course, that depends upon whether or not it would work for you and Jon."

"I think it's a great idea, and I have no doubt Jon will feel the same. He recently mentioned he and Harry have become good friends, and he values being able to kick around thoughts with him. Work thoughts, of course."

"Of course. They definitely have that in common. Let me nail down the plan with Harry and I'll get back to you."

"Sounds good. Talk to you later."

I walked out of the kitchen with a spring in my step, placed there by the news that Julie might be coming to visit soon. Of course, that meant I'd need to prepare the upstairs space for them, plan meals, and make a trip to the Red and White to stock up on groceries. None of that could make a dent in my happiness at seeing her, and I was sure Frankie, and most likely Jon, would feel the same. I realized my face had been stretched into a permanent smile since I hung up the phone.

Ebie ambled into the living room, and I scooped her up and danced around the sofa while I hummed a tune. She pushed her front legs against my chest and gave me a startled look. "I know. You're wondering if your momma has gone crazy. Well, no she hasn't. I'm just feeling happy." Her expression softened, and the edges of her mouth turned up into what could only be described as a smug smile. I hugged her to me before placing her on the rug. She sat on her haunches and continued to stare at me. "I'm going to get the guest rooms ready. Even if it turns out they can't come, at least it will give me something to do while I wait to find out." Before I could take a step, she sprinted up the staircase ahead of me. I shook my head in wonderment. Ghost sightings, conversations with the dead, and now a psychic cat! I hurried to catch up with her.

By the time Jon and Frankie arrived, Julie had called back to say that she, Harry, and the twins would be arriving on the island on Friday afternoon. Since that was only four days away, I set about making a list of everything I needed to do before then.

Frankie was elated to hear about Emily and Ashley's visit, and Jon commented it would be good to see them all.

I placed a pot of water on the stove to boil and set about peeling and deveining the shrimp. Jon walked up behind me and looked over my shoulder.

"What's for dinner?"

"Fresh shrimp, corn, and tomatoes. I ran into Josephine today, and she told me there was a farmer's market at the Cherry Hill School. We ran into Mary there, and she gave us each a bag of shrimp."

"Sounds great. Want me to do anything?"

"Make us each a drink? Then you could slice the tomatoes."

"On it." He opened one of the cabinets and took out two glasses, setting them on the counter.

"How did your meeting go with Robert Quinn?"

"Pretty good. At least, he was open to the idea of helping establish a nonprofit. He wants to talk it over with his board of investors, but he seemed to think they would be amenable to the idea." His words sounded hopeful, but the frown on his face said otherwise.

"That's great, isn't it?"

"I thought so, but after I left him, I stopped by to see Henry and he was less enthusiastic. He brought up the fact that Quinn has never included a black person on any of his boards or committees. He's worried he won't have the best interests of the Gullah community at heart."

"What do you think?"

He finished making our drinks and set mine where I could reach it. "I'm not sure what to think. Quinn seemed genuinely interested, but now it occurs to me his interest may be strictly motivated by money, or more precisely, the profit he stands to make from such a venture."

"Wait a minute. If you're asking Quinn's help in setting up a nonprofit corporation, doesn't that mean he wouldn't be allowed to make a profit?"

"Not necessarily. Since nonprofits are designed to serve a government-approved purpose, they're accorded special tax treatment. As long as the nonprofit's earnings are generated from activities related to its purpose, there's no problem. That could include something like holding a fundraiser to aid with the restoration. Monies earned from such an event could legally be used to cover operating expenses and employee salaries for the project in general, and those earnings would not be taxed. If, however, the corporation generated income from an unrelated activity, such as selling t-shirts that have been donated free to the nonprofit, that income would be subject to taxation. It's an accountant's nightmare trying to sort it out, and not something we need to worry about at this point. I just want to find out what's really behind Quinn's apparent interest."

"But you've already said that money is the bottom line for Quinn. If that means he's on top of what it will take to make this project successful, and he earns a little extra in the process, is that necessarily a bad thing?"

He took a sip from his drink. "I really don't know. Henry's concerns have raised some of my own. You know that gut instinct you and Julie are fond of talking about?" I nodded. "Mine's been working overtime since I left Henry. I guess I just want to make sure we don't lose sight of the real purpose in seeking the grant, which is to bring attention to the fact that Hilton Head was the home of the first self-governed community of freed slaves, predating the Emancipation Proclamation by several months. That's an amazing story that has mostly gone unnoticed except by the descendants of those slaves who are still on this island. The real profit will be measured by how well the story is brought back to life. If we don't learn the history of places like Mitchelville, we'll never understand why race relations are the way they still are in the United States."

I never realized until that moment that Jon's interest in restoring Mitchelville represented more than just a good business deal. His compassion touched me. "I agree completely. Did Henry have any suggestions?"

"He thinks I need to have a frank talk with Quinn to find out what motivates him to even consider getting involved in this." He stared off into the distance for a moment. "You know, Harry's visit couldn't come at a better time. He indicated he has some ideas he's mulling over. Hopefully, I can get him to hash them out with me."

I stood on my tiptoes and kissed him firmly on the mouth.

He gave me a silly grin. "What's that for?"

"Sometimes you just amaze me."

He pulled me toward him and deepened the kiss. "Mmm. You're pretty amazing yourself."

"What's ah-may-zen mean, Daddy?"

We both pulled back with a start at Frankie's question. I smiled at Jon, who quickly grabbed a dishcloth in an effort to cover the evidence of his interest in carrying the kiss further.

"It means something, or someone is extra special. Like you," I replied. "Because you're such a special, wonderful young man."

He puffed up his chest and placed his hands on his hips. "Like superman!"

I reached to caress his head. "Yes, just like Superman, only sweeter."

He scrunched up his face. "Superman's not sweet. He's strong!"

I placed my hand on Jon's arm. "Sometimes men are both sweet and strong. Like your daddy.

Jon rolled his eyes. "Okay, okay. Enough about that. Frankie, why don't you wash up while your mom and I finish making dinner?"

"'K, Daddy." He jogged out of the room.

Jon looked at me with a sigh. "He does have a way of showing up at the most inopportune times."

"Yeah, he does at that. Rain check?"

He grinned at me. "I hear they're predicting rain for later this evening."

October on Hilton Head Island is typically known for its warm days, cool nights, and little rain. That held true for the time Julie, Harry and the twins spent with us, allowing ample opportunities for outdoor activities and meals on the deck. Our house had plenty of room for the seven of us, as long as we spread ourselves out. But whenever we congregated in one place, it could get too loud, too fast.

Julie and I spent a lot of time walking on the beach with the three kids while Harry and Jon were immersed in something in Jon's study. They had been doing a lot of that the past couple of days, once Harry was free from the business he had to attend to in Savannah. I was becoming increasingly curious what they were talking about, but so far, I managed to curb my impulse to push Jon for details. I expressed my frustration to Julie, who indicated she felt similarly piqued.

"I think it's time for an intervention," she remarked.

"What do you have in mind?"

"Once we put the kids to bed tonight, we tell them we want to know what's going on. A couple of cocktails over dinner should help loosen their tongues."

"Good idea. Maybe we should increase our odds by fixing one of their favorite dinners." We glanced at each other before simultaneously shouting out, "Fried chicken." The dish was a Southern staple sure to show up on a regular basis on pretty much every table south of the Mason-Dixon line. Harry had been a die-hard fan of the dish his whole life, but it took some serious persuading on my part to get Jon to give it a chance. Early on in our dating relationship, he spotted some in my refrigerator and swore his hatred for the dish. Since then, mostly due to it being the only thing available on more than one social occasion, he swore it was one of the best things he'd ever tasted, especially when it was accompanied by mashed potatoes and coleslaw. None of those foods had been popular in Cincinnati where Julie grew up, but she quickly learned to like them once her family moved to Nashville. In fact, I hated to admit it, but her fried chicken recipe was better than mine, although my mashed potatoes and coleslaw won the prize. We quickly divided up duties for the dinner that night and hustled the kids back in the direction of our house, making a detour to the Red and White to pick up what we needed.

Dinner turned out to be a huge success. The platter of chicken was emptied, along with most of the potatoes and a good portion of the slaw. A last-minute decision to add in an apple pie topped with vanilla ice cream proved the pièce de résistance.

After we put the kids to bed, I looked around at the assembled adults and wondered if the dinner had been too much of a good thing. Both Jon and Harry looked half asleep, and Julie's eyes kept opening and closing as if she was trying to force herself to stay awake. I went to the kitchen to put on a pot of coffee before returning to the living room.

"Hey everybody!" I clapped my hands loudly. "Who's up for a game of charades?"

Harry looked stunned, while Jon glowered at me. Only Julie rose to the occasion. She pushed herself up into an erect position on the sofa and nodded happily. "What a great idea! We haven't played that game in ages. What do you say, Georgia? Woman against men?"

I could see the strategy behind her suggestion. "Absolutely. Especially since these two don't look like they could come up with a good clue if their lives depended upon it."

Jon and Harry glanced at each other. "I seem to recall the last time we played, the men made twice as many successful guesses as the women, in the same amount of time." Jon rubbed his hands together and leaned forward. "You're on. And the losers do the dishes."

Suddenly everyone looked totally awake.

I first learned charades in high school. It was a favorite choice for slumber parties, as well as mixed gender gatherings. The rules required one player on each team to come up with the title of a book, movie, song, or famous person's name, and then pantomime the word or phrase to the other members of the team.

I removed a notepad from a drawer in the kitchen and tore off several pages. "Let me remind everyone of the rules of the game. The phrase that's to be acted out should be written on one of these scraps of paper by the non-participating team and given to one member of the other team. Titles must be acted out in silence. No lip syncing, humming, clapping, or pointing to objects permitted. Three minutes will be allowed for the other member of that team to guess the answer. One point will be awarded for correct guesses, or one point will be given to the opposing team for missed answers.

"It is permissible to hold up a number of fingers at the beginning of the time period to indicate how many words are in the answer. Tugging on an earlobe means sounds like. Moving the hands closer together means shorter, or moving the hands further away means longer. Holding the hands close together without moving them indicates a short word, like the, a, or. It is permissible to spin the hands in a circle to indicate you should keep guessing. 'I' is suggested by pointing to your chest or eye and touching your nose while pointing to the guesser indicates the answer is correct. Any questions?"

No one spoke up, so we flipped a coin to see which team would have the first shot at guessing. Jon and Harry won, so Julie and I quickly put our heads together to come up with a title. We chose the movie "One Flew Over the Cuckoo's Nest", hoping it would be a hard one to guess. Julie wrote the title down on a piece of paper and handed it to Harry. She glanced at the clock and announced the time had begun.

Harry began by pretending to crank an old movie camera and then held up six fingers to indicate the number of words in the title. Jon easily guessed the first word when Harry held up one finger. The rest of the title came just as quickly thanks to Harry's innovative ways of acting out flying and cuckoo. They were finished in just under two minutes. They hooped and hollered before huddling together to come up with a title for us. Julie and I looked at each other in dismay.

"I thought that was going to be a lot harder!" she whispered. I nodded my agreement.

Harry handed Julie a piece of paper and our turn began. She pantomimed that she was looking for a song title that contained five words. She then held up three fingers to indicate she was looking for the third word in the title. She folded her arm across her chest and wrapped her blouse around it. It took me a minute to figure out she was pantomiming a broken arm, and I answered "broken". She pointed to the center of her chest to indicate the word heart, and then held up two fingers to suggest she was now looking for the second word of the title. I correctly guessed "go" but was stopped from guessing further by Harry's proclamation that the time was up.

"We can't be out of time already!" I cried.

"'Fraid you are, my dear. The correct answer was 'Don't Go Breaking My Heart'," Jon said. "It's our turn again."

The game went on for another twenty-five minutes, at which point we decided to call it a night. The tally stood at four points for the men and two for Julie and me. Jon walked into the kitchen and returned with two dishrags. "Here you go. Be sure to scrub the fryer extra well so Ebie doesn't decide to take a poke into the chicken fat."

Julie and I each took one of the rags begrudgingly before kissing the guys goodnight. I was up to my elbows in soapy suds before I realized we'd never gotten around to asking them what was going on in their private talks. I slapped my forehead, causing soap bubbles to splatter over my face.

"I can't believe it! We didn't even bring up what we wanted to talk to them about!"

Julie's mouth fell open. "You're right! How could we possibly have forgotten?"

"I guess we got too wrapped up in the preliminaries and forgot about the main event. What do we do now?"

"There's nothing we can do except find a way to bring it up tomorrow."

"Shesh! How stupid! Well, let's make a pact with each other to broach the subject as soon as we get the two of them together again."

"Deal." She held out her right hand.

I dried my hand on the dishrag and took hers. "Double Deal."

Our chance came the next afternoon when Betty offered to pick up the three kids and take them, along with her son Tommy, to a matinee showing of "The Muppet Movie". It was playing nearby at the Coligny Theater, and the kids had been begging to see it ever since they saw it advertised on television. She invited Julie and me to join her, but I explained over the phone that we really needed to talk to our husbands about something without the kids around. She understood, although I suspect she hadn't considered what a handful four little ones would be without another adult present. I made a mental note to return the favor in some way in the near future.

After the kids left, I suggested the four of us walk down the beach to the Tiki Hut. The tide was low, making our walk along the wide, packed sand, easy. We strolled along at a slow pace, enjoying the brilliant blue sky and warm temperature as we watched other beachgoers engaging in a variety of beachy pleasures. There were a handful of bike riders, numerous shell seekers, and a good number of folks spread out on colorful towels intent on soaking up as much sun as possible.

The Hut wasn't too crowded when we arrived. The lunch crowd had dispersed, and the happy hour bunch were yet to arrive. We grabbed a table near the entrance and settled in. Jon waved at a passing waiter who stopped to take our order. Harry ordered a beer in a frosty mug. Jon chose his customary scotch on the rocks, and Julie and I decided on Pina Coladas. I reminded myself of the tendency of these frozen concoctions to cause brain freeze whenever I drank one too quickly and asked for a spoon.

Julie looked at me curiously. "A spoon?"

I nodded. "Whenever I try and drink something frozen, it ends up giving me an excruciating headache. I'm hoping by using a spoon I can avoid that particular dilemma."

Harry looked around cheerily. "I like this place. Do they always have live music?"

The band had just finished playing a tune, and announced they were taking a short break.

"Yeah. Unless the weather is really bad. Otherwise, there's a set from 1 until 5, and another that starts around 6 and goes until 10."

The waiter arrived with our drinks. Jon told him to keep the check open and raised his glass in a toast. "Here's to another great day on this wonderful island with special friends."

We all raised our glasses and clinked them together. I dipped my spoon in my glass and took a small sip, careful to press my tongue against the roof of my mouth to ward off a headache. "That was a nice toast, Jon."

Julie agreed. "Yeah! You kind of surprised me. You're not usually prone to such sentimentality."

He scoffed. "Don't get used to it. I guess I was just affected by what a great day it turned out to be. It's nice to share it with friends."

I leaned forward in my chair. "Speaking of sharing, Julie and I have been wanting to ask you and Harry what's going on. The two of you seem to be having some serious conversations about something, and we wondered if it had anything to do with the Mitchelville project?"

Jon glanced at Harry before answering. "We didn't want to say anything before we had more information. One of the people Harry's been meeting with in Savannah runs an investment firm. He's had a number of dealings with Quinn and his group. Harry was trying to discreetly get his take on whether or not joining forces with Quinn would be wise. Apparently, the guy thinks Quinn's a solid citizen: not prone to making careless investments, but with an eye for unique opportunities that others might overlook. Harry didn't tell him what we were considering, but he got the impression any project with Quinn's name on it would be well received by other investors."

His words sounded encouraging. "So, it's a go then? You're going to approach Quinn about helping set-up a nonprofit?"

Harry spoke up. "Probably, but we're considering another angle, as well. There's a program called the National Trust for Historic Preservation that has established the Black Americans Cultural Heritage Action Fund. Grants from the fund are designed to advance ongoing preservation activities for historic places that represent the cultural heritage of black people. I've been doing a little digging into the history of Mitchelville, and I'm fairly certain a project to restore the site and preserve its historical significance would qualify for one of those grants. Only nonprofit organizations are eligible, so we would still need to set that up."

Jon joined the conversation. "Quinn is a likely choice to be involved in setting up the nonprofit because of his contacts. But we believe, as does Henry, that our chances of being awarded a grant would be improved if we also include a significant number of black members. Henry knows all of the local blacks, and he has their respect. We think it would be a good idea to get him in the same room with Quinn and see if their interests are compatible. With Quinn's contacts on the financial side, and Henry's on the personal/cultural, we should be able to put together a winning team."

I smiled at his use of the word "team". "Sounds like you're planning a baseball game instead of a preservation project."

"The approach is the same: choose the best possible players so our chances of hitting a home run are 100%, or close to it."

Julie laughed. "I think Harry Simpson has been rubbing off on you. He loves to use baseball analogies to explain everything from financial deals to relationships." She looked at Harry fondly. "Who's the coach, and who's the pitcher of this team you're imagining?"

Harry and Jon exchanged another poignant look. "I guess if we continue this baseball analogy, Jon would be the coach, and Quinn and Henry would both be pitchers; or at least co-captains."

My amulet began to throb insistently, triggering a thought to pop into my head. "What about you, Harry? Do you have a position on this team?"

He grew silent as he sipped his beer and glanced at Julie. "I'm hoping to become the General Manager. That is, if I can convince Julie to leave Nashville and move here."

Julie's eyes flew open. "Move to Hilton Head? But what about our jobs?"

He gave her an apologetic look. "I'm sorry I couldn't say anything about this before, but the whole reason your dad's been sending me to Savannah is to oversee a plan to open a branch office of the bank there. It would specialize in investment dealings, in particular, start-up companies. Quinn's Rose Hill project would fit into that category, and your dad's been talking to him for some time about how the new branch could be involved in providing funding. Nonprofits obviously don't fit in the same category, but we could manage the expenses involved in running one. Especially if Quinn is at the helm of both."

His decision to withhold such important information as a possible relocation from his wife struck an unpleasant chord in me as I remembered how Jon had done the same. However, our situation certainly turned out even better than I could have anticipated. I decided to give Harry the benefit of the doubt. "How does one go about creating a nonprofit?" I asked.

Jon set his drink on the table before answering. "The process is similar to creating a regular corporation. You choose a business name, appoint a board of directors, then file the formal paperwork to incorporate and apply for tax-exempt status. After all of that is taken care of, you just need to make sure the nonprofit has all the licenses and permits required by the federal, state and, local governments."

Julie turned to Harry. "Let's go back to when you said we'd move here. If the new bank branch is going to be located in Savannah, doesn't that mean we'd have to live there?"

He squirmed in his chair. "That's part of what I'm still trying to work out. Technically, I'd need to be in Savannah to oversee the start-up of the investment branch. But that doesn't mean we couldn't spend a good deal of time on Hilton Head, as well. I thought we could start out by renting a two-bedroom place in Savannah, and have Jon help us look around for a house here. My hope would be that if we are able to realize our idea of the nonprofit, I could eventually make a convincing case for my need to be physically available to keep a close eye on things.

"I've been talking to Jerome about coming along as my second-in-command with the long-range plan of having him take over direction of the Savannah office. He and Gloria are getting married as soon as she finishes nursing school, which will be at the end of this semester. After that, he said they're game for moving anywhere interesting. Savannah, Georgia has been on Gloria's wish list for some time, and Jerome thought it would be a nice graduation/wedding present to surprise her with." He studied Julie's face for a response. "Of course, all of this hinges on how you feel about it."

I smiled at the thought of seeing Jerome and Gloria again. Jerome worked at the same bank as Harry and Julie, and his girlfriend, Gloria, worked as a hairdresser in the Cain Sloan department store while she went to nursing school. I remembered the story of how they had "crashed" the dinner at the Belle Meade Plantation by being the only black faces in the room, aside from the wait staff. Julie had been impressed by how gracefully they handled the potentially uncomfortable situation. After that, they became a regular part of our group gatherings.

Julie was unusually quiet after Harry's announcement, causing me to wonder what she really thought of the idea of leaving Nashville to relocate to the East coast. When I turned to look at her, I noticed her face forming an ear-splitting grin which could only mean one thing.

"When can we move?!" She shouted her question, causing the three of us to jump with surprise before breaking out in laughter.

"Harry put his arm around her shoulder. "I take it, that's a yes."

"YES! I love the idea!" She looked at me. "Do you know what this means, Georgia? We'll be able to see each other all the time again."

My eyes filled with happy tears. "I can't believe it. It's something I've been wishing for, but never dreamed could really happen." I looked at Harry. "Do you really think this is possible? I don't want to believe it unless you tell me it's a certainty."

"I've never been one to count my chickens before they hatch, but I'd say the odds are in our favor. There are just a few loose ends that need to be tied up."

I shook my head in wonder. "Wow. I was expecting some news about Mitchelville, but I never would have guessed this new turn of events in a million years. Maybe I would have wished it, but I never would have predicted it." I was so distracted by Harry's announcement I forgot to use the spoon with my drink, filling my mouth with a sizable amount of the frozen swirl. When the icy cold hit my brain, I pressed the palm of my hand against the pain that assaulted me. "Oh, my God! I'm so stupid!" I pressed my tongue against the roof of my mouth in an attempt to halt the discomfort and waited for the headache to ease. I wiped tears from the corners of my eyes and looked at Jon, who was studying me with a worried look.

"Are you okay?"

I nodded. "Brain freeze. Gets me every time."

He shook his head in wonder. "Then why do you keep ordering those frozen drinks?"

"I don't know. I guess because they taste so good." I knew what I was saying was illogical. Why keep punishing myself in an attempt to capture a fleeting pleasure. I chuckled to myself. Isn't that the way things often go in life? We take a risk on being hurt because the chance of finding pleasure is so beguiling. That pretty much summed up what happened in my relationship with Jon; in my work at the newspaper in Nashville; in my dealings with the Belmont journalism program; in my communication with Miss Bessie; in our decision to move to Hilton Head. Once again, we were sailing uncharted territory. Only this time, our closest friends were at the helm.

I glanced around the table at three of the people who were dearest to me and felt a swelling in my heart matched by the growing warmth of the amulet. I laid my hand over the top of it.

"I have a feeling everything is going to work out just fine."

Julie looked at where my hand lay. "Just a hunch, or is it a palpable feeling?"

My smile told her my answer.

CHAPTER TWENTY-FOUR

Over the next several weeks, everything that had been hanging in limbo for months began to undergo a metamorphosis. Henry's reputation as a man of honor and trustworthiness helped him convince four members of the Black community to join the board of directors of the Mitchelville Preservation Project. They were joined by Robert Quinn and three key players from his investment group, with Jon and Henry making it an even ten. Subsequently, the MPP, as it became known, submitted a successful proposal to the Federal government to create a nonprofit association, allowing them to secure a sizable grant.

Three months after our fateful gathering at the Tiki Hut, Harry, Julie, and the twins moved to Savannah so Harry could supervise the opening of the Southeastern branch of the investment department of the First National Bank. Jon went to work immediately to help them locate a beach-oriented home on Hilton Head, which ended up a stone's throw away from our house. Julie and the girls moved into the house while Harry worked zealously to shift his work focus from the investment branch to the MPP. They were able to make the transition from living in two cities to full-time residency on Hilton Head in just under two months. Jerome and Gloria relocated to Savannah a short while later, moving into the Simpsons' newly vacated apartment.

Jon continued his work with Robert Quinn, divvying up his time between the Rose Hill project and the MPP, with occasional forays into island real estate opportunities. I couldn't recall a time when he seemed as happy as he was with his fingers in those three proverbial pies. Seeing him that way warmed my heart both inside and out as the insistent throbbing of the amulet continued in earnest. I remained puzzled over the messages I'd received from the spirits of Miss Bessie and Ida; messages repeatedly telling me to trust my heart. Eventually, I decided I needed to set aside time for a thorough exploration, Georgia, and Julie style. That meant outdoors, cocktails in hand, with a pen and paper close by to jot down our thoughts.

We finally found the time one Sunday afternoon a few months after they made the move to Hilton Head. Spring was just beginning to return to the island, as evidenced by the warmer days and blossoming foliage. Jon and Harry were off on a golf outing with a couple of members of the MPP board. The members in question had consistently been the dividing voices on pretty much any discussion involving expenditures that would enable the Mitchelville restoration to move forward at faster than a snail's pace. Harry convinced Jon that time spent on a shared round of golf would be more effective at hashing out their differences than meeting in a stuffy conference room. Golf was still not Jon's favorite pastime, but he had grown a little more tolerant of it once Harry moved close by. Hilton Head was known for its pristine courses with breathtaking views of the island coastline and towering trees, as well as frequent alligator sightings alongside water traps and lagoons.

Jerome and Gloria quickly became regulars whenever we gathered together with some of our closest friends on the island. They made friends with the Sanders and formed a special bond with Henry and Mary. I wasn't surprised. That was pretty much everyone's response to the Palmers. On this particular Sunday,

Henry and Mary invited them to lunch at their house after attending service at the St. James Baptist Church. It was a long drive from Savannah to Hilton Head, but they didn't seem to mind. As Gloria remarked, it was worth it to spend time with the couple she dubbed "my substitute parents".

Frankie was over-the-moon with joy since the arrival of Emily and Ashley. He and Tommy remained the best of friends, but the boys made room in their entourage for the girls with barely a missed beat. Even Ashley seemed pleased, or at least tolerant, of having the boys around more often. As a result, the four of them were in and out of one another's houses every weekend, and at least a couple of afternoons a week. Betty phoned a few days earlier to invite the kids to a picnic at Fish Haul Beach on Sunday afternoon. Several other children would be present from the Daycare Center, and some of the parents had agreed to help supervise. I accepted her invitation after insisting she allow me to reciprocate sometime soon. She readily agreed, which left the afternoon free for Julie and me to get together.

Julie and Harry's house was on the other side of North Forest Beach Drive from where we lived, on a street called Heron. It was an easy walk between our houses, which made regular visits a cinch. Their house was all on one level with an attached carport and backyard patio. It was further from the beach than ours, but still required only a 6 or 7-minute walk to reach the sandy shore.

We decided to meet on her patio this particular Sunday. I brought along a chilled bottle of white wine and a Tupperware full of CHEEZ-IT crackers and grapes. Julie added slices of ham and some strawberries, and a jug of ice water. We settled around her patio table and sipped our drinks and enjoyed the warmth of the sunshine. The weather was perfect for sitting outside; not too hot, but warm enough for short sleeves. A slight breeze was blowing, which carried the scent of Azaleas, Jasmine, and the ocean. I breathed deeply and smiled at my friend.

"This is nice. I still get surprised when I realize you're not just here for a visit, but you actually live here now."

"I know. It seems like a dream sometimes. So much has changed in such a relatively short time."

"Do you ever regret it? Leaving Nashville?"

She thought for a moment. "I miss my family sometimes, but they're all so busy these days that I really didn't see them that often. I thought I'd miss my work at the bank, but I have to admit, I don't. Is that crazy? I mean, it was the first real job I ever had."

"I don't think it's crazy. I haven't really missed working at Belmont either. I do miss being involved in journalism in some way, but I'm not sure what I want to do. Jon has suggested on more than one occasion that I get involved in the MPP. The idea appeals to me, but I haven't done anything to make it happen yet."

She gave me a studied look. "What's holding you back?"

I considered her question. "That's one of the reasons I wanted to get together with you today. Something Miss Bessie, and now Ida, told me has me puzzled. I believe if I could figure it out, I'd be closer to knowing what I want to do about a lot of things."

She reached for the pen and paper that lay on the table. "Then let's get at it. Tell me exactly what they've said that you find puzzling."

"From the first time I met Miss Bessie, she told me I should trust my heart. At first, I thought she was just referring to my relationship with Jon, but eventually I understood she meant in every aspect of my life. She sent a message through the root doctor to remind me of the same message, then Ida stated pretty much the same thing. Ida also told me to remember how she and I met."

Julie began writing. "Okay. Trust your heart and... what do you think Ida meant?"

"We met because she worked at the Metropolitan Historical Commission. I thought maybe she was suggesting we should follow through on trying to restore Mitchelville."

"Makes sense. Or maybe she was referring more to your potential role with the project."

I frowned. "You think so? That's an interesting idea."

She glanced down at the paper. "Let's go back to the first point. When they keep telling you to trust your heart, how does that make you feel?"

I smiled as I took a drink of wine. "You sound like Dr. Blackburn." Dr. Blackburn was the psychologist Julie introduced me to, who helped us both through some difficult times. I thought about her question. "I guess it makes me feel like I'm not doing something right. That I'm getting caught up in my head instead of listening to my heart. It also occurs to me it has something to do with the amulet. Maybe I'm not letting it guide me as well as it could."

She jotted the word amulet next to trust your heart. She tapped her pencil against her cheek and stared at the sky. "Let's try something. I'm going to ask you a series of questions, and I want you to place your hand over the amulet and tell me what response you sense to each thing I ask."

"Okay, although I have to admit it sounds a little spooky."

"Just give it a try. First question: Do you miss journalism?"

The amulet grew warmer under my touch. "Yes."

"Do you want some sort of work to do that feels satisfying?"

It grew even hotter. "Yes again."

"Does the MPP sound exciting?"

As the heat intensified, a rapid throbbing began. "Absolutely."

"Are you afraid to start working again?"

The amulet grew cooler. "No."

"Is there something that's holding you back?"

The heat returned. "Apparently so."

She stopped, as if considering what to ask next. "Do you believe that returning to work would interfere with the possibility of having another child?"

Her question surprised me. We hadn't discussed it in a while, and I thought I had successfully pushed it from my thoughts. The amulet suggested otherwise as it began throbbing insistently. "I would have said no, but the amulet is saying otherwise. Do you think that's it? Is that why I've been dragging my feet on getting involved in the MPP?" Before she could reply, the amulet grew so hot I had to lift my blouse to fan cool air on the spot where it touched my skin. "Whew! I guess I have my answer. That's what puzzles me though. Why haven't I gotten pregnant? Maybe another baby isn't in the cards for us."

"Why don't you ask the amulet? On second thought, ask yourself, first."

"Ask what?"

"Are you certain you want another baby?"

The idea of voicing that particular question frightened me. "I'm afraid to answer that because it's something I haven't been able to decide."

"What are you afraid of?"

I filled my mouth with crackers to delay the need to respond. When I was finally ready to answer, I spoke up. "I think I'm afraid it might change my life in a way I'm not prepared for. We didn't plan on Frankie, as you know. What if I have another baby, then find out it's too much for me to handle?"

"What does Jon say about it? Does he want another child?"

I nodded. "He hasn't been pushing me in one direction or the other, but it's obvious the thought of adding to our family makes him happy. He loved having a little sister when they were growing up. I guess he imagines it would be the same for Frankie."

She began drawing circles on the paper. "Do you believe you could work and raise a second child?"

"I suppose so. A lot of women do, but I really don't know." I realized I may have just reached the crux of the issue. "That's it, isn't it? I don't know, and not knowing has been stressing me out and keeping me from making a decision."

Her scribblings changed from circles to hearts. "Maybe when Bessie and Ida told you to trust your heart, they were referring to the thing that sits on top of your heart." She looked pointedly at where the amulet lay. "Why don't you try asking it a direct question and see what happens?"

I drew a deep breath and let it out slowly. "Okay." I searched for the right words to state my question. "If I have another baby, will it prevent me from realizing my dream of getting back into journalism?" The amulet gave no response. "Hunh. No answer. Let me state it another way. Should I pursue working with the MPP?" The heat began to intensify. "That's a firm yes. Let me try again. Can I raise another child and work with the MPP?" A steady throbbing beat joined the heat. "Yes again. Do you think I should ask it if I'm going to have another baby?"

"I don't know. Maybe you should leave that one up to the gods."

I giggled at her use of the word "gods". "The gods? Plural?" We looked at each other and said in unison, "What would the nuns think?" When our laughter subsided, I considered her response. "You know, I think you're right. I don't need to ask the amulet whether or not I'll have another baby. I just need to be clear in my head; in my heart; that I'm okay whichever way it goes. In the meantime, it seems apparent that I need to get off my duff and see how I can become a part of promoting the MPP. I find that idea exciting, and the amulet clearly agrees."

"Great! I really believe what both Miss Bessie and Ida are trying to tell you is you need to get out of your head and into your heart. The amulet is a messenger from your heart. It reflects what your heart is honestly saying. You just have to allow yourself to listen to it."

I felt as if a burden had been lifted off my shoulders, and more to the point, off my chest. "I feel better already. I'm going to talk to Jon as soon as I can and see how I can start working with the MPP. I love the idea of helping bring attention to what Mitchelville stood for and should still stand for." I could feel my heart beating more rapidly in tune with the amulet. "My heart is speaking to me quite clearly now, and not just through the amulet. This is what I want to do. And if a baby is in our future, I'll just have to trust I can find a way to do both."

She clapped her hands and then raised her glass in a toast. "Here's to facing the unknown with courage and grace." We clinked glasses and took a sip. "You know you'll never have to face any of this alone. You have a wonderful man behind you, not to mention fantastic friends."

"I certainly do. It's not that I forget that. I just tend to allow doubt in myself to crowd out what I know to be true."

Julie replied with one finger in the air. "When the wisdom of the heart replaces the chatter of the mind, the power of love flows forth."

"Did you make that up? I like it."

"It's not original. I read it somewhere once, and it just popped back into my mind." She stood and stretched. "All this sitting has made me stiff. What do you say about a walk to the beach?"

I began to gather our things from the table. "You'll always get a yes to that question."

Later that evening, we gathered at our house for a burger cookout. The guys were in stellar moods after a successful golf outing that resulted in mended fences with the two board members. As a result, Jon felt certain they would be able to move ahead soon with the plans to begin construction on a mini-Mitchelville town prototype to be dubbed the "freedom park". The park would include a Gullah heritage center, praise house, store, two model homes, a garden, a statue of General Mitchel, and panels describing the history of the town.

The board had been successful at procuring a sizable grant which both Jon and Harry felt would be sufficient to carry out the planned restoration. Their enthusiasm was contagious, and I found myself growing excited at the prospects they described. At one point, Julie nudged me and raised her eyebrows in question. Jon noticed our exchange and looked at me for an explanation.

"Julie and I were talking earlier today, and I've decided I want to become involved in the MPP. I thought maybe I could start by interviewing a few of the key players – maybe Robert Quinn, Henry, and Harry – and write up an article for the local paper. I would like to describe the history of Mitchelville and emphasize why it's important for us to preserve its memory and intent, not only for the descendants of the freedmen and women who resided there, but for all of us who have been touched by the battle to overcome racial inequality." I looked at Jon for a reaction. "What do you think of my idea?"

He grinned and pulled me into a hug. "I think it's about time! I've been hoping you'd come around to seeing the potential in this, and what role you could play in helping us make it happen."

For some reason, his reaction brought tears to my eyes. "I've been intrigued by the project since you first mentioned it. I just had to get out of my own way first. Julie helped me with that earlier today." I smiled at her across the table.

A flush began to spread from her neck up to her cheeks as she dipped her head. "I just helped you listen to your heart. Like Bessie and Ida have been telling you to do. You just needed a little help to learn how to do that."

I wiped the tears from my eyes as I looked around at my husband and dear friends. Life was always going to be ripe with challenges, but as long as I was surrounded with loving support, I knew I could weather any storm that came my way. Apparently, even when it took the form of a hurricane! I blew out the breath I had been inadvertently holding and took a sip of water. "Y'all are the best. Now, why don't we put aside the heavy stuff and just enjoy the rest of the evening? We'll be joined by three little ones before long, and I, for one, could use a little levity before that happens."

The others chimed in their agreement. Harry refilled our glasses and raised his in a toast. "Here's to us: a formidable team, whether we're tracking down bank robbers or mapping out a strategy for restoring an ancient village."

We clinked glasses and laughed at his toast. He was referring to several years earlier when we had successfully helped thwart the illegal actions of two brothers who were attempting to commit bank fraud in Nashville, although the real hero in that story was Julie's dad. Our coup in organizing the MPP seemed like small potatoes compared to that scandal, but I had a feeling we were seeing the tip of the iceberg when it came to the impact the project would eventually have.

I could feel my excitement growing by the minute as I imagined what lay ahead, and I gave a grateful look to the three people around me. They were my family. Maybe not in the biological sense, but at the deepest level I could imagine.

I settled back in my chair and allowed the silly grin that had occupied my face since my decision to become involved in the MPP to flourish unbridled.

EPILOGUE

"Daddy, come on! We're going to be late!" Frankie stood at the door and frowned at his father. We were on our way to celebrate his fifth birthday; a celebration he would be sharing with his best friend Tommy. One of the first things they learned about each other was that they were born on the same day, the same year. Since that discovery, they chose to celebrate their birthdays with a joint party. Last year we hosted the party at our house, and this year the Sanders would return the favor.

"I'll be ready in a minute, Frankie. Why don't you take that box down to the car?" Jon gestured to a carton holding various party favors.

Frankie lifted the box and headed out the front door.

"Just leave them on the ground next to the trunk," Jon yelled to his retreating back. He turned and looked at me with a chuckle. I can't believe how big he's grown. Pretty soon, he'll be driving us around."

I looked at him in dismay. "Oh, let's not rush things. He still has a lot of childhood ahead of him."

He placed his hand on my stomach and rubbed gently. "Yeah, and he has to learn how to be a big brother soon."

I lay my hand on top of his. "Eight months, 25 days, and counting. I sure hope this baby has a good sense of time. I feel like I'm about ready to burst." By the doctor's estimation, our baby had been conceived sometime in July which, by my recollection, most likely coincided with the post-Fourth of July celebration Jon and I had enjoyed after returning home from the fireworks exhibition at Shelter Cove harbor. The harbor opened the previous year and was a popular spot to listen to live music, watch the sunset, and catch the fireworks over the Calibogue Sound.

"I can't wait to meet her. Or him."

We decided against learning the gender of the baby before it was born, opting to be surprised instead. As a result, we chose gender-neutral items to decorate the nursery. That meant, instead of a color theme of blue or pink, we selected pale green and yellow. I was pleased with our choices. It gave the baby's room a happy, restful atmosphere, and blended in well with the beachy surroundings. Jon offered to convert his study into a nursery so it would be close enough for us to hear the baby. It's location just down the hall from Frankie would also allow the siblings to share a bathroom as the new arrival grew older. Frankie was already making plans for the things he wanted to teach his new brother or sister. The list included: dolphin spotting, building lego villages, collecting shells, and riding bikes. We tried to tell him it would be some time before his new sibling would be able to do any of those things, but our words fell on deaf ears. Frankie was a perpetual dreamer, with a healthy dose of optimism mixed in, and I was proud of the little man he was becoming.

We pulled into the Sanders driveway and parked behind a row of cars that spilled out onto the adjacent street. I spotted Julie and Harry's red station wagon and the Palmers old Chevrolet. I didn't recognize the other cars, but suspected they belonged to some of the neighbors or families from the Daycare Center. Jerome and Gloria would be driving over from Savannah a little later, and David from the Red and White was bringing the birthday cake.

Jon offered me a hand getting out of the car before collecting the box of party favors. Frankie ran ahead of us, shouting he was going to find Tommy. The commotion he caused must have alerted Betty to our arrival because she stuck her head out the front door.

"There you are! Ready to get this party rolling?"

"Ready as we'll ever be," I replied. "Although, the only thing I'll be rolling will be me." I caressed my midsection with a groan. "I don't remember the last trimester being this uncomfortable. I guess that's a good thing. If women remembered every detail of pregnancy, they'd probably never opt to go through it again."

"I have to agree. That certainly played a part in our deciding to stick with one. Although, if Hal had his way, we'd have a few more. I guess ignorance is bliss when it comes to men deciding whether or not to have babies." She held out a hand to help me up the steps. "We've got a full house inside, but I made sure to cordon off a special place for you to sit."

As she warned, the house was bustling with a small bevy of three-, four-, and five-year-olds, and their assorted parents and friends of parents. The volume was loud, and I looked around for a place to position myself so I'd be out of the way of traffic. Hal gave me a wink as he entered the room and clapped his hands loudly.

"Hey everybody! Let's head out back where there's more room to spread out. Betty and I loaded a couple of coolers with beverages, and there's a stack of plastic cups on top. Kids, be sure to let your parents get your drinks for you."

There was a rush for the back door as most of the kids made their way outside. The only hold off was Ashley who sauntered nonchalantly a few feet behind the others. I caught Julie's eye and smiled as she walked to where I stood.

"Some things never change."

"That's true. But luckily some things do." I pointed to where Frankie was circling back inside to join Ashley. He took her hand and grinned, and the two of them walked outside together.

"Well, I'll be! I always thought Emily was his favorite."

"I suspect she still is, at least when it comes to playing games and stuff. I imagine his interest in Ashley is more primal."

She looked at me askance. "They're four and a half and five years old! Surely you aren't implying there's some sort of romantic interest between them?"

I laughed at her shocked expression. "Not the way you mean, but I think there's definitely a boy-girl thing going on."

She shook her head. "Don't even think it! Those days are a LONG way off; at least I HOPE they are!"

Harry came bouncing up behind us and pecked Julie on the cheek. "Hey, wife. Want to go outside and supervise a game of tag?"

She gave me a parting look of exasperation. "Anything to get me away from what Georgia just said." He gave her a questioning look, to which she responded, "Don't ask!" Harry shrugged and led her outside.

Betty joined me again and motioned in the direction of an overstuffed chair placed next to an open window. "I thought maybe you'd be comfortable sitting there. You can see everything that's going on without having to be in the middle of it."

I looked at her gratefully. "Thanks. I'm feeling a little out of sorts today. The baby's moving a lot, and I could swear it's butting its head against my ribs."

She winced. "I remember that feeling! Well, you just relax, and I'll tell Jon to bring you something cold to drink."

After she left, I looked around the crowd more closely to see who was there. Josephine and Samuel were talking with Isaiah, Aileen, Evelyn, and Joseph – the six neighbors I'd first met at the Sanders moving-in party. Henry and Mary were standing nearby laughing with Jerome and Gloria who'd just arrived. Frankie's teacher, Vanessa Browne, stood in the middle of a group of parents and children I didn't recognize, but who I assumed were classmates from the Daycare Center. David Martin from the Red and White was chatting with an attractive blonde who he seemed to have a more than casual interest in.

I noticed another man walking up to join Henry and Mary, and I squinted to see who it was. Benjamin Scott! What in the world was the root doctor doing here? Jon walked up and handed me a plastic cup.

"Betty gave me strict orders to bring you this and see what else you need."

I took the drink and nodded in Henry's direction. "The root doctor's here. You know, Benjamin Scott. The man we met on the beach after the hurricane. He's Josephine's brother, but I can't imagine why he's at this party."

Jon looked at him quizzically. "Maybe Henry invited him. They seem to be pretty chummy."

At that moment, he looked up and nodded in our direction.

"He's seen us staring at him," I said. "What do we do now?"

"I don't think we have to do anything. It looks like he's headed straight for us."

My breath caught in my throat as I watched him approach. I don't know what it was about the man, but just seeing him made me nervous.

He stopped directly in front of us and gave us a friendly smile. "Mr. and Mrs. Barnett. I hope you don't mind me crashing your party. Henry thought it would be okay considering the circumstances."

His statement confused me. "What circumstances are you referring to?"

His eyes sought Jon's as he paused before answering. "I've had another visit from your friend. The one you called Ida. She told me to give you this." He handed me an envelope.

"Are you trying to tell me the ghost of my friend gave you this? She physically put it in your hand?"

He smiled. "Not exactly. She appeared to me a while back and told me where to find it. It took a while to locate, but she clearly said I shouldn't give it to you until today. I got in touch

247

with Henry and asked if he thought I should bring it here or wait for another time. He suggested I bring it today."

I turned the envelope over in my hand and studied both sides. There was no writing on it, and it didn't feel very heavy. I started to run my finger under the sealed edge, but Benjamin Scott stopped me.

"The other part of her message was to tell you not to open it until the baby comes. She said she knew waiting would be difficult for you, but to ask you to trust her."

I sighed. "It feels like all I've been doing lately – at least for the last several years – is trusting in things I don't understand."

"I can only imagine how frustrating that is." He glanced around the room. "Well, I'd better be going. I'm just going to find Josie and say goodbye."

"There's no need for you to go." He started to walk off but stopped at Jon's comment. "Why don't you stay a while? At least until we cut the cake."

He looked pleasantly surprised at Jon's invitation. "Why, that's awfully kind of you. Maybe I will." He tipped his imaginary cap at me and went outside.

I looked at Jon curiously. "Why'd you do that?"

"I wanted a chance to observe him more closely. See if I can figure out what he's really all about. Plus, I imagine if Henry invited him, he must have a good reason."

I fingered the envelope he had given me. "I wish I could open this now. I'm dying to know what it says."

"Better not. He said Ida's ghost made it clear you should wait. It never paid to ruffle her feathers when she was alive, and I sure wouldn't want to cross her now." He winked at me playfully. "Can I get you anything else before I go back outside? Maybe something to eat?"

I shook my head, and then reconsidered. "Would you ask Henry and Mary if they could come say hi?"

He nodded. "I know what you have in mind. I hope they can help shed some light on things."

He walked off, returning a few minutes later with Henry and Mary in tow. "I'd better check on the boys. Those two have a way of getting into double trouble whenever they're together."

Henry moved two folding chairs in front of me. Mary sat with a sigh. "Dere's uh lot ub folks here tuhday. 'Min' me w'en lil Mary turn t'ree."

Henry sat next to her and looked directly at me. "Jon say oonuh hab sumt'in' tuh ax us."

I nodded. "It's about Benjamin Scott. He said you invited him today. I was wondering why?"

"Didn't inbite 'e. Jes say 'e kin gib oonuh wha' 'e hab f'um oonuh fren." He looked at the envelope I was holding.

"He said Ida told him where to find this, but I shouldn't open it until after the baby is born. I'm dying to know what's in it."

Mary spoke up. "Bes' do wha 'e say. Nebbuh smaa't tuh cross de sperrits."

I tucked the envelope into a pocket on the front of my blouse. "I'm sure you're right. I guess I'm just feeling frustrated in general. I'm ready for this baby to get here." I rubbed my stomach, eliciting a kick in response. "Oh! She kicked me! Or he, since we don't know if it's a girl or boy."

Mary grinned. "'E surely be one or odduh. Fin' out soon nuff!"

Jon returned with Frankie in tow. "Frankie wants to know if the three of you can come outside. They're about to cut the cake."

"Tommy say if we don't cut it soon, he's gonna stab it with his sword." He brandished a rubber sword from behind his back and waved it menacingly in the air. Jon caught it with one hand and lifted it out of harm's way.

"We'll be right there, sweetheart. Why don't you go tell Aunt Betty we're on our way?"

"Dat boy git mo' smaa't ebry time uh see 'em!" Henry said. He stood and offered his hand to Mary.

"Jon, why don't you go ahead? I just need to stop by the bathroom, then I'll join you all." As I began walking down the hall, I was startled by the sensation of water dripping down my leg. "Oh, surely not!" I glanced at the floor where a small puddle had formed.

"Is that what I think it is?" Julie walked up beside me and looked down.

"I think you'd better get Jon. It seems my water just broke!"

Harry offered to drive us to the Hilton Head hospital which was only a few miles from the Sanders' house. We pulled up to the emergency entrance where a nurse hustled me onto a gurney and instructed Jon to go to the admissions desk to sign me in. I clasped Julie's hand before they wheeled me away. "Don't leave."

She squeezed my hand in response. "I'm not going anywhere. I'll just wait here until Harry comes back from parking the car, and then we'll come find you."

By the time Jon returned, my obstetrician had been located, and I was settled into a private room. The doctor informed me my contractions were about fifteen minutes apart, which he said meant the baby was not likely to arrive for several hours. I remembered I had been in labor with Frankie for at least 24 hours before I reached the final stage. A nurse told me labor was often shorter for second births, and I silently crossed my fingers hoping she was correct.

Julie and Harry stayed with us for the next few hours until we shooed them away, promising to call as soon as things progressed. Frankie, Emily, and Ashley were still at the Sanders, and they wanted to go back and help clean up after the party ended. They also offered to take Frankie back home with them. We had managed to slip out with only a few people becoming aware of what was happening, and I hoped the party had gone on without a hitch for Frankie and Tommy's sake.

Jon stayed dutifully by my side through the night. The staff brought in a chair that converted into a bed-of-sorts, allowing him to sleep in the room. I was sure he wasn't very comfortable, as suggested by his cramped position, but he never complained.

For my part, I dozed occasionally, until a new contraction forced me awake. At one point, a nurse came into the room to inform me the contractions were now three minutes apart, and it was time to get me ready to go to the delivery room. I was hooked up to an IV that would deliver relaxing drugs into my system. Luckily, the drugs also created a state of amnesia, so the next thing I remembered was being handed a tiny bundle wrapped in a swaddling blanket.

I gazed down into the face of my baby with an overwhelming sense of awe and delight. Jon leaned down next to me and kissed my cheek before caressing the baby's head.

"It's a girl," he whispered.

"A daughter! I know we said it wouldn't matter, but I was hoping for a girl."

"Me, too." We both stared at her for a couple of minutes. "I called Harry and Julie to let them know. Frankie wanted to come right away, but they convinced him to wait until they could feed him some breakfast. They'll probably be here in about twenty minutes. They're going to drop the twins off at Betty and Hal's first."

I lifted one finger to push the baby's hair away from her forehead. It was light brown, like mine, but her eyes were dark brown, like her daddy's. "She's beautiful."

Tears filled his eyes. "Like her momma." He swiped at his cheek. "What are we going to call her?"

"I have an idea, but I don't know what you'll think about it." He looked at me questioningly. "How about Ida Elizabeth Barnett?"

His face scrunched up into a thoughtful expression. "Ida Elizabeth. I guess that's in tribute to your two ghost friends."

"Um hum." I looked down into our daughter's face. "What do you think of the name?" Her eyes opened slightly as she made a sucking gesture with her mouth.

Jon laughed. "I think she has more important things on her mind."

The door to the room swung open as Frankie rushed in with Julie and Harry close behind. "Sorry! We tried to slow him down, but he got away from us." Julie frowned apologetically.

"It's okay." I shifted the baby, so she was more visible to them. Frankie stopped in his tracks and gazed open-mouthed at his little sister.

"Wow! She's so tiny!"

"Yes, she is, just like you were when you were born. Do you want to come closer so you can see better?"

He nodded and began walking slowly in our direction, stopping when he reached the edge of the bed. "What's her name?" he whispered.

"Ida Elizabeth."

He leaned close to her ear and said, "Hi, Lizzie. Happy birfday." And from that day on, that's the name she was known by.

After Julie and Harry left with Frankie, I urged Jon to head home where he could take a shower and get something to eat. The nurse took Lizzie from the room in order to collect her weight, length, and head circumference, and change her diaper. A second nurse arrived to give me a "bed bath" and help me change into a fresh gown. While I was waiting for Lizzie to return, I remembered the envelope Benjamin Scott gave me, and fished it out of the blouse I had been wearing. I removed a single, typed page on an official looking stationary that bore the name of an attorney's office. I recognized the attorney's name as the same one who handled the transfer of Ida's house to me. I felt as if my heart stopped as I scanned down the page. The words described a trust fund Ida had set up to cover college expenses for Lizzie or living expenses should she decide to forego that path. Lizzie wasn't addressed by name, only described as "the daughter of Georgia Ayres and Jon Barnett". Frankie wasn't mentioned at all, and I couldn't help but wonder why she would have excluded him, or even have known Lizzie would become part of our lives.

The fact that Frankie was left out of the trust overshadowed any happiness I felt from Ida's generosity. My heart felt heavy as I pondered the meaning of the gesture.

"Don't overthink it, dear girl."

My head jerked up at the sound of Ida's voice. "Ida?"

"Yes. I thought you'd be happy when you read what I set up for your daughter."

Her image came into focus at the end of the bed. "I am, but there are several things I don't understand. How did you know I'd have a daughter? And why did you leave Frankie out of the trust?"

She smiled at me warmly. "We have a way of knowing things on this side that aren't clear on the other. Besides, do you really expect me not to provide for my namesake?"

"You knew that would happen, too?"

"Yes. Just before I passed, I dreamed you would have a daughter and name her after me. When my lawyer asked if there was anything else I wanted to address in my will, I decided to cover all the bases in case the dream became a reality. You know you've always been like a daughter to me, which means Lizzie is like my granddaughter."

Her words touched me. "But why leave Frankie out?"

"I didn't know about him. The dream only showed me a daughter. Had I known Frankie would also be a part of your life, you can rest assured he would have been included in the trust."

Her explanation made sense. At least, as much sense as anything involving messages from ghosts, or the prophecy of dreams, could make. "Have you seen her yet? Lizzie?"

Her eyes grew misty. "Oh, yes. She's a doll. Beautiful and with a kind heart. Bessie and I could both see that right away."

I glanced around the room. "Miss Bessie's here, too?"

"Not right now. We were both with you through most of your labor and all of the delivery. We held your hands while you were in the recovery room. When you started to wake up, we left you and went to see your newborn. Miss Bessie said she looks like her when she was a baby, but I told her that's impossible. She got all uppity, too, when she heard you're calling the baby after her – Lizzie. She said that meant you liked her better than me." She shook her head in a gesture I remembered from when she was alive. "I told her that's just silly because you gave the baby my name first. She left in a huff after that." She chuckled. "I expect she'll be back after she settles down a bit."

I looked longingly at her fading image. "Ida? Do you have to leave?"

The image grew stronger again. "I'm always here, dear girl. You just have to hold me in your heart and trust I will come to you when you truly need me."

Her words struck a chord in me. "I've been trying to do that more. Trust. In my heart, and in myself. I believe it's starting to work."

"I know it is." Her image began to fade again, but this time I decided not to try and hold her back. She asked me to trust she was always with me and would be here for me when I truly needed her. I also knew she was trying to tell me it was time for me to be strong and depend more on myself.

The nurse returned with Lizzie and placed her in my arms. I looked down into my daughter's face with a smile. "Well, Miss Ida Elizabeth Barnett. You have quite a wonderful life ahead of you, with more people who love you than you could ever imagine." As I said that, I remembered Frankie's ability to see Miss Bessie and Ida, and wondered if Lizzie would have that same gift. "I guess that falls into the *I don't know* category, doesn't it? And as I spoke those words, I heard Ida's voice respond, *But it will be a wonderful journey finding out!* And once again, I decided to trust she was right.

ANNELL ST. CHARLES

Following a long career in the medical profession, Annell St. Charles turned her attention to writing fiction and producing photography. Her first two novels, "The Things Left Unsaid" and "The Choices We Make", were published in 2016. Her third novel, "The Chances We Take", was published in 2020. It is the prequel to this novel, which is the fourth and final in the *Georgia Ayres* series. She also has two books of photography, "Sunrise On Hilton Head Island: Coligny Beach" and "Island Life", and a book of poetry, "The Clam Shell", also published in 2016. She has been a member of the self-proclaimed "Greater Nashville Book and Wine Club" for around 20 years (who she describes as her toughest critics and greatest friends) and holds a certificate in digital photography from the Shaw Institute. She is an avid walker and can usually be found roaming the streets and beaches around her homes in Nashville, Tennessee and Hilton Head Island with her camera slung over one shoulder while she ponders her next work of fiction. She is married to Constantine Tsinakis, and visits her friend's "Ebie-like" cats every chance she gets.

Review

Reviewed By Deborah Lloyd for Readers' Favorite

Hilton Head Island is the idyllic setting in this thought-provoking novel in the Georgia Ayers series. Georgia loved being a mother to her three-year-old son Frankie, being Jon's wife, having many friends, and frequent walks along the island's beaches. Two of their closest friends were Henry and Mary Palmer, descendants of the original Gullah people brought from West Africa in the 1700s. They greatly missed their best friends from Nashville, Julie and Harry. At times, Georgia felt unsettled, not sure about professional aspirations or having a second child. While Jon was generally happy with his real estate career, he often had feelings of restlessness. Georgia always wore an amulet as a result of a previous spirit encounter. More strange things were happening, including her son's visions of spirits. The main message was always to trust her heart which led to the title of this captivating novel written by Annell St. Charles – The Hearts We Trust.

This book is especially interesting for readers who like history and culture; the information regarding Mitchelville, a Gullah, freed-slave community on Hilton Head is intriguing. The spiritual aspects are also fascinating – Frankie's fascination with "dolfs," his word for dolphins, an animal known for spiritual meanings; the amulet's energies; messages from spirits of deceased loved ones; the intuitive abilities of Henry and Mary. All can be challenges in trusting the wisdom of the heart! The author's writing skills are also outstanding, especially in the way she interweaves several different storylines into one easy-to-read plot. Author Annell St. Charles has written a charming story in The Hearts We Trust. A wonderful read!

CPSIA information can be obtained
at www.ICGtesting.com
Printed in the USA
JSHW041914060522
25540JS00007B/196